THE FARM
WEST OF MARS

THE FARM
WEST OF MARS ·

JUSTIN ISHERWOOD

HEARTLAND
PRESS

Heartland Press
An imprint of NorthWord Press, Inc.

Direct all inquiries to:

Heartland Press
P.O. Box 1360
Minocqua, WI 54568

ISBN 0-942802-90-X

Designed by Moonlit Ink
Printed in The United States of America

CONTENTS

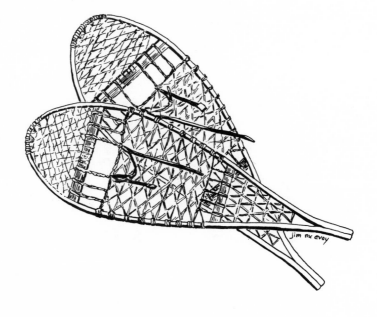

LETTERS ON THE WIND OR
HOW I CAME TO BE

I WAS BORN TO A FARM THOUGHT IN THE INNOCENCE OF my youth to be both distant and separate from the rest of the planet. Mars was closer to the township than Philadelphia. Mars seen red and portentous in the bell jar of farm country night. Mars, red barn Mars and the J. C. Whitney jeweled shift knob Venus. They, Jupiter and the Moon were next-over towns.

Uncle Jerome died in the Second World War on the volcanic beach of Iwo Jima. He died in the worst possible manner according to the code of my family. The insult wasn't war or Pearl Harbor nor was it his innocence and youth. Even Grandma must have known he wasn't really innocent, for when he embarked from San Diego he was almost a father. The tragedy of Uncle Jerome was he died away from his country. Estranged from gravel hollows and purple moraines. No, the separation was more violent than that. Uncle Jerome was disemboweled, cut off from clay-silt farms and the horrid stone-boats. War is all right, of course war is necessary and even righteous, my family told themselves in the plow-layer of their consciousness. War was useful in their Calvinist, republican, capitalist, Methodist, farmering, yankee imperialism and "don't let the flag touch the ground" turn of public dirt. Beneath their plough layer was a private stratum, a separate ground, whose existence and meaning only applied to those of dirt permanence. Like farmers who dig postholes and wells, and foundation-diggers and grave-shovelers and generations of diggers. It all went for nothing if a man, woman or child died in the distances. What was the theological aftermath of such a conclusion, I could only guess. My family did not talk theology. They lived it, alloying the biblical with the spiritualism of farmers and farm country. They weren't sure their god was in Philadelphia or Iwo Jima. The preacher at the funeral for Uncle Jerome said god was over Iwo Jima and maybe over Japan. My family doubted him in their hearts.

A coastal mine killed Uncle Jerome. The family doctor who opened the coffin to verify who it was said, "It didn't leave a mark on him." But they knew it wasn't him. Not really, almost but not quite. They heard of the undertaker ships for all those dead Marines. Embalming them and slinging the guts into a hot sea. Maybe Uncle Jerome did die for his flag but his family knew they had lost him, his vitals spread in an unconcerned ocean before a separate god.

A stone is for him at the Liberty Corners Cemetery; over on the south edge next to Uncle George's alfalfa field, but the stone can't cure it. They bought the plot from the Association when word came in July '44 their son had paid the supreme sacrifice. What do governments know of sacrifice? Governments don't die. Families and farmers die but governments are like gods, they will take what they want, if they want it bad enough. Let 'em earn 'em, Eugene Fletcher said. Let government earn sons like farmers earn sons and work them and try and get them to love ya at the same time. Mister Roosevelt should try to keep "his boys" with a stoneboat.

Grandpa Fletcher was mad the rest of his life because Uncle Jerome got killed in the western sea. Though he had four sons they weren't enough. Why Kingsley followed Jerome into the Marine Corps he couldn't say. He spoke against it. The family was taking a risk the way it was. You think he'd listen? No sir. They had them fool four-color posters just about everywhere from the high school cafeteria to Charlie Webb's store and grocery. How could a brown-cow-farm compete? he asked. Government don't know nothing about survival—what morning means when you got boys and some of the best valley land in the whole north except for a few stones. If he promised anything at the buryin' it was to stay mad, gawd-dammit-mad the rest of his life. Uncle Jerome's plot is at the outside of the Liberty Corners Cemetery so maybe he could win him back. To this land. To this god. And conjure up a new soul for his boy, lost 300 yards out from a black pumice beach.

The outposts of my childhood were Plainfield, twenty miles to the south of Liberty Corners; the metropolis of Stevens Point ten miles north where the river turned hard west and they had street lights, two movie theaters and one whole set of stop-lights; and Plover village, five miles over and the chief source of commerce with the Cash & Carry hardware and Plover milling across the road. Not that my father was loyal to Plover General Milling, 'cause it was a Union Mill, and the cousins belonged. Anything the cousins did pretty well tainted the objective for him. Instead he drove the eighteen miles to Amherst Junction on the Green Bay and Western track, and there purchased his hundred pound sacks of bran and soybean meal, his salt blocks and milk-cow cures.

South and west lay the city of Wisconsin Rapids. Not we or anybody we knew had ever been there being twenty miles distant and that across the Buena Vista Marsh unless you took the state road over from Plover. The west wind was knowledge enough of Wisconsin Rapids. Rapids was a sulfide process papermill town and with a direct wind Wisconsin Rapids told all it needed to say about itself to farmers who knew enough about the extracurricular taints of existence but still couldn't abide Rapids. Calf pens left a month over-long weren't as bad as Rapids on a breeze. We imagined the natives of that city to be badly shrunken by the vapors, probably no more than three feet tall. Too, we heard the river was gray and gelatinous from all the leftover wood-pulp and acids dumped into the stream. Foam so thick, bergs of it caught in the underbrush and formed bridges that wove and collapsed with the wind. Heard of kids who thought the bridges real because they had seen spiders and butterflies crossing and when they went at them drowned in the shallows and the sheer rupture of dreams. But these were distances not parameters, to the township, even Plover village was remote. My world was bound by more important and civil institutions.

North, the kingdom held as far as the Community Club named after my great grandfather's bequest of two acres for the club building and school. The school remained until 1954 when the enlightenment of the consolidated school system replaced it and I began a succession of love affairs with the various city girls that were to coarse and lacerate my heart. The road to the Community Club lay between Wiggy's Woods on the west and Altenburg's to the east and was a good township road except for the one stretch where a hard right angle suffered an unusual sand wallow. A bicycle had to be pushed by hand through the two hundred feet of openly consumptive sand. Pushing a bicycle was less chore than a demotion to a kid who had the distinct faith he could, if liberated from chores, propel his bicycle of genuine Schwinn manufacture around the world and back without once getting off. The sand wallow was an embarrassment. To be seen pushing a bicycle was the worst of social disgraces. Yet none of memory could avoid it. Not even Dickie Eiden who could ride a bicycle backwards and besides had the best bike in the whole town what with the fenders off and those modern tires. But Dickie lived on the state route which was concrete, and ultra-thins didn't work for nothing on the town roads.

North was mostly Wiggy's Woods. Joe and Teddy lived in the house over. Retired bachelors, they had moved to the township in the thirties.

Joe was seen often enough, even coming to crews for barn-building and silo-filling and down-cow-butchering and what tendencies remained yet to crew, what with threshing gone in the wake of the combines. Teddy was not seen much. It was known he had been married to an eastern lady of real society and she'd been killed in an automobile accident. Most folks said Teddy was crazy, that being sufficient reason for our caution. Still Wiggy's Woods was handsome. Being pastured, the undergrowth held back so there was no fear of losing the trail as in a wild woods which had the confounding tendency to whirl the four cardinal directions around so if you entered from the west and perceived yourself bearing east, somehow you ended up on the south. You could almost see through Wiggy's Woods. Nor did Joe seem to mind the neighbor boys coveting his woods as a handy ground to carry on the diplomacies of those approaching puberty. Wiggy's Woods was the first place beside the apple-grove and the cow-pasture we pitched what then passed for a tent.

Seven dollars worth of green canvas and two wooden poles shared between three boys and two dogs. The company formed on the previous union of the two dogs, one a highland collie the other a handsome country rogue who had populated the female with its life-strand. The offspring were to be sold to the highest bidder whereby the five principals of the company would grant stock shares in a two-man green pup-tent from page 711 in the Monkey Ward catalogue, shipping weight 7 pounds 3 ounces, $6.54 plus shipping. The thesis seemed reasonable enough but a market in hybrid dogs was lacking in our township. When we persisted, my father who had his own motives, decided to buy the whole batch for seven dollars even or the pup-tent on page 711. On the birth of the puppies, Pa was given immediate custody and advanced their careers to the backside of the granary from where they were never seen or heard from again. We knew exactly how much that pup-tent cost and while moral indignities swirled through us, the consequence was to place this event in the category of bull calves and October chickens. We did not allow the puppy pail to impinge our delight when the item, #760243B

green arrived and we, on a rainy night in July, attended the first extra-
territorial venture in our lives.

Tommy Soik lived north by a forty. Tommy was Catholic, uncir-
cumsized and fatherless, Leo and the middle daughter having been killed
in an auto accident when a semi-truck smacked them broad as they returned with groceries. This was where federal route 51 and state road 54
join below the hills at the Moore Barn tavern. The truck driver was
reportedly under the influence, cementing the worst temperance fears of
my parents that alcohol was the center of ruin and damnation. My father
sensed a territorial shift when Leo died. He could talk to Leo even if he
was Catholic and he knew Leo could talk to him even though he was
Methodist. They both knew as long as they were each other's neighbor
the world would be right. Leo someday might even have persuaded my
dad to try a cool stock-tank beer after haying and flop in the front yard
with him. After Leo's death my father took a whole new stand against
alcohol. Alcohol had ruined his fenceline and his sense of symmetry with
the world. There were lots of other folks God could have killed instead
of Leo—his brother Edmund, for instance. Edmund raised potatoes on
the forty east from Leo's. Let the cows stretch that fence reaching for a
morsel on Edmund's side and the phone would be ringing in the hour
and Edmund using language every farmer knows is reserved for only the
most severe of occasions, and don't take the chance of wearing it out
beforehand or it won't work when it's supposed to.

I loved Tommy as my brother, better even. Tommy was uncircum-
sized and showed me so, and I showed him mine and he wished mine
was his 'cause it had a more dangerous look. You can't help but love a
friend who looks at you that way. I told him his looked the more secret
and if we could I'd trade even-up. And he told me about catechism and
I told him about methodee Sunday School and we figured it was pretty
much the same god between us. He dreamed of a BB gun some day and
wanted to be a cowboy when he grew up, just like me. Or maybe a pilot,
just like me. He lived in the little house Leo built after the big house

burned in '47. I could make it to his house in less than three minutes when the road had been sprayed down with a solution from the papermill that smelt bad for a couple days but made a sand and gravel road almost as good as pavement. Any time after dark I could pedal the distance in under a minute due to older brother's casual inference of a saber-toothed tiger in the woods west.

East was bounded by the Liberty Corners Methodist kirk on country trunks J and JJ exactly in the middle of what natives call the prairie—the whole place the geological aftermath of the Wisconsin glaciation of 20,000 years previous and its kinsman another 100,000 winters before. In the hollow of the two moraines, standing like fossil waves of an ancient tide, were some of the finest upland soils in the entire north. You could see the church from Grandpa's place over by the stage-road. The term stage-road had been an antique expression for a generation but Grandpa held on to it for its sense of pageantry. There was something biblical about that road being called the stage-road. 'Cause, he said, nothing was a thing without coming from someplace. Not even creation born out of a six-day fit came from nowhere. People oughta know, he said, the world hadn't always been pneumatic tires and winter plowed.

Rare in that time was the man or farmer permitted to forego Sunday churching. The sheer sum of reasons precludes cataloging. Modern sensibilities cannot understand when a man or farmer went to church it didn't mean he was in due consequence its believer. To my ancestral grandfathers the two could be and often were mutually exclusive. A man could church from the time of his confirmation to his funeral oration all without unduly stretching his mental torso. Faith was a suit of Sunday blues. You wore it. Sunday was the preacher's god. Monday to Saturday night, maybe even right up to the doors of the kirk itself on Sunday morning, was the field-god. Sometimes they were the same god, sometimes not. Related, Grandpa thought, anyhow it didn't really matter. The Sunday god had to be democratic. You couldn't have the deity of hill farmers mixing with the sovereign of muck farmers and expect any consensus. The preacher was thence allowed his passions to proclaim just about any worship he desired from the Sunday pulpit. It didn't matter in the least and none took umbrage 'cause, well, just 'cause that was the think of it.

A good sermon lasted twenty minutes, a better one went thirty. Better because thirty minutes of nap was better than twenty minutes. Twenty minutes left a man groggy and the last hymn two-thirds past before he could work his mouth right. The Liberty Corners Buena Vista Methodist Church had been designed for the churching of farmers. The oak pews had wing-back end boards that a man could settle up against and it would hold his shoulder up without his paying any attention. A like brace was carpentered to the middle of all the center pews so the divine aspects of side pews was not lost on center pews of double length. With practice a man learned to hold his head up and sleep thirty minutes solid. You'd see 'em winding down from the third verse of the second hymn on past the Apostle's Creed so by the time of the sermon their legs were wobbly and some almost tipped off standing up.

Celluloid collars remained a fashion at Liberty Corners long after they had disappeared in the outside world. With high collars a man didn't need balance to maintain an acceptable perspective. Of course there were preachers who took insult to the majority of the adult males in the congregation nodding off at the handsomest occurence of his theatrics. Preachers who were over-loud or slew beyond the standard rim of the pulpit were not long countenanced at the Liberty Corners Buena Vista Methodist Church. Not that the congregation had any full right to escape the errant behavior of clergy. The ministry was shared with the village but what was acceptable in the village of five work days and eight hours per diem was not determinant at the juncture of J and JJ. A preacher given to indiscriminate bellars, screechings and flailings of prophetory aspect was simply not bestowed the classic township gratuities. Free chickens, free potatoes, free calves liver and first serving at the church supper and fall bazaar. The lobby could be carried on even more diligently if the cleric was resistant, such that if mired in a spring road the route became suddenly untraveled. In due course the menfolk could count on a thirty minute nod.

The fragility of the system was exposed when preachers in a new fashion had sermons lasting only ten or fifteen minutes. Took too much practice to have any useful benefit from a ten minute nod. None of it would have happened if it hadn't been for television and football. It was television, football and Paul Hornung that extinguished the thirty minute preacher. Churching went from an affair of a good hour and a half to one hour complete, from the front steps and finding dry matches to light the candles to blessing, evacuation and discussion of corn prices.

Grandpa's place was east, Eugene Fletcher, #2 son of Charles who farmed in the Valley Down as separated from the Valley Up and Valley Over, which was Albertie's and MacLaren's. Grandpa's brother Don was planted in the lee of Moore Hill, George on Valley Up's prairie, Claire and Earl in the flats of Valley Down and Eugene spread both ways. From my perspective these brothers owned 90 percent of all creation or of what parts as mattered. All were members of the Liberty Corners Buena Vista Methodist Church and any two of them could not agree over any one object of discourse no matter the selection of the topic involved. If one bought war-bonds the other accused him of being a war-monger while another thought the enemy of instance weren't such bad fellows in the first place. The others weren't even willing to admit the last war had finished satisfactorily.

Grandpa's house was situated at the hump of the hill where County J rises out of the Valley Over and the stage route issued over the berm and hedge cairns of Valley Down. It was a conversational strategem. Every rig, tractor and engine seeking relief after the hills found it at the stock-tank of Eugene Fletcher, just two rods off the road with an overflow pipe spilling into the ditch. Any neighbor headed for market, hardware or funeral turned in at Gene's for a last topping of the radiator before pending Moore Hill another half mile beyond.

Was it his desire, Grandpa Eugene could attend the various news services passing through the township by going to skim the stocktank. Hot mornings, shot to pieces by neighbors in a mouth mood, defined Eugene Fletcher and his farm biggings. The house of Eugene always stood in a delicate balance between prime and dismissed. The clapboards needed paint, eventually getting it at the precise moment when they would have gone from fallow to weedy. At the precipice of graying wood gone to dark rot Eugene Fletcher managed his farm and biggin'. A weld delayed, a broken window pane, a mend of the wrong size, or sock stuck in the offending fissure. A winter wind smuggled through the vacancy of window froze the pulsators of the milking machines so they had to be het-up on the stove and milking lasted till 10 o'clock in the morning. Eugene succeeded exactly where he wanted to and pretty much at his own speed.

He was acknowledged as the best surviving woodstove cook on the prairie, an honor given to the enduring tenure of the last wood-fired stove. His specialty was raw fries, sliced ham, eggs, toast, welsh marmalade, a side of pancakes with silver maple syrup or comb honey. His faith was in two meals a day except when laying to, such as haying, rock-picking or dehorning calves. Otherwise noon was a slice of bread, a glass of milk from the can-cooler and ten minutes of yesterday's newspaper before twenty minutes of nap. Supper was boiled tatees, roast, canned corn, salt pickles, squash, sauerkraut, home bread, gravy, two helpings of pie with ice-cream and maybe a pan of popcorn before bed. He was long and slim and his bib overalls hung on him with enough shim for two others of his dimension on the inside. His cowlick came from the side of his head rather than the back. No matter how he wetted and brushed, it bloomed. Eugene had a doctor's prescription to take glasses but held off until the last years of his life. The circumference of things he chose to see was about all he wanted to deal with anyway.

South, a mile exactly, was the north branch of the Buena Vista Creek, labeled on the map the Isherwood Ditch. My cousins called it ditch and were in the habit of calling it ditch because one of 'em had been on the

Drainage Commission since the turn of the century. Ditching, they held, was to the general health and environment of the Buena Vista Marsh. Since first light on a Sunday morning attempting to circle heifers I have been at blood odds to drainage. Drainage to the marsh was what Sunday School was to my soul, an attempt to tame, straighten and otherwise ruin the last fully free and wild resource on the planet. No philosopher of laissez-faire had to teach me there was already harvest enough, and I and every farmboy since the piney days knew that. The swamp was the one timeless center of our lives. There we took our first smokes, panned gold or what we allowed as gold, wondered at the purpose of girls, and questioned the distributional circumstances of creation.

South was Ted Jensen's place at the old muck experiment station, the cottage house set well back from the road along with the cream-colored barn and machine shed. Every fall we filled Ted's silo and took dinner at Mrs. Jensen's table and smelt the tangible vapors of what it must have been like to crew a threshing, the one lingering residue of a hunting society and clan.

South was Bannack's sawmill at the spring head and the buildings of their first settling hard-up against the swamp. The deserted house still had lace curtains at the windows and doilies on the cabinettes. A wool-felt rug on the floor and austere ovals of ancestral Bannacks hung on vintage wallpaper. The house had the look of recent abandonment; ice-box, parlor stove and rug duster, a case of empty beer bottles in the corner, the kind with bottoms three-quarters of an inch thick. The window bay was the exact measure and purpose for laying out a coffin, with purple velvet drapes and tassels. We never knew for sure the logistics of the Bannack evacuation. The place was handsome, not dangled clapboard or a rotten porch step in sight. What could have driven 'em out? The swamp? Murder maybe? Something to do with the Courtwrights who were lynched just before the turn of the century, they saying the Masonics done it and Bannacks were Masons once, then a peculiar and sudden switch to Catholocism?

Not two hundred yards from the Bannack place was Myron Wood's junkpile. Myron was the local electronics and radio repairman. So the pile consisted of radio tubes, motors, rheostats, carbide headlights, headsets, antenna insulators, miscellaneous horns and dials. We were sure the dials were connected to the V-2 rocket base at Peenemunda, which had come into Myron Wood's possession because he was in reality an agent for Winston Churchill himself and as a reward for his tapping Mister Hitler's phone with built-in translator had received war spoils personally from Winnie for what advantage it might give to the American allies-perhaps rocket-propelled tractors. If Myron would wire it, we'd ride it. That junkpile had possibilities, if assembled just right, that would permit voice transmission to Mars and beyond to the folks of Alpha Centauri and if we did contact them we had our questions ready, like what were girls for? Myron Wood's junkpile was the primest of junk. The esteemed materials were lugged home in sacks, packs, wagons and barrows to be redistributed to a thin veneer of rocket engineers, space cadets and bomb scientists.

Myron's second cousin was the barber in the village and detailed to Myron his overstock of Police Gazettes. In course these, too, found their way to the junkpile, after which the first rain cemented them together. This ruined the epidermis of any sensational enlightenment but preserved the interiors for future archaeologists.

West, Harold Edwards' place, his sawmill, his four daughters, his Case Model 7 tractor. West was Whittaker's Woods which my dad bought in '51. It came into our possession as Garth was setting up a sport shop in the rivertown. He needed money. My dad needed land. A farmer with three sons has an expansive nature. He had just bought, for 1100 dollars cash, an Allis Chalmers Model WD with a wide-front-end. Whittaker's Woods is where Gary, my younger brother, lost his finger—the second joint on the right side, middle finger—to a wagon hitch. Losing a finger was the most rapid sort of advancement a boy could wish on himself, a station ordinarily achieved by only the most lofty chieftains. Harold

Edwards was missing the first and thumb on the right, Harrison Newby was without a right thumb and no left middle, Rob Berry vacant for all but one on the right, Bob Steinke down to the last two on the right. Dad had the joints of two set stiff from a sawmill. Winny Altenbourgh was decapitated. A missing finger was a mark of distinction and the little brother had it at the age of five without hardly even trying. I learned early fate wasn't fair. That the same finger in later years voided for him the whole Vietnam debate was but a continuance of destiny in a desultory mood.

West was Puznach's, a forty opposite Whittaker's woods with relic house and barn. Pa rented the land for $15 an acre for five years then bought it in a series of payments lasting ten years. It meant 80 acres square counting Whittaker's. Handsome ground with a white pine grove, blueberries and jungles of blackberry and bear track. Lasted but ten years when the Wisconsin Department of Transcience decided to renovate federal route 51 by taking it out of the hills and running it smack dab into the heart and lungs of the Buena Vista. Drove due-north through Whittaker forty and the best alfalfa patch we owned or dreamed of.

Shortly after we bought the Puznach place, County Welfare asked whether there'd be interest in renting it as subsidized housing. At $18.50 a month my dad was interested. For five years Charles Bentley lived at Puznach's, in the half of the house we didn't use to store oats. Bentley, two cats and his three-quarter ton Dodge truck. Chores ordinarily detailed us to Puznach's for fifteen sacks of oats on Saturday mornings after barn cleaning. Our old man never wised up to the sudden occurence of his sons noting it was both proper and fitting for all of them to sack oats when a year previous the same chore was considered among the worst of the possible choices. Except for the three miles total in a half-ton brown Studebaker, likened in our minds to Enzo Ferrari's machinery, Phil Hill at the wheel; a four-wheel-drift may have been an easy thing in a Ferrari, it was quite another attainment in a half-ton four-lung "Stoodie" with fifteen sacks of white oats.

Charles Bentley's age was somewhere in the low seventies. He had seen a world which was thereto none of our experience. His list of achievements included a little time in jail for some social faux pas, enlistment as a bouncer in a Chicago speak-easy, a number of relationships loosely labeled marriage, and in general, a perspective which was then to us the very embodiment of an anti-matter universe. And he shared cigarettes. Called 'em butts. Ma pronounced the word, cig-gretts, two syllables, like regrets. Smokes and coffee he offered. We pumped his water, shoveled snow, disconnected his truck battery and put it behind the stove where he stashed it like the essence of survival itself. As a result of a visit to Bentley's we found ourselves grinding feed, forking out the calf-pen and pitching silage with considerably more honesty and faith than we otherwise achieved, partly to cover the volatiles of cigarette smoke we knew clung to our hides like sin. Pa never seemed to notice the new efficiencies of the farm after his three boys from 11 to 17 years spent two and one half hours on a Saturday morning bagging fifteen sacks of oats. If he suspected, he said nothing.

Ma, we weren't so sure about. Not at all certain she couldn't detect the pheromones of cigarettes beneath fermented silage, calf-pens or feed-mill dust. Ma had a nose for that degree of trespass. Mouth odor was our defensive weakness. We had strategems, if not guaranteed to work, at least gave us time to cement a defense or acknowledge a week in her purgatory. "How could you?" "What would your grandma think?" "You know very well smoking is just the beginning of all sorts of bad habits, just look at Uncle Ray." It was always Uncle Ray. Uncle Ray really wasn't so bad but he did suffer the distinction of being the first in our line in something like two million years to get a divorce. And that didn't even begin to include his political opinions. Uncle Ray voted for Roosevelt, the first time. Not just the second and third try as did a lot of township Republicans who went FDR once the war was off the ground. Uncle Ray served as the prime example throughout our educative years of what not to be, or think. He ran a general grocery, taught public school at the Lac du Flambeau reservation, and finished out at a filling station. Uncle Ray knew everything. When my dad oughta sell corn instead of bringing in more heifers. Or that he ought to sell the pulp out of the woods 'cause the papermill in Rhinelander is paying 11 dollars a cord and what good was the woods doing him the way it was?

Steeping a handful of silage in your mouth for ten minutes was a pretty good defense against an Uncle Ray lecture. Onions worked too but were a dead give-away. Soybean meal was also known to cover the tongue tars of Kool cigarettes as could a pint of warm milk from a fresh cow, if it didn't glue your mouth together entirely.

West was the Maine School and the Maine Cemetery at the physical diameter of our liege. West was Willie's place. William Tech lived two forties up from Harold Edwards. His folks had traded steads with my Grandpa Isherwood so consolidating their acreage with their habitations. Architecturally Willie's house was of the muck-prairie design, a square frame house, thirty foot on the side with a central chimney. The south and west face each had an enclosed porch for winter insulation. The west porch was the sleeping porch once summer had honestly arrived. The south porch started slow calves, piglets and tomatoes.

Willie Tech had a singular calling. He could pass the time of day with a 12-year-old kid as well as he could with any other township citizen, without acute embarrassment. Nobody knew better the ways of trout in the swamp back the Buena Vista. Whether the hulking browns under Eckels' bridge, brookies at Cold Meet, or rainbows at the bridgehead of the old Coddington Railroad Line. Nobody else but Willie filed a #12 brass hook so the barb didn't catch without him deliberately setting it. Was like a man using a crank-starter for the sake of art. Willie was not above offering a beer to a 16-year-old. Taken out behind the house and the lilacs, on the bench in front of his two-holer with six feet of a fox snakeskin nailed to it and license plates going back to '19. Willie planted hedgerows the length and breadth of his property on May mornings by getting up an hour early, milking the cows and before breakfast setting out fifty white pines with space for wild crabs, sumac and whip oaks. Willie Tech was the most holy man of my existence. Willie knew the earth was not so much the center of something as it was kindling to another energy. He had schooled with my grandma when she was 16 and he at 15 had a sudden boom for script. Grandpa Isherwood often kidded Adah that he should have traded her off to Willie when they swapped land back in '08, he getting Alice, she Willie. It was about as smutty a joke as my grandpa told or Adah imagined. Willie told her he didn't think much of the idea if maybe borrowin' won'ta been half bad.

Those were the marks of my ken. Like letters on the windvane, I had my directions. I was free to roam, after chores or in between. I do not think a Sioux boy had more liberty. There were wildlings and there were cultures in that township and they served me and I served them and they were responsible for the accidents and adjudications of humanity that were to follow.

PICTURES FROM A FAMILY ALBUM

MA TOLD US NEVER TO SAY THE WORDS 'IWO JIMA' IN earshot of Grandma Fletcher. We didn't, except it got said by someone else. Her body jerked as a bullet of remembrance lodged in her and as it turned, dislocated her balance. I saw her peeling potatoes with tears dripping off the ends of her fingers into the sink. God almighty, didn't know so many tears could run out from a person.

I knew they were brothers because I was told they were brothers. And because a picture of them stood in the tilted fashion of photographs on the top of the piano in my grandparent's living room for 35 years. A black and white photograph, color retouched, of two brothers in Marine Corps uniforms. One wearing a cloth garrison hat, the other in the beaked parade hat worn in the characteristic twist of Fletchers and not according to the uniform code. They were brothers, one Jerome, the other Kingsley, in fact they looked like brothers. The photograph on the piano was never moved and rarely touched. Grandmother dusted with a damp cotton rag as the custom among farmwomen. Them, she dusted with a peacock feather.

The photo was common and perhaps classic of the early 1940s. Handsome boys smiling at an unknown photographer who made his fortune capturing ghosts of soldiers told to smile for "the folks back home." The smile grew haunting. Seen every Christmas, every holiday, winter Sunday afternoon and Saturday night spent at Grandpa's house.

They were ordinary boys, they were me and my brothers in a different time, same but for time. Buena Vista farmboys born near the end of an eleven-member family; one in 1921, one in '24. Born at a distance from power they had little idea of, or use for. I wonder if even then the drums must not have begun the slow roll and muted cadence that would one day get farmboys to turn in step to a single holler.

Their task was to go for cows in the morning, in the 6 o'clock morning only hillcountry and summer produce. Like me they went for mud puddles, could throw stones with their toes and found comfort on an October morning standing barefoot in a fresh dropped cow-pie. Don't suppose they ever answered the queries either. Of why they stopped at the pump and washed their feet on such a frosty morning. They learned, as is custom of Buena Vista boys, to pick stones and as is custom to hate stones. A matter of farmboy pride, to hate stones, hate the stone-boat and hate the glacier-ruined fields. They knew how to hoe corn, milk cows, smoke corn silk, tend hogs, chop chickens, curry horses, split stovewood and the thousand other chores a farm inflicts.

I cannot remember them without remembering the piano. A William J. Ennis player-piano of Boston and Fall River. Grandpa bought it new and heavy from the Daly Music Company of Grand Rapids in 1922 for the incarnate sum of 500 dollars even. Was a crazy purchase. Five hundred dollars in 1922 was a herd of cows, a parcel of 40 acres cleared and 40 acres wooded. Five hundred dollars was a motorcar and a college education.

And that player piano was $500. It was music; music even a farmer could catch. Grandpa Fletcher wasn't the only farmer to buy a player, half his neighbors had too. The player was the one chance they had of filling the house with the elixiral stuff called music. They all bought players; Berrys of Valley Down, Whittakers, Alberties, even Eckels. Did the salesmen wonder what was in these people that made them so hungry for music? Their lives? The work? The stony fields? Perhaps it was style. Style bought and sold ninety percent of what any drummer had to offer. Salesmen did not philosophize out loud or to any length; instead they rubbed their hands and sold their pianos.

The piano had come a long way to make it to a Buena Vista farmhouse. John Isaac Hopkins of Philadelphia invented the space-saving upright piano. He sold the first to a T. Jefferson of Virginia who returned it because it wouldn't stay in tune. The union of piano and the parlor waited on an invention of an Alpens Babcock of Boston, who poured the first cast-iron string bed, iron doing for pianos what it had already done for jail doors and windows. The tune, so to speak, kept in place. No matter a Wisconsin winter able to crack elm stovewood and give creak and groan to every floor and chair in the house. Or the perversity of summer to swell a door shut as if secured with nails. No matter. The piano stayed in tune, or at least approximate tune. This was good enough music for farmers and Buena Vista boys, like the approximate warmth of a fresh October cow-pie. Approximate music is better than no music, and Thomas Jefferson would have been pleased.

The encyclopedia says H. B. Tremaine invented the player piano in 1886. Invented is a word you have to use with caution, nobody really invents anything. They borrow and pass on borrowings. On Grandma's bookshelf, "Heroes of the Civil War," it says John McTammany invented the self-playing piano and also had the claim chiseled into his tombstone. George B. Kelly developed the windmotor and Elias Parkman Needham manufactured the first perforated music roll. What H. B. Tremaine did in 1886 is nothing more than apply a blacksmith's bellows to the windmotor. The bellows pumped air out of the piano causing air to be drawn through the holes in the music roll which admitted atmospheric pressure by way of tidy rubber hoses to individual key bellows, 88 of them, which struck the corresponding key with the right force. The aeromotor rotated the paper roll and two levers controlled the direction of the roll and speed. I always thought a player piano was a lot like people, the way air is breathed into them, a steady chore, whether of music or life.

Pianos acquire inertia, that word I found in "One Thousand Science Experiments", meaning some possession of energy of place or energy of motion. Grandpa Fletcher's player piano had place. Once a piano is in the house they rarely get moved out. Houses are destroyed before a piano is. When the tornado unhinged Albertie's house and exploded Mrs. Albertie's dresser drawers and we went and tried to find most of it and embarrassed 'cause as it were mostly her under-stuff and window curtains, the piano remained. Hadn't moved an inch in spite of 500 miles an hour and ten tons of suction. Pianos, I think, must have a soul. Anything that is one place long enough is going to have one whether it wants to or not. Pianos steal the leftovers from the souls of flesh and blood members in a house and folks seem aware of the particular solidness and affirmation they get from a piano. On pianos they place the photographs of the honored dead and the family Bible, entrusted to something constant, something immovable like a stone altar.

Music is not easy. A man will swear in public before he will sing. Most farmers don't sing in church. They just stand there. I don't know if it's the words or what. Pa said he didn't have voice Sunday morning 'cause of dust and he weren't used to it. Is a lie. I heard Pa singing "Just Beyond the Sunset" a hundred times when he thought he's alone. Soon as you come in he shuts off. Pa could vibrate a silo.

A player piano let them out, the secret singer. Pumping the bellows after supper kinda got a man in the mood. The music so infective he is swayed by it. In the evening after a spring in the fields and fried potatoes with horseradish for supper, Grandpa couldn't keep the music down.

Saturday nights music shook Grandpa's house, reverberated around the parlor, bounced off the family, and like high-energy bomb-blast went right through them.

Pa never went to war. Neither did Grandpa. Whole family missed out on the Civil War. Grandma Isherwood said she had a great great uncle who almost got to Waterloo but it was over by the time he got there. Other kids had war stories, Arlyn Clark, Louis Simmonds too, stories for the schoolyards. Of uncles and fathers who went to war. Stories of wounds and medals. Stories made awful and real by parts of carbines, and Louie's dad had a German luger and a letter found fluttering across the broken ground, written in German.

Uncle Jerome wasn't any help. He was killed ten yards up the pumice beach of that volcanic island. Ma said it was a land mine, killed everyone bang-dead in the landing craft. February 20, 1945. As a schoolyard story the death of Uncle Jerome didn't have any appeal. What kind of hero is that? Saw the letter Grandma Fletcher got and the purple heart and a gold star for her. Said something about valor and courage. More like the killing of kittens with a ballpeen hammer if you ask me.

Uncle Dean, Aunt Audry's husband, said the hospital ships stayed about ten miles offshore, depending on the accuracy of hostile shore batteries. The wounded were ferried back to the hospital ship and hoisted over the side with a cargo net. Dead or alive, they were all taken to the same ship. Part of the hospital ship, he said, was for embalming. A tube exited the ship below the waterline, a black rubber hose six inches in diameter and three hundred feet long. Sharks constantly prowled the end of the tube and the ship had to circle to spread them out.

Encyclopedia says embalming began in the Civil War. Invented by Thomas C. Holmes, called himself the father of modern chemical embalming. Claimed he embalmed 4,028 soldiers and officers in 1863. He also invented modern root beer, it said.

When Jerome Fletcher was shipped home in the summer of 1946, Doc Winfield opened the casket to verify identity. Later he told Pa, Jerome was "quite perfect, not a mark on him, you'd think he was just sleeping."

Embalming is a kind of hibernation; it is different from regular death. Regular death is clumsy, ugly if left out in the open and you don't want the skull for a birdhouse. Ma never liked when I used cow skulls for birdhouses. Already had holes about the right size, the brain case the exact amount of room for sparrows and tree swallows. Don't see what Ma had against skulls, didn't need paint either, and hunters leave'm alone. A skull gave a fencepost a soul better than barb wire. It kept something off that barb wire couldn't defend. And when a skull fell off the post, it didn't leave nails behind to wound feet and hooves and paws, it just went off, went away with the wind, the dirt and its allies.

The player piano in the parlor corner wasn't used much after 1941. With the boys at war the piano seemed too noisy. Evenings they wanted nothing more than the clock and the fire in the stove. Piano music might cover up the sound a farmboy whispers in the darkness a world away. Grandma listening for him while knitting or candling eggs and Grandpa listened, too, with his head against the flank of a milkcow. Did they know the moment he was killed? You'd think they would. They made him, most of him was connected to them. Ma knows about things in me even before I tell her.

After awhile mice got at the player. Seen mice empty the bottom three feet of a corn crib just 'cause it was covered with a snow drift. Someone tried the piano. Pulled out the stool, flipped down the pedals, slipped the lever to forward and nothing happened.

A piano tuner told them repair cost too much and besides, player-pianos weren't in style any longer. He cleaned out the piano for them, so they could use it like a regular piano, and it wouldn't attract mice. Charged them just a tuning fee.

So the piano fell altogether silent. The rolls were lain in boxes, hauled to the attic and put away with other stuff. His parade hat, some bullets he sent home to Uncle Curtis, the flag and the bow and arrow he made when he was fourteen and almost like me. The piano took up the new function. The pure function of monument. Was like going to his grave, that piano. Exactly like his grave, even the smell was the same.

ACHIEVABLE MIRACLE

THE CONGREGATE OF THE LIBERTY CORNERS BUENA Vista Methodist Church comprised of all the practicing or liberally documented Protestants in Buena Vista Township. Its membership spread haphazardly into Plover Town and extended its tentative theos into the Stockton Townships and Arnott village. Liberty Corners had long served the community as a public school, a store of general merchandise, as well as the church and attendant parsonage ten rods back. Most Sunday morning worships gained the witness of approximately twenty-five parishioners, this numerical population being neither the fault of the particular congregate or lack in the epistle's delivery. Essentially the Liberty Corners Buena Vista Methodist Church shared the fault of all Protestantism. A failing not over-looked by the Catholics, Baptists and what few specimens of Lutherans known to exist. The difference was damnation whose act and transport was directly hitched to church attendance. The Methodism as practiced at Liberty Corners did not subscribe to the principle. As a

25

consequence the Liberty Corners Methodist was less popular on Sunday mornings than the Catholic institute on the high road. This numerical disloyalty did not sit comfortably within the bosoms of itinerant preachers serving the church. Despite the repair being obvious, Methodism never picked up on this cue and never in its existence knew the swollen and appreciative audience as those filled the walls of Saint Martin's Catholic below Keene and the Buena Vista Creek. The only distinctive adjustment to this situation was Easter Sunday morning at Liberty Corners when attendance to the Liberty Corners kirk blossomed toward a favorable comparison to attendance-minded damnation. Why local clergy did not reform the obvious cue will be left to further researches.

Casual notions can be forwarded as to the cause of Easter morning's popularity. It was, after all, spring in a farm country. Seeding being the fragile novitiate it is, and cold ground, and the skies gray with threat, besides winter licking at the windowpane every night. If religion can aid the yeoman who can use all the cheap labor he can get what with seed up a dollar, the drill in need of a new set of drab links and the wheel bearing yodeling, then that religion has some direct utility, hence an appreciative audience.

Easter is a movable feast. Spring is pretty movable too, the connection is not lost on farmers. All others Christmas, the Fourth of July, Valentine's—are all immovable observances. Village folk might well accept as holy a solid event, but that class of event is suspect in the rurals. The reason revolves around the heart of farmers, faith as they know it is less in solid magnificence than slippery sovereignty. Farming and its habitant are fragile, they aren't always where the calendar or ledger says they ought.

Easter, too, is elastic, exactly like everything else that is real in the universe. Easter hobbles across the calendar from a Sunday in late March to almost May. Easter thus is real, same as frost going out. A vagrant, along with the other affairs of cosmo-mechanics, thus gaining a considerable say with the rest of what counted at Liberty Corners.

First Sunday after the first full moon after the vernal equinox there is Easter, right in there with stars and orbits and when to plant oats and red clover. What the event has to do with resurrection didn't matter, least not at the Liberty Corners Methodee. Not that the local preacher understood this facsimile of theology, neither could he explain the factors involved when Easter morning attendance at the Buena Vista Methodist soared all out of previous pattern. What he did know was a new pride and sudden glory inhabited the plain white church on the corners of County J and double J. He could feel the hot breath of the congregation, the smells of scrubbed children, the sweet lacquered womenfolk in pillbox hats, and working men rigidly sacred in their one dress shirt and polished shoes.

Those were the days before clerical robes came in Protestant ranks; then a clerical robe on a Methodist preach smacked of Catholicism. Granted, the preacher well might have traded his dark wool suit for a clerical robe if it was device enough to fill the church like what went over at St. Martin's Catholic every Sunday morning. Still, the Methodee preachers must have known Easter Sunday was satisfactory enough and, to tell truth, if the populace spilled out every Sunday in a like manner, there'd be no pleasure in it anymore. In course, the preachers to this rural park and parish came to view the world like their farmer-kind and offer reverence for its seasons.

Liberty Corners kirk is a typical country church. Farmers of the domain constructed it a hundred years previous using square nails, virgin white pine boards and clap. Painted white, it had six stained-glass windows in abstract design in blue, yellow and red. The leaded panes cut in geometric shapes often were more pleasing to the eye than the sermon was to the ear. Entry to the building was offered by a set of concrete steps leading through double wood doors. The double doors were of course all out of proportion with the normal demand, but the church couldn't admit folks with a single door and feel very proud of itself. A small side-table guarded the vestibule where the Lenten banks were placed and parishioners who had not recently attended were duely noted by the layer of dust allowed to accumulate on top of their banks. The procedure was meant to coerce those who did not to attend; it failed. Citizens of the valleys were not, for some reason, embarrassed by geological accumulation. As time passed, the vestibule table came less to represent condemnation than a catalogue of all persons thought members of this elect body of the faithful but chose to keep the distance until the severe moment.

On the north wall of the vestibule hung a framed record of those of the congregation who served the Armed Forces during the Second World War. The banner read, "Those in Service," below was an illustration of sailors, pilots and helmeted soldiers looking off to the distant horizon where stood a single illuminated cross. The names were listed by rank and branch of service. Every Sunday the congregate trooped past this list of names. I looked to them as if they were some sort of saints. My Uncle Jerome's name was there, Lance Corporal, United States Marine Corps, dead ten years previous. Grandma Fletcher rarely attended church, and when she did someone discreetly removed the framed list. The blank of unfaded paint made it ghastly obvious the implement was missing. I looked to the blank out of habit, and his name seemed there yet. Grandma Fletcher always left the service weeping. Even as a child I knew well enough why, that wall was awful obvious.

Easter Sunday served an important function in Valley Up, Valley Down, Valley Over for a variety of reasons, none of which can be substantiated. A sudden propulsion came over the farmers of the moraine, its source, the preacher felt, was a new perspective on their mortality and worldliness. They wished to know Jesus again, he thought it was his passion, death and the miraculous resurrection which brought them out. That he was at the epicenter of the event and promoted it with his mouth served his thesis admirably. He was wrong. Most preachers were and had little power to be any else than wrong. Preachers came awkwardly into the lives of the Buena Vista townsmen. They licked the cherry off the ice cream, they married them, buried them and baptized. From this, the itinerants took the succor of the importance, sensed their community position and their spiritual profundity. Buena Vista was the humble flock and they were bringing them to pasture.

When the preachers mentioned their version of belief in the realm of Valley Up, Valley Over and Valley Down, the congregate neither complained nor censured. Menfolk nodded knowingly at the preacher's words, a nod composed of 90% loss of consciousness and 10% affirmative behavior known to keep the man from raising his voice just when a farmer had a good somnolence going in the warmth of the red oak pews. The preacher for his own sake noticed only the saintly congregation drifting deep into the bliss of his words. If he valued his survival he left them so and gained what gentle godliness was available from these people and their country.

The pattern deviated with Easter. The Berrys from over on the hill road came to church as did four sets of Bardens and six extensions of the Newby-Precourt alliance all the way from Stevens Point. All the hired men of the valleys were boosted up in hand-me-down suits and kept sober by several different conspiracies. MacLarens, Alberties, Orgish, MacRaths, Gilmans, they all came, along with any camp followers and mercenaries. The kirk so swollen that every established pew pattern was overthrown. Even if the men felt any ambition for a morning nod, the sunlight fell wrong in a strange pew, and he couldn't get the thing going. Besides, the preacher could not be bound. Suddenly he possessed an enormous congregation. Brought, he wished, by word of his majesty when in the hands of the Lord. His only thought was to give them the most divine measure of his righteous noise. The congregate knew punishment was in store, escape was impossible and they had to manner through it as best they could.

At Easter the congregation got up its biannual choir, Christmas being the other instance. The reason was less the desire to sing as it was for womenfolk to show off a new dress and for what menfolk as could be enlisted to have a reserved seat for the affair.

Over the generations, three Easter anthems were known to the populace. The reason was not original in so much as these were the only three songs they knew how to sing with any steady pressure. To learn another required at least a generation of indoctrination, and since the hymns had served their own childhoods, they were good enough. Besides, they knew the words and some of the, if inexact, harmonies. A new anthem would have severely limited the choir numbers. None wished to chance the elevation of the choirstand on an unexplored tune when 95% of the Protestant community was gathered in witness below them.

The choice of the Sunday anthem at the Liberty Corners Buena Vista Methodist Church was a source of suspense the week before the actual event. The selection of the music was kept secret from the membership, the preacher going so far as to rehearse all known choices so any spies within earshot were no wiser of which was the real item. The object of this ploy preserved the betting system which had evolved around the Easter morning anthem. The entire community knew the possibles; "Oh, Jerusalem," "On a Hill Far Away" and last, the all-time favorite known by every tink, hired man and Moore Barn drunk, "Holy, Holy, Holy." Dimes, quarters, tobacco and sweet money were wagered, a half day picking rock or potatoes for the heavy hitters.

"A dime on Jerusalem."

"Naw, tit'll be Holy, Holy, Holy."

"I say Jerusalem 'cause Fanny is on this year and you know they always use her to blow when it's Jerusalem." Fannie did have the tendency to be audibly immodest.

Fannie Fletcher and Uncle Claire lived in mid-swoop of the road curve toward Valley Down. The farm one of those E-class varieties. Farms of the region were known to be of four different types, then and yet. D-class were the dilapidated specimens. Reasons varied, some simply so classified for want of paint. Mathematically two out of ten farms were D-class. Some husbandmen simply preferred life unencumbered by enamel, varnish, latex or even a milk and blood splash. Pine boards were supposed to be unadorned, and truth is some biggins are more handsome. They held a near-earth quality because of the enamel forebearance. Others were classed because they went habitually without window glass. Or because any death-taken cows were given no more formality than to be dragged into the field or barnyard, there to evaporate by native processes, relying on black fly, pale maggot, kit fox and moonlight dog. Oddly, D-class farms were equally distributed across the fiscal vistas. Some were among the wealthiest, some the poorest.

E-class were ekers. E-farms contrived a living and not much beyond that. They pivoted on luck, tenuous balance and heavenly intercession, a change in wind seemed enough to collapse their institute. Of all farmers, ekers are the happiest. They delight in every crop, every live-birth. Failure comes in the guise of milk-fever, Bangs-disease, tuberculosis, hardware, bloat. A calf born healthy was a special delight. When their potatoes ran 60 bushel they couldn't contain themselves and spoke handsomely of it at every intersection.

G-class farmers were gung-ho. They bought the latest mowers and enamel paint hay-crushers. They traded tractors every other year. If the barn needed a new roof, they put on everlasting steel instead of shingles. Before their peers, they explored irrigation, milk parlors, diesel engines, cash-crops and Florida vacations. To some, they were less farmers than entrepreneurs. Which is not to say they didn't love the land; they did but in a sense of foot-pounds per square inch, pH and plow horsepower. They loved their children and their women from an equal momentum and pride for their usefulness. Their children went to college and the farm institutes; their wives were the presidents of the March of Dimes or Extension Homemakers. Was bad karma to be born to a G-class farmer. The chores never ended, trout-fishing never won. These were the first farmers converted to leisure suits. When the old barn no longer suited them, they tore it down. They built a new ranch style house with a den, a built-in bar and two car garage. They did not wear their farming on their sleeve. This is not to say G-farmers did not know the spiritual release in a well-done boast. They knew they were getting 195 bushel an acre. They could prove it 'cause they were using the experiment station's test results on trace elements. They knew they themselves fed Chicago, Detroit and Minneapolis, they knew it and loved it. Why get involved with the intimacies when there was so much fun playing with the observables. G-class farmers were mostly by and large Republican and equally distributed between Catholocism and the Methodees.

The remainder are SS-class; steady-state. Farmers as their fathers had been farmers. Sons will be farmers and daughters will marry farmers. Easy as that. They existed, they survived, on occasion they were exalted. Once or twice in the while of their existence, steady-staters got a new tractor and tried the new feed-ration. Ekers and Steadies knew the intangible absence when Neil O'Keefe from Badger Breeders took over insemination duties from the divine hulk of sexual congress in the corner pen. They knew the rapture of spirit that sometimes visits a farmer, an entity quite beyond profit. Generally they were embarrassed or too shy to openly call it love, this alloy of man and a half section of dirt. Privately they knew, whether in the bodies of their sons, or in their heart bound to muck ground, or to the yellow sand and gravel moraine. Privately they could imagine making love to Earth, and a willful desire to put arms around her and hold her. A son went to the sand-pit and in a fantasy of lone adolescence sculpted the damp shape of woman. Prone, as he imagined her to be. If like most boys, he wasn't exactly sure of what gargoyle to put where. His only recourse was to extend the logic of his own reference to the anatomy of a bull, subtracting various measures, and do the same with the cows to get what in his mind was a reasonable facsimile to the female worship. Then he made love to it. A post-pubertal male can, will and does make love without reference to Linnean demarkations as long as he keeps himself above reptile. Existence for him is a study in restraint when his own chemistry is awful and implicit. Researchers would do well to find methods of moving puberty to a later address in the human span. Lives will be saved, education benefited, the safety of streets and roadways improved.

After spending himself for the sixth time since Sunday he found a love for earth. The smell of earth rose in him and he knew then his destiny. Perhaps evolution is responsible and provides the avenue of endearment at this particular moment. If so, then evolution is wise. Different results can be imagined were other resources at hand. While chic, these fates are impractical and perverse, and ruin any chance at tribe. To the landchild, all the distinction between what he loves is lost. Never as long as he lives can he escape. His ardor for spring is the same at 80 years as at 18. Again he feels the old distaff tug and the desire to go to her, to lay near and hold her. His passions extend to all things once he decides this central love. Differentiation is no longer his prerogative. Those who know him know his abandon, they'd not ask him the difference between love and lust. Twenty years married and she still will catch him watching her dress. The leer unmistakable, wanting to see again how her legs join the body, she knows he is seduced repeatedly by the geology of her shape. On Sunday morning he takes her to bathe in a spring he knows in the swamp, the one heated by sweet mold. There he watches her shed her clothes as though they were leaves, he faithful as ever to her image, naked in his woods. For him biology is transfigured, she is the source, the navel and womb of all things. Here the virgin meets the godhead, here the stars kneel and the planets touch. The radiation sears him. Here the fire, here the spark, here the hub and bearing to the turning wheel of light. She will understand, perhaps she will not, but she will know genuine adoration.

Claire didn't like to mix pig pasture with cow pasture. Others thought it a waste, seeing as an extra lane is necessary to serve the new distance from here and thence, besides, pigs can be rough on fence when corn is in milk. Claire didn't mind and had a somber five-strand all the way.

The real problem was how to tour the pigs across County EE without all the bother of minding gates every sow out and sow home. Claire answered the dilemma by building the lane fence right up to the corrugated road culvert. The town chairman, brother George, didn't think pigging was an appropriate use of the town's right-of-way and drainage. Neither was it specifically countermanded by the statute book so Claire had his long-ways pig pasture and the divisions of his domain.

The problem being to get the pigs home at feeding time. Ordinarily they'll come of their own accord, a relationship with no adroit recognition of clocks, which is the problem. The solution was Fannie. Fannie called the pigs from the curve on the state road to past the nether side of County EE headed south. Fannie brought 'em. Starting with a minor D in 2/4 time, escalated to a high C in 4/4 time. H......ere pigeeeee, pigeeeee, pigeeeee. All the living members, and as likely a few not living, between Valley Down, Valley Over and Valley Up knew when Fannie was lungin' after pigs. The energy in her voice wonderfully supersonic in character. Fannie could stop a pig in half crunch of new corn, bring genuine gleam to its eye and another half curl to its tail. All on one lungful of pure Buena Vista air.

Fannie was the soloist at the Liberty Corners Buena Vista Methodist every Easter Sunday morning. Whether the anthem was "Oh, Jerusalem," "On a Hill Far Away" or "Holy, Holy Holy;" Fannie struck the first chord. The village cousins who had innocently advanced to the Easter services of the Liberty Corners Methodee were astounded by Fannie. Transported might be the better word. Fannie saw no difference between calling pigs and Easter morning. She sat in the first chair across from the pulpit. The preacher knew and if he had any sense, backed around the corner of the podium when the choir stood its ground just previous the sermon. Some congregates collect the offering before the anthem but that was found the less liberal at Liberty kirk. If they waited until afterwards, half the congregate was so stunned as to no longer recognise the difference between the dollar note and the ten. Fannie became the major asset of the faith, she had a like effect on new fillings and dislodged any starlings nesting in the belfry. Liberty Corners Methodist didn't have a bell and didn't need one. They had one once but it came down. Went halfway through the maple floor before it rightly stopped. Everybody knew why the bell came down. Wood and nails stand only so much stress. Wood can be kinda psychotic that way, holding up, holding up, then at a sudden letting smash. They didn't blame Fannie. Besides, pigs won't come to a bell but they will come to Fannie. Let their own hogs flood loose in October and have 'em in the oak woods when they want to ship and the only way to bring them out is Fannie. Something in a pig's brain is inclined precisely to the oscillations of her voice. A fit that would no more leave a pig alone as whisky to stay from the lips of John Bushshey or Frank Bintner.

Frank, that was Mabel's husband, she sings in the choir too, shot himself on a Sunday morning six Easters previous. He was farmer enough not to do it on Monday with all the day's work to do. Used a 30-30. We always wondered what Frank looked like with a 30-30 dimple in his head. Davie Johnson from Keene said it would splatter the whole thing all over the ground and there'd be nothing left but a collection of eyes, teeth and nose holes. Roger Precourt said it weren't so. More liked to cow death with hardly any more evidence to show than running into a door. We thought that was too bad considering the trouble Frank took with having his shoe and sock off to reach the trigger.

The Liberty Corners Buena Vista Methodist Church was built 24 feet wide, 36 feet long including a two step altar, pulpit, communion table, baptismal font and the nine wood folding-chairs of the choir stand. Wide enough for two aisles and four sets of pews across, a dimension approximately five times the congregate's population. The builders, who included my great grandfather, should have known and probably did but a church built solely to match utility would not look like much of a church. Anyhow, this way there was room to maintain theological decorum. Tradition dictated a shim-space between the pulpit and the membership. Sitting close to the pulpit was considered uppity cosmologically speaking. As they saw it, someone else did the pickin' anyway and it didn't make any difference where you sat. Besides, distance nicely mulled the preacher's drone and harmonized it with the window flies.

Except on Easter. On Easter with the village cousins, the wayward Bardens, Precourts from Milwaukee, three flavors of Eckels, all the Johnsons from Keene, any surviving Bushsheys, a Pardou, the MacLarens and the Liberty Corners Buena Vista Methodist Church was full. Folks had to turn sideways to position all their hams in a common row. Such was the fit, when a majority in the pew stood up, everyone else did too, whether they wanted to or not.

Charlie Whittaker suffered a sawmill accident. A sorry story when but 22 years and new-wed, his right leg was cut off at the knee. The incident also took his left foot out of meanness. Charlie wasn't blameless. Folks say he was teching the bottle and being new at it, got carried away on the log-carriage right into the grin of a set-tooth 60 inch saw-blade. Others say Charlie weren't so innocent in regards to the bottle and had nearly died of mayhem a dozen times before.

Charlie came all the way from Amherst Junction to partake of a Liberty Corners Easter morning. Charlie had been healed years before and wanted to recount the new and holy grace in his life. You can see from where you're sitting the sense of it. Weren't no miracle like the preacher said it was. Was that Easter Sunday morning fit. When everyone stood up, Charlie in the middle of the pew did too.

It did look impressive. Charlie shoulder-to-shoulder with Claude Newby, he is from the village and his brother-in-law Harry Precourt. If you got down and looked under the pew there was one set less of legs than the number of folks standing. Straight as a second year mullein plant Charlie stood. Most people had seen it often enough as not to bother with it but any new client were taken by it.

You could watch as the event wetted through 'em. How they sucked spit past their teeth when Charlie came into the church using two crutches and Esther Precourt to steady him up. Never wore his formal foot on Easter Sunday morning, just rolled up his pant legs and took out his Easter Sunday crutches. We thought after a while the preacher ought to pay Charlie for going to the trouble he did. Seems only right, Charlie being the draw he was.

You know how people mind a gimp once they're in the ripples of one. Why, they can't leave their eyes off 'em, needing to see how they prosper in the ordinary act of things, like standing up. Right from the first hymn on the new folks take to tugging on each other's sleeves, whispering to each other right in the middle of the music and pointing, pointing at Charlie Whittaker levitating.

Charlie, if he plays his part right, doesn't take no notice. Miracles are supposed to be that way, unobtrusive, which is why they happen mostly to humble people. That's supposing they happen at all. I figure all miracles are Charlie Whittaker miracles. Maybe there tain't no strings or such but there's a reason for it somewhere. Which my dad says is why we're Methodist. 'Cause there's always a method. I don't know if Pa has researched it or if it's in a book somewheres but it sounds reasonable.

Charlie and Fannie are good for the collection plate and the preacher knows it and Esther Precourt knows it. One year Charlie had to go to Rhinelander, upriver a hundred miles, and Esther had to find a substitute, meaning their hired man's brother who lived west on the tracks from the village. He was missing a significant acreage from his leg. Anyway, she tried to talk him into attending with a promise of a warm Sunday dinner. He wouldn't do it. Wasn't till Harry went to him on the sly that he agreed to come to the Liberty Corners Methodist for its "spiritual" sake. The man wasn't practiced and when someone coughed at the first hymn, he teetered badly, but by the second hymn and the Apostle's Creed he was steady enough.

Charlie Whittaker's cure did have its effect. For awhile there was always two or three extra limpers and hobblers at Easter Sunday morning. If they sat at the outside of the pew they went off disillusioned. If properly sandwiched they rose off their sorry limbs and knew the sweet flower of joy the preacher said was in jesus the christ who hung till he died and then three days later rose out of the dead stench of herbal dressings and bad ventilation.

I always wonder about that. Not so much in church as in the woods. How jesus, who seemed regular enough if given to promises you have to take without guarantee, could get off from dead. Or why he even wanted to. Three days dead is a pretty legal dead, flies, maggots and warm country being what they are. I'd seen calves, lambs, chickens and deer three days dead and weren't no resuscitation for them, no matter where they sat in the pew.

A blind man came once and in the middle of the first hymn started going off by himself, thanking God and puttin' his hands up in the air and waving them. God is supposed to live in the air somewhere, the air accorded as the necessary and regular place of gods. Why they didn't live in the ground I didn't understand. Isn't the ground as good as sky? Sky can't do a lot of things ground can, people are biased toward sky, thunder and lightning mainly. Thunder and lightning is eloquent, I'll admit. But so is dirt. Sky, once you get past thunder and sparks, don't have anything over dirt. Dirt is 99% of beauty. Ground is the seed of mountains and when you want it nice and quiet, it's the root cellar where you go. Nothing scares you in the ground. If it was my religion I'd make the ground the holiest place. I don't know what I'd do about that jesus fellow kitin' off into the sky. Think maybe I'd just leave him dead, kinda unfair to single him out the way they did. Yah, I'd leave him in the ground and if his words meant anything, let them stand a thousand years and regulation death.

The reason the blind fella carried on was because he saw light. They didn't find it out till he got calmed down enough to stop pumping holies. The preacher's name that year was Ulig and he built balsa model airplanes and had the best P-38 and P-40 I'd ever seen. The P-40 had a plexiglass canopy with a leather cockpit, shoulder harness and joy stick with a tiny red button in the middle of the handle to fire the Browning machine-guns and 50 cal. cannon. Ulig was a good preacher which he ought to be with a P-40 like that.

Ulig got the man calmed down and when the words evened out he said he'd seen lights. Ulig kinda stroked the man and petted him with some words so he could go back in the pulpit and finish the service.

The blind man came back every Sunday for awhile but never saw lights again, at least didn't speak of it. The miracle stood to reason. He saw lights because he was in the middle of the pew along with Claude Newby, Marvin Fletcher and a cousin of the Hilmers. Taken together those three people could squash the lights out of anybody. That's what he saw. The concussive sparks of all that meat standing up at once.

I liked Easter Sunday morning at the Liberty Corners Buena Vista Methodist, even though we never got our regular seat at the back where we could throw paper airplanes down the stairwell. On Easter there were other things to watch. Buddy Berry came with his mom sometimes. Buddy Berry is the pitcher for the Moore Barn Tavern baseball team. Buddy Berry once played with the Milwaukee Braves and breathed the same air as Warren Spahn and Hank Aaron and the only thing better was the atmosphere of Satchel Paige. Some Paiges lived right next to the church, they collected cars, but those Paiges were the wrong color. Buddy Berry was the only pitcher the Moore Barn Tavern had or ever needed. He farmed just beyond the hill cut of the state road to Valley Down. Sunday afternoons he pitched. We'd sneak through the swamp and watch him from among the white pines on the other side of the road. Buddy was so fast we never saw the ball, instead just a linear white blur with red stitches. If Buddy wasn't pitching for the Braves it could only mean Warren Spahn was so much faster. Imagine that blur. Which is the way of miracles. If you don't know how it's done it's a miracle. Buddy Berry could put horse hide past white ash without the grain even getting close. I think that's pretty close to miracle and more useful than a three-day-dead kind of trick. Never ever see the ball, just the blur.

THE BARN

T HE BARN IS THE CENTER. THE BARN HAS THE SAME POWER
of the seed. Barns are the passion, the faith, the long bones of farmers.
Grandfather built the great barn in 1909. A small, temporary barn existed
before, it was little more than a shed with a slope to the west. It was a
frightened structure, it quailed before the wind, snow violated it, rain
penetrated. Grandfather knew, his neighbor knew and his god knew if
he was to really be the farmer, the land's husband, then he must have a
sign. A thing before all other things, a sign to his livelihood and damn
the expense, this an omen, a barrier against the foul season, the bitter
winter or incessant rain.

Grandpa read Mister Hoard's Journal. Read and reread how good
husbandry is borne on the part of barns. Efficiency, economy and eu-
clidean fields matter; but the barn is the center. Barns improve the quality
of milk, promote cleanliness and calf survival, barns retain animal heat,

protect hay quality, provide ventilation. Barns all but hold back the night, such was their special space and light.

Hoard's Journal told exactly how to do it. How the purloins joined to the girts. How to use a notching stick if a store-bought measure wasn't at hand; one mark for the depth, one for the width, one for the center hole. How to put the beams together on the ground, didn't need nails on the beams. Nails last a hundred years, maybe two. Use hickory, use white oak, use ironwood; peg the beams. Grandpa was looking for a thousand years kind of barn. The barn was his mark, his pyramid. A well-done barn didn't require more than a keg of nails, eight penny commons out of Cleveland at twenty-eight dollars. Otherwise the barn was free. Sure there were windows and the hardware for the sliding door and ventilator tube, like Hoard said.

He dreamed it a thousand nights, ninety-seven feet, six inches of barn. The length aimed into the west. One big sliding door on the south, two, three, four Dutch doors. He dreamed himself in the dawn of those doors. Swallows venturing in the crystal morn, he in his heaven.

You mean you're thinking silo? Gawd Almighty man, y'gonna feed right cows rotten corn? Why, dear fool, it's chemical alkeyhall and alkeyhall is poison enough to kill a man much less an unhardened cow. It'll poison yer milk, why do you give ear to them scientisters? You want wobbly cows? And to think of feeding them bubbly corn twice on the day? Mon, you're a leer. Listen to common sense, otherwise Journal gonna ruin ye right off your stead and ye'll be begging just like a heathen injun. Fly from silos, I tell you. Give 'em clover and tim, give 'em good marsh hay and they stay even sober those kye. Silage is satan's work, friend, the deeval's own brooth if ye ask me. Fly from silos, it's good coin ill-spent, ill-spent I tell ye.

Grandpa read of silos, wide mows, the benefit of a separate milkhouse and ventilation tubes. How to string lantern lines and never have a light in the barn unkempt from the safety wire and it never fail and never to see the barn burn. Cool the milk in a tank constructed of stone or cement. Keep the profile low so lifting the cans over the edge is not an undue strain. Near-by, sink a pitcher pump.

"...at a convenient height the water inlet is positioned. Though a hand-pump is more laborious, in winter it is less likely to freeze. Install the overflow pipe below the rim of the tank, allowing surplus water to discharge as full cans are placed into it. A drain in the floor of the milk-house is a favorable addition allowing utensil cleaning in the most modern and sensible manner. The result is high quality milk gaining a premium with the local creamery and whole milk buyers . . . "

Nine hundred and forty-six dollars and fifty-two cents, that's what it cost him, including paint, cedar shingles and fifty-six feet of ventilation pipe. Nine, forty-six, fifty-two for fourteen 9-lite windows of the Vetter Pinewood Manufacturing Company, hinges to four Dutch doors, a set of dolly-wheels and hang track. And six of the finest Moss Hardware special order lightning rods with detection globes. One with a wind vane of pure virgin copper mounted on a stainless brass swivel guaranteed for a lifetime. A wind vane capable of minding the wind direction in any excess of three miles per hour.

The silo of the finest clear cedar shipped special delivery from Seattle. The diameter was seven feet even, twenty-two feet six inches tall warranted from rot, blow-down, premature leak and lean. A ring adjustment manual was included with the shipment along with a special box-end wrench solely for the purpose.

Two years Grandfather worked the woods, January to March. Skidding white pine logs, white oak, red oak. He ignored hemlock, black oak, tamarack, even red pine. This barn was the supreme act of his life and he weren't going to cheapen it with basswood boards. He knew there were tithe barns in England three hundred years old. His dad, James, drew in the dirt what the beams looked like. James told him to go climb overhead at the village kirk, see there how the king posts and queens were a measure of carpentry for something permanent. Wood is to the

English way of doing barns, wood and lots of wood; it's wood as gives a barn the advantage, whether of wind or frost heaves. Set 'er lean-ways in the wind and take heavy timber into the mow else the wind'll have it before your grandson. I know your brother says to aim it south but dearie, no English barn goes south if it can find fit going west. A landsman needs a sea eye much as a sailor. Hark darling, send her right west. Mark ye own calendar if you're mind to. Count the days she comes west over days she tends other. West'll win I wager. No matter they say the howlers come out of south. Cyclones of southwest, but I tell ye darling, if it's God's howl you think to muster against, fly off of it. No barn stand out against the smashers and don't think you're even gonna try. Aye, south has its blow, but she is of a wit to reform. West, darling, is whereof set the shoulder your barn. How much I hear they say you spent?

A thousand! Lawd darling, ain't you a sweet for cowies. A thousand gold dollars on a barn! Ye ain't on credit are ye? Don't spill a barn on banker's blood, darling, or they'll own your hide till they cork you up. What? Ye sold another brace? Who to? Shoulda known old Boston the undertaker couldn't leave off them horses. As pert a set of harness charmers in the territory. I was of the thought maybe Boston have 'em for his funeral wagon. How much ye cut him for? Three hundred! Darling, he'll squeeze your purse of you. What's a three hundred dollar brace of horse do even for an undertaker? 'Course I seed 'em. Sure darling, they's proud beasts and aye and the step you trained to 'em, that's royal. They's look mighty enough to haul God to his bury ground. Still, you know the buryin' price be up. Them's three hundred dollar goina come of our hides; Boston fill his creel a thousand times over for them horses, you can count at that. Still, if going to ground behind them beasties don't settle a grin in your bones then you're too sorry a dark plug to plant in fertile good ground anyway.

Your grandpa spent six months at the woods. Spying out the straightest and widest trees for the sake of tight grain. Staying off of wind-shook logs, woodpeckers, too, were sign of faithless wood. Was March of eight he hollered the townsmen over to Holliday's mill. Uncommon warm day even for March. We lumbered them trees well as any. Sang them true and squa'. Could tell from the logs the time he spent snaking logs. I's of the bet he spent more time eying them than shucking them out. They were most whi' pine. Pity's they's the last of it. I's of the bet ain't an equal child of them to come off in another thousand years. Oak is the test of the mill. Oft times it'll pinch on the blade and bind tight as harness glue turned into the hired man's drawers. Oak's swell for barns. Oak's got spirit enough for queens and carry posts. From the lumber we knew. George had his pride going, knew Freddie spill over it.

Freddie Taylor was carpenter and none better could we expect in the north. Took it from his pa, many as three pa's before were carps and wood fitters. Oh lad, there was no better man with saw set and chisel. He had an eye for wood. Knew wood like a dairymaid knows cows. He'd follow grain and if there's spend in a log, he'll cut the notch where wood grain pinched, something in the log made grain close in one place, stronger there than anywhere else in the length.

George hired Freddie in spring of eight, full year before he knew to have the boards cured. Had to have Freddie. Coulda used Silas MacInise or Archibald Pince's cousin Abner Weise. No, had to be Freddie, if Freddie couldn't George said he'd wait till 1910. 'T'were Freddie told him two years earlier what the sort of trees and logs to look for. No hemlock, no tammies. Not even black oak if he could avoid it.

You knows the whole muck once were tamerackery? Whole thing. Tammies and poplar, birches, tag alder, willars and wire grass. Rude ground the marsh was, and all government parcels right into the modern century. Why, there were injuns in the Buena Vista; Menomeenees and Hochunkes right up till 1940. Even a little after. Guess the war done it, killed them off forever. Came to the muck moor for ash and baskets. I heard them. Chist, what'd we want ash for? In the night we'd hear them pounding the bolt logs. Knocking the fibers loose so as they could peel strips away.

'Cause it was government it didn't matter. Highlanders used the marsh woods like was our own. We cut meadow hay and took bark of tammies and hemlock. If need of a quick shed, tamarack were quick. Hand axe be enough of tool. Lotta folks got their start with tamark rafters. The bark were for curtain money. If hadn't been for tammies a farmer been hard put to keep a woman. Bark money was culture and civilized life like in the direction of village folk. Tammy bark was hard money that keeps a woman in blue curtains, calico, gingham check and real china-man's tea-cups. A week barking trees kept the farm in money all year. Stovewood besides. Though care is well spent on tammie in the stove. I'd seen a tamarack fire blow a stovepipe clean outa the socket. Ye don't beat winter with tamarack, but they's good to fry eggs. Still, care to see it don't sag the chimbly from the much of draft.

Government was itching to move them marsh parcels. Woulda been there till Second Coming if Hiram Haycroft hadn't lit on measuring window curtains. Hiram knew us too right well. I thought it cheating for a government man to be married into the town the way he was. Shoulda kept one way or the other. Not fair, since being married to the Holidays he knew how we all used the muck moor.

His solution being to note which biggins had window curtains, which didn't, and when he had a list, took his rig by and ask them if they like to buy a parcel or two on the Buena Vista seeing as they had had use of it already.

Was a shotgun wedding. Weren't no surviving farmer who didn't take tammy bark of the Boney Vieux. He says right up we'd been bedding the marsh without benefit of matrimony. He made it sound like we was all adulterers! We all played innocent for awhile, your grandpa too. Regular theater it was. Heck no, we says, weren't us freeing bark off the marsh. 'Course we did have to admit the hay. Everyone north of Nekoosa took marsh meadow hay. Sometimes the marsh was the only grass left if the summer went evil minded hot. Highlands had heck to pay in a dry summer. We had him on the grass issue and he knew it. Every livery and hotel barn depended on marsh hay and if he were criminalizing marsh hay then we were all pokied. From Holiday, to Commins at the bank, Warner at the hotel and Boston at the parlor. Moor hay was a nice fit for horses with some of the nicest bluestem, sweet grass, wild brome and sweet fern. Nothing made a better tick than marsh hay. Didn't need any more of bathing than the Saturday night before Easter if ye slept your nights on marsh hay. And it was a way to tell if a lassie was freeloving, if she had that smell of marsh hay about her bloom. Burns your ears does it lad? Your ma'd snip me off if she knew I were tell ye of peckering. Ye'll not tell will you lad? No, not thee. I sees your ears lay back and you's right inquisitive. Darling, there's always more to say about the territories of womenfolk. You'll know well enough in your own time. 'Tis the finest country a man can lay claim to and when it comes to your time, don't fear the pinch of lugs like some fools. It's God-given and near the sweetest pleasure in life, and if God didn't intend it, then he woulda made us elseways. You be a proud man, hear! Be proud of your hams. Be proud of yourself and your fine animal and ye can lay a Sunday summer under the tent of a lassie's tit and feel right.

'Course we all bought muck when the price got right. Your grandpa, he bought four forties and your Uncle Jim a full six. Holiday and Boston had to buy too, to be sure of their marsh hay. Sudden boom in mucks for awhile there.

Darling, you shoulda been to a barnin'. Tain't nothing in wide creation the more lovely and grand as a barn getting born. You'd think it was more than mere board and beams the righteous way it lifts up over the land. Freddie Taylor run it, he run every great raising in the country. 'Cept for your Uncle Jim's. On account George had Freddie, Jim had to have someone else, was that Tom Richards out of Waupaca. You can tell from the outside. Freddie never run a barn south, Richards preached south on account Waupaca is back in the hills and in the hills they can get away with south.

Freddie run it; hardest part were the frame and the raising. We got there, musta been near 9 o'clock in the morning. If I remember, we was going to do it a week earlier but it rained and we had to wait for the ground to dry. Was a Friday morning. Freddie always raised barns on Friday morning, it was his way. Two or three days before, he was into the boards and beams, sorting them out, marking the angles, cutting the notches and tongues. All the crew had to do was fit it together like a big puzzle, save for the mow stringer; that had to be cut right there in the morning while we held it, otherwise the fit wasn't fine enough to suit Freddie.

Freddie did barns English. Meaning ground up instead of mow up. Mow up were easier but then the barn had top and bottom halves. Mow up were lighter too. No, Freddie had to cast the whole thing one piece except the rafters. That was another difference between Freddie and Thomas Richards; Richards built mow up. Richards were the more modern, even Hoard's said so. Freddie and George didn't see it that way. A barn weren't fashionable, a barn were not even necessarily modern.

Time we all got there, Freddie had us laying out the timbers. Six or eight of us slide bolts under a beam and carried it to where he said. A couple men he set to augering holes. No kid's job augering those holes, they had to be true. Freddie come by just to see if you were minding it. Was the only chance we got to use his tools. Took an edge to sink perpendicular in oak. "True hole," he said, "always takes more time than a foul hole." We laughed at him for another reason and knew he were right about that too.

Didn't take long to set a mow together owing as Freddie had it notched and tongued already. He did have to size the thrust beam to its mate. Used a common eight tooth rip-saw. We watched him cut the thing with no more to guide him than two lines either side of the beam. When we set 'em a mosquito couldna drawn breath in the space left behind. Freddie was tight even for a carp.

48

'Course we weren't strangers, barn raisin' or no. Same crew as threshed, ditched, graveled the road and tended Sunday at the kirk. There's always a few quits and drags in any crew. Some's you gotta have, like Skyllar Whittaker for one. Skyllar couldn't work a whit and none really wanted him seeing as he'd lost his mitt in the Civil War. Shiloh, as I remembers. In his good grip he carried a walk stick and handled it like it was a cavalry sword. Handsome blue beech stick it was, with a wolf's head carved on top. Wonder what ever happened to that cane, I'd pay ransom for it now. None minded Skyllar, he was worth his plate at the table if only for when he'd drift off "...thirty thousand of us from the new territories, Wisconers mostly, few Michigans. Oh, we were fancy pants we were, in blue shirts and hats and gilt buttons. Not a one of us ever killed a man afore and now we were harnessed to war and they was expecting us to do to a man what we only done before to squirrels and whisky bottles. Before Shiloh I ain't killed nothing much above a chicken and any fool knows a chicken weren't war...thirty thousand of us, that were April '62, under Grant. Confederates hit us when we didn't know they was even close, whole blooming Confederate army under Johnston. Those with Prentiss had to fall back and if it weren't for dark we woulda gone swimming in the Tennessee River. Next day the 14th Wisconsin Volunteers up and took the New Orleans. They says we won. Maybe. 25,000 dead men in two days ain't exactly winning..." Then Skyllar'd come back, kinda shake and restore himself. Skyllar was worth a dinner plate all right.

And the preacher came. Came toward the end of the forenoon so as to have place at the board, which is what he really came for. If he was real he woulda come early and helped or even prayed over the barn, we coulda stood that. Problem was, coming at the forenoon as he did, he didn't get passed around so everyone didn't know he was there. So when the lady hollered "Dinner," he thinks God's grave is enough to save him a dinner place. Weren't. We burnt out the wash basins and flour sack towels in less time than it takes to say it. Him standing there thinking polite counts. Manners at a barn raising board is extinguishment. Preacher oughta knowed that and set himself according. Time the dust settled he was without chair-leg and dinner-set. Much less how he imagined it, him at the high chair of the first table from the kitchen. Skyllar were there and Freddie, George and Winslow Herman who brought the hickory pins special all the way from Sauk City.

Folks don't ordinarily say words over the dinner at a raising or threshing but the blamed fool stood forelorn in the doorway looking like an orphan. We's about to open fire when Missus says, "Oh Reverend Longs, you're here, could you ask the blessing please." Warp of a man, he looks surprised, "Oh, oh yes...God, ah, ah, our almighty maker and ah redeemer..." all the while them taties is sitting in front of us mellowing their sweet pastures under our noses, new beef and what must've been thirty chickens. "...Grant us thine, ah, protection and, ah, ah, see us to heaven, in Jesus' name. Amen."

Fool. Couldn't he talk to his God any better than that and paid every Sunday and buryin'! You ask me, Freddie Taylor be more preacher than him or most preachers. What matters is precision. Gawd damn preachers anyhow.

Missus found him a corner in the kitchen and he ate three courses of stewed potatoes, string beans, half a chicken with biscuits and three inches of roast beef without a lick of work and not a half cent's worth of words. Gawd damn preachers!

And that only after she took him a clean towel as he came back from the washboard saying all the towels were dirty. The turd! And he had the effrontry to eat like a man. After, you think he'd help us? No siree. Was in his buggy ten seconds after dinner with no more than a tip of the hat. You ask me, the reason why them creatures are itinerant is 'cause nobody can stand 'em long enough to let them perch. Preachers come in two versions, only two. One is a preacher 'cause they've got the holler of God inside them so bad they have to preach to settle their sanity. Don't let one of them kind get between you and your soul else he'll have you repenting and spending money in the collection plate like it was cold water. Other kind comes to preaching 'cause their pa done it, or it seems the easiest thing to do. Only Sunday and funerals and weddings to climb over and all they have to do is act the part. Better the preacher who is a little god-crazy, whose soul pinches every time he turns and wiggles. Real god-man ain't comfortable. That's his whole object, to take the slack of godlessness and fetch it right on top of their own backs and carry it for us. That's a fair man of god I think.

Ya ever been to a long board? 'Tis the clambake to end all clambakes. 'Tis payground, potlach, giveaway, all tallied up in one ripe occasion. Never raise a barn out of garden season. You didn't know it had season? Did. Wait on the barn till the tater patch can stand it, till the coop gets to fryer size. Barns, if they're not to ruin ya in buildin', might ruin you of your grubstake. Green beans, peas, sweet corn, little summer squash. George, I know for sure, killed a heifer special. Dressed out at four hundred pounds. Your grandma took on an extra 150 chickens. With two extra rows of taties. 'Yond that all he needed was pass the word 'round and the neighbor ladies took up their own competitions. Adah sent them couple hundred pounds of taties and maybe two or three roasts and they set to seeing who of them cold spill the finest fix of digestive luxury.

Tillie, that being Jim's missus, weren't fair to potatoes; left off mashing them too soon but sweet lord, was she the divine instrument of pot roast. Couldn't even cut it it was so tender. Now I ain't saying it's true, and we never believed it ourselves, but some folks said Tillie wrapped the meat in a couple layers of paper bag and buried it in the sun two days before she cooked it. Wherever it come from it was a loose billy jesus.

Gracie, that's Jesse's wife. She couldn't handle meat. Actually Gracie weren't any length of cook. What she could do was strawberries and shortcake. Theodora Whittaker was the archangel of taters, mashed, fried, stewed, scalloped, she could enshrine them. Were like eating cake. Adah herself was God's gift to chicken. Fried chicken is the test. Any pair of tits can make chicken and dumplings. Fried chicken takes charm. Most drive it either to fossil or leave it bloody. Adah could pan-slap chicken.

More menfolks coveted another's queen at the dinner table than any other time save maybe church suppers. After eating, we stagger out the door and loll on the porch, some fell asleep under the trees. Quick enough though, Skyllar after cobbobing with the ladies, came out waving his stick, roaring at us to fetch our hides to the front lines. Funny, if weren't for him we'd have slept an hour which is why every barn raising had him. So's to keep up the storm. We figured it was the same for barns as it was for war.

George's barn took two days. Most did till the truss and hutch barns of the '40s and '50s, they'd go up in one day. George's barn took two days. 'Cause of the notches and 'cause Freddie wouldn't be rushed. By evening of the first day we had all the mows built, the first placed and ready to lift. Sometimes we did the first mow that first afternoon. It was at risk if the wind came up and shook the pikes loose. Freddie never chanced it. Meant starting over, but some folks wanted something new against the sky the first day and chanced it.

First mow frame is the worst. Heavy? Lord of my wattles, it is heavy. Timbered barn took upwards of thirty men and two steady horses to lift off the ground. Near thirty feet from cow-floor to hip, not including rafts. No barn raisin' is ever without a worry. Been men killed building barns. Smashed blood and guts flat. Ruins the barn, they say. Never seen it myself and wouldna want to.

Rolling up the mow, that's what we called it. When everyone got there, Skyllar line us up. Boys to the inside, biggest men at the walls, couple scooters with the pikes and poles. Hardest part is to get her off, up from the ground and going. Skyllar chant, "OK, ye fairy pipsqueaks, I want to set your girl-thinking out of your brains and gets your anger up. Mad dogs is what we want to lift a barn." He wave his cane. "OK now, on three ye white-assed lumoxes, get her off. One." We got our fingers under it. "Two." Find gear for our feet. "Three." Gawd she ain't even moving, oh god damn is she heavy, then the first crack. Off-right you don't think it was possible. But suddenly she moves and starts climbing. Once there is an angle on it the horses and ropes start to help. All the while Skyllar shouting and giving orders, "Mind the blocks! Mind the blocks!" he yells, so the mow piece doesn't slide off the foundation. He swings that cane out and is willing up the beam. Like the cane is levitating the thing off the ground through magic alone. Before the horse gets it good, the weight leans back and we feel that white oak mow piece coming straight back at us. Gawd damn your oak mow, George Isherwood. Skyllar bellows, "Get it up, get it up, boys, now's no time to wet your pants sonnies. Suck in your purse and git her up."

You know he didn't move. If we was to lose that mow piece, Skyllar Whittaker woulda been smashed flat as white flour. His voice didn't change, calm as you want he says, "Git it boys, git it." His stick swinging. Then the horses had it and the weight lifted off us. The pikes leaning up and dug into the timbers, catching and gentling the piece like it was a wild thing. Freddie was over by the foundation with his brass-square. One hand telling Skyllar when to ease off, "Little more, little more, that's it, whoa." More pikes rise to hold it on the other side. The mow piece hangs there quivering. "Hair west," Freddie yells. One set of pikes lean, the other set relax. "Put her in iron." Couple boards are nailed hurriedly to the foundation and the beam, the ropes are tied to trees or fence posts.

'Tis a kind of feeling seeing the first frame against the landscape. Think Skyllar let us gape? "Hells bells, this ain't a bawdy house window lads. We've three mow pieces to go and here it is half way to noon." In half an hour we have two. They are nailed together. A couple boys are sent up with pulleys to hang over the drift pins. The small timber is hoisted and nailed on, tying the two mow pieces. In the next hour the last mow frame put up and cross beams added. From the hips a set of rafts are cast and touch, then a rowdy climbs the peak and throws boards across, tying rafters with rafters. Then we hear the Missus holler, at ten minutes yet to noon, the barn looking like a pile of lumber resembling geometry.

That afternoon we pound nails; roof boards, the rest of the rafters, siding. Most of it already cut 'cept for the short boards around the windows and doors. Boards are the fun part of barning. Always seems we get divided up into a couple teams and try to see who can get their side done first. Some farmers won't have it 'cause the contest don't always include square fit. But with Skyllar and Freddie and old George, they kept the boards going on straight. All they did was watch us and walk around with a square. Skyllar made us go back six boards when his square won't sit.

Those who can't stomach the roofing did walls. Funny what happens in the hollow the boards make of the barn. Regular acoustic, first just of folks hammering then the hammering finds a variation, a swoon in time with hammer swing, it's a sort of music. Makes your skin crawl. Wouldn't think hammers had it in them; they do though, hammers and eight penny nails. The noise kinda swoops you along, I bet if the barn were a thousand feet long folks keep right on pounding and pay no attention to the time of day. The noise has you in it and you feel part of it, like it were a pond and we all was living in it, buoyant on the noise.

Ain't ever been to a barning that when they started boards they didn't finish boards. I think it's 'cause the hammers hypnotize. Then, then it finishes, the sound dies out and folks know how sudden tired they are. The barn she is done. Somewhere after mow-beams and boards the barn becomes a she. Her shape has conquered a piece of landscape. It is the greatest thing on the near horizon and we built it. With Freddie's barns one roof board is left out. Next day being Sunday, the man climbs up at his own want and hammers the last board home.

First night it weren't regular custom to stay for supper at a raisin'. Second night it were; cold chicken, potato salad, dill pickles, layer cake, coffee, tea, pump water. Served informal-like. You go eat when you want after the boards' done. Some string for home after that and some don't stay for supper. Other folks have their missus and kids come over with more cold chicken and potato salad and deviled eggs and lemonade, hot new bread and biscuits and dill pickles and pickled beans and early onions. And someone always brings a quarter barrel from the village. George were temperance, and if a man were temperance the barrel stayed on the back side of the barn.

Folks come by just to look at the new barn. Kids want to go inside and smell it. Young boys go to slosh water over each other at the water trough. 'Bout everyone goes for a look at the last board-hole. We don't know why we done it. Maybe 'cause we don't want to master whatever it is, not to catch that much sky without hesitation. Maybe it's a kind of telling there is always something left undone, or something that don't like to be tamed or covered over or something that shouldn't be and you hadn't ought even if you can.

With dark the folks are gone. Even a temperance man been known to walk around back to the beer tub after a barning, but he better mind his singing before he gets home.

Barning was about as good as it got. We didn't have the Green Bay Packers at the Super Bowl and we didn't have hard roads or penicillin, but we had barns.

I heard about barns about once a week. I wondered what a raisin' was really like and maybe it was as good as they said. Sometimes when it rained and the mow is at summer empty, I went to look at Freddie Taylor's joist. Pa said it weren't no more than a handsaw that he done it with. You know you still can't slide a dime in the space between the two oak beams each of them twenty feet long and a hundred storms to their credit.

Freddie Taylor died at Whiting Village. I don't think all of him is dead, and what isn't is in the keeping of barns. The barn is the only scent folks leave behind, like of Skyllar Whittaker swinging the barn up with his blue beech cane carved with the head of a wolf.

Soul, I think, is not what you take but what you leave behind. If done right it's all used up and there ain't nothing for the grave to corrupt or the preachers to argue over. Nothing to damn and nothing to bless and nothing for a breeze to haul off. Sometimes in a storm I go to the mow. Listen how the wind meows at the dove window, or splashes like a sea over the roof. Listen how the heaves of west wind try to reach under the barn and tip it and how the barn leans back trying to teach the wind a thing or two. What you hear is the sound of good oak and good white pine, same way a grin sounds inside your own head on a cold day.

THE MELT

IN THE ELECTION OF FARMERS EXIST TWO SECTS; THOSE WHO will plow snow, and those who will not. In the first sect are the denim druids who will not venture a field if a snowbank advances the sheerest gossamer within the asylum they pay taxes on. Whilst the neighbor hitches plow to tractor for a vengeful turn of gristly snow into lubricious earth.

The husbandman who will not disturb the snowdrift at the field edge is the more whimsical of farmers or perhaps the more cognizant of his own hazard. Which of the two sects of plowers or abstainers is more solvent is difficult to say. Each believes in the derivation of his statistics and hence his odds. One lays claim to history in the long pull, the other bets on efficiency. Each then has its god.

Some hold plowing snow into a furrow is queer, a savage enlistment, a blasphemy against theological mumblings not worth the risk of insulting. The same as sitting to Sunday dinner without saying words over it. Those who plow snow believe in early luck, August and July and early crop luck. Credit is the bank's not the snowbank's to give; all else is mumble-jumble compared to the price per hundredweight of who gets to market first.

April's first installment, All Fool's Day. There are farmers who will plant twenty acres of oats on March 30, another twenty on the 31st but avoid the field altogether on April one. The pedigree is mixed. The practitioner who will mercilessly slice a white snowbank, spilling its soft organs into loam won't even go in the tractor shed on April one. His neighbor, who waits another week before venturing the field, spends the day frilling the tractor. Sitting on the seat, practicing the throttle and hydraulic lever, smelling in his memory the must of first furrow, the groan of shares slipping into the brown jugular. All the while in the shed.

April tractors are brides. Garnished with new oil, blemishes painted over, squeaks located, if not cured at least talked to, bearings packed and wheels lent the smugness of a parts manual torque chart. The tractor is aligned with what they remember or believe of old luck. If the year previous was solvent and they carried a ten-inch crescent wrench in the toolbox, they will carry a ten-inch crescent wrench in the toolbox this year, wrapped in the same oil rag. Farmers have a vital sense of "something borrowed and something blue."

The town-road is the cipher of the melt. A field isn't even paced till the dip in the road loses its mire. Blacktop roads, while adoring shoeshine, have ruined farmers who'd venture a field a gravel road would have counseled against. When the road no longer interrogates each passing car for the amount of lug tread left, the field is not far behind. These farmers know of permafrost and semi-permafrost, and know exactly how the mastodons died and have an equal fear for the fossil of their own bones.

The melt has this same insidious significance with rural children. The cause is puddles. Such glazings as a kid can smash and be perfectly comtemptuous of. Childhood is an arduous citizenship, it has no legal territory. Without resources it can corrupt and derange. The recourse to the

The Melt

kid is a puddle and the explorations that should return our kind to sea; the galosh is not far behind the flipper and the gill.

A puddle can be smashed, stomped, kicked and violated, then heal itself so the whole process can be repeated. Name one other thing in the orders of creation so portentious of psychological health. An adult passing a puddle looks at himself and straightens his hair. A kid distrusts this or any such mirrors. To smash this puddle is to cleanse the mind, and send a splash like gamma rays through any idiotic enough to stand within range.

The melt sends me and every kid with a sudden passion for barn doors, hub caps and shingles, anything as'll float, tied together with wire, twine and shingle nails fashioned into brigs, barks, corvettes and man-o-wars. The zeal was to start at road edge and follow rivulet to rivulet, field puddle to meadow pond and by barrel stave, fencepost and broom handle entertain visions of a true Northwest sea passage. 'Tis a penchant of spring and farmboys, fascinated as only midlanders can be of a thing so distant and unimaginable as to be unbound by solid ground.

At the melt, circumnavigation seems both appropriate and natural from the issue and ekes of last year's corn field. Only a matter of connecting the tributaries deems the farm-childe who has yet to see the county line.

Without subtlety my intent was piracy. Bluebeard would have recognized the thirsty germ, of barnboard, oil drum and a sibling's doll lashed to a lath spar. A lovely evil evoked with no more corruption than a pocketful of cookies and a jar of blackberry jam, then hoisting the flag of youth and bloodletting on the odd chance of the spring melt.

Tom the Terrible was lord of the north sea. Circumstances had been fair to neither of us, so plain-named, yet we both knew our true leige and baptism. Beyond the bounds of the back door he was no longer Tommy but Tom the Terrible, the perfect and true dissection of his twelve-year-old person. He was my neighbor and my friend and only I loved him in sufficient enough detail to call him neat things like terrible and he loved me with a mutual brutality.

On an equidistant puddle we launched our voyages and our wars. By energy unavailable to chores we compiled between us a quarter ton of materials suggestively buoyant. Each with a pilfered doll reduced to nudity for a bowsprit. Why naked? We had no idea, having not yet anatomically evolved any resident appreciation of that state.

Provisioned with snowballs we embarked, our tender craft less floated than treaded water. Beginning thus the taunt and stalk.

Ahoy.

Ahoy what?

Ahoy is how pirates say hello.

Oh...ahoy.

How go ye, stranger? Where from and forthwith?

Huh?

What's your name?

Tommy.

No, you dumb ass, your pirate name.

Oh, yah, Tom the Terrible.

Don't you know to be decently terrible you got to talk like it, loud and mean. Like they do at the Union Mill when corn is up and milk is down, or talk like the guys who come with the meat truck with language foul enough to give a cow the shits.

I am Tom the Terrible. Who be ye stranger smelling of calf pens, brown splattered surcingles and stinking of cow pee who trespass on my sovereign sea? (A pause here to savor the enormity of the utterance.) How's that?

Good, really good.

Our progress through humanity had yet to advance to the pinnacle of direct cussing. The miscellaneous go-to-hells, geedamns and sons-of-things had not yet been properly deeded to us. Besides, we were not sure hell was nearly as bad as advertised. Infernal temperatures did not seem such ill fate to boys who bucked wood on Saturday from breakfast to sundown in knitted mittens ten degrees colder than the rest of January. Nor is hell any equal measure against calf pens after the slurry of scours. Or the right hook of a Holstein's gutter-dipped tail. Or cleaning a chicken coop with its cloud of air-borne nitrates, which we found too late for our salvation to be explosive.

Pull astern, ye miserable wet pee pup, or I'll bucket yer hide and feed ye to Chinese swine who'll dance their hard toes into your sodden corpse then slobber ye up in a rattle of soft bones.

Lower your own cloth matie or I'll blast you to smitherines. A devotion here to the installation of scarves on broom handles. His was blue with red tassles, mine a thorough red, eroded to pink in the middle of the windings.

Hold Mumpy, you've entered the lagoon of the most truant cutthroat west of 'eland who'll gouge your eyes and wax your skull to hold toothpicks.

Preliminaries installed, the cannoneering commenced. Poignant at first, conservative of economies known only to snowballs. The perfect snowball is a marvel of slush and compaction. At a range of ten yards such an armament can concuss the victim and reduce their IQ for a week. Inside of twenty yards it inflicts both earache and nosebleed.

The aim like all evil has to be reconnoitered and tendered on the remaining stock of snowballs. Terrible Tom's third shot neatly clipped my scarf from the broom handle, delivering it to a sodden condition beyond resuscitation ten feet to the starboard.

Escalation is natural to wars. What began as polite splashes became U-boat sinking of passenger-liners and machine-gunned infants. His hat was no longer of this world and one mitten had followed the bore of a snowball twenty feet then sifted into the melt pond, lingered a moment and was drowned. Between us occurred the last true blizzard of the season. Fifty snowballs each, at 55 feet apart in 30 seconds. I doubt whether our obituaries would have listed the cause of death as shrapnel. More likely drowning, a failure of those who've never felt the hard murder in a spray of cold melt water.

In silence and variable condition we retired, pretty much given up on piracy as a profession. At least a cannonball death is warm.

One farmer in the neighborhood groused every spring why his field should always collect the most curious assortment of rubble. He was said to be divided over whether to call the sheriff. Evidence suggested a felony of kidnap or a crime of mutilation had taken place somewhere upstream from the melt.

ALLIS CHALMERS AND THE HOLY GRAIL

I NEVER DROVE HORSES; MY DAD DID, HIM AND ALL THE generations before. I wondered why I, of all those generations of farmers, was spared horses. Never did decide if there was a reasonable why, think I would have liked horses. Pa did, and at some turn of moon or mood recounted the glories of horses.

Uncle Jim loved horses. He was my grandpa's brother who lived and farmed down the road, 160 rods. Had been four brothers; Ed, Henry, George and Jim. Uncle Ed farmed on the Maine School Road, Henry cured houses of termites in St. Louis, Missouri. They had sisters but they got married off and belonged then to other families.

In my years, Uncle Jim was the only old man available for inspection. Except maybe Mister Eckels, but I only saw him on Sunday and he was dressed up, and you can't tell anything real about a person on a Sunday morning. My own grandfather had died so far previous I had not gotten a fix on what purpose age serves in a person. Maybe if they had left him around to mildew I could have drawn some conclusions, but they buried him in the township cemetery. I touched his face when he was in a coffin in the bay window of the Boston Furniture and Funeral Parlor Company. They sold furniture at the front of the store. He was hard. Told brother Gary to touch him too 'cause I was worried that maybe death rubs off. Like stone Grandfather was, if a little painted. I wondered afterwards if the furniture of the Boston Funeral Parlor Company wasn't more than genuine leather.

Uncle Jim and my grandfather looked alike. They did not think alike; least not for fifty years. To my inspection George and Jim exercised the full range of hostile forces anywhere in the world. They acted civil enough on the outside, like at the Community Club, but by mutual agreement kept to opposing parties, opinions and methods of agriculture. If they did meet the salutory words were simply, "Jim," "George," combined with a nod.

Wasn't hate; was horses. Jim loved horses like he loved the Republican Party, even when it was hard to love the Republican Party. On horses Uncle Jim was absolute in his faith. Since righteousness is measured by vigor, any lack is equally apparent. So it was necessary, it was obligatory, that what Jim and George had to say to each other was righteous and vigorous and about as extreme an utterance as possible to communicate. This crease of dissimilarity ran the full length of the lives of George and Jim.

If George read in William Dempster Hoard's Journal that the silo method of corn preservation was the best source of winter feed and happened to mention it aloud or to an intermediary, then Jim, within the week had proof and direct quote from the Grange Journal that silage is the cause of hard calving. The conflict of their personal passions extended to every mechanical object and philosophical treatise ever given the reality of words or cast iron. Should one take a position on any topic, tool, trend or touchstone, the other was obliged to assume the opposite.

Somewhere over the lip of the twentieth century George offered a favorable opinion as regarding internal combustion. Jim, though nearing that conclusion himself, had to take the antithesis. The clinker being horses. For the next fifty years these two brothers of Isherwood Road, extending from the sandstone ledge of Bancroft to the state road, battled the politics of horses versus tractors as if all human purpose and destiny depended on the outcome. Each side spent its propagandas, propelled its slanders, bought spies, assigned saints, gathered holy objects and provisioned for the defense in case of sneak attack.

They argued over when to plant oats, whether it might by October rain or freeze, argue whether winter had been long, short, warm, cold, all the while it was the self-same winter. Each took, as statistics would have it, a fair share of the prognostic victories. The only object on which they agreed was bib overalls. Everything else was up for contest, not bibs. Both recognized the purity of overalls, but vainly believed each had worn them before the other.

Typically the farmer is a lean-loined creation. A fat farmer simply did not and could not exist. The offshoot of this was not lost on the manufacturers of bib overalls. They didn't offer sizes. One size fit every farmer from the Ohio Valley to the wheat flats of Saskatchewan. They marketed three sizes; large, extra large and medium. In fact, all were precisely the same cut. What farmer who could lug twenty sacks of white oats two stories in the hour between milking and dark wanted to admit to a sneeze of a store clerk he was small. Not on your life. The manufacturers of bibs knew all about farmers. 'Course it did present a minor problem, as anatomy will have it, folks are different. Some got shoulders which is no problem, bibs don't prevent shoulders. Hams could be a problem. What bibs did, and rather brilliantly, was to anticipate the revival tent and make it into a set of clothes. By pulling the tent-stakes out a little, the overflow crowd is accommodated.

On a medium man the leg holes on a medium pair of bibs was exactly three times the circumferance needed to fit the foot through. The result was a man could put his work shoes on first and not have to worry whether the shoe and sock fit through the pant leg. The reverse was also true. The farmer could withdraw from bib overhauls without taking his shoes off. Smart manufacturers fit as much democracy as possible in a suit of clothes, they don't ask what purpose folks might put their innovations to. They don't want to be responsible; they don't want to be sued. If a man wanted to put his shoes on before his bibs, it was his business. If he wanted to leave his shoes on but shuck his bibs in a hurry, that, too, was his business. Bibs were multi-faceted, multi-floral, multi-moral. The manufacturers of bibs knew they were designing men and men's hearts as much as their clothes. They knew bibs on a victim of medium format got in the way of medium trying to tie his shoes. If he could put his shoes on first he might be more inclined to start the fire in the stove. If he had to put on the bibs before the shoes then he'd be less inclined to catch the stove before morning chores. An early catch in the stove promoted marital harmony, it raised the honor of breakfast, ultimately it invigorated civilization. Every manufacturer of bib overhauls knew this. Oshkosh knew better than the "Ladies Home Journal" what style really meant in the wilds of the middle north.

Uncle Jim remained loyal to horses throughout his life and hated tractors the same length. Tractors were an abomination of purpose and sense. Horses were the true destiny and perfect use of farm talent.

Pa bought his first tractor in 1940, a used WC of the Allis Chalmers Company. The price, two hundred and sixty dollars. The first trajectory my father offered at the world with his new tractor was a casual deployment down the road. He drove past Uncle Jim's house, crossing over at the bridge meaning a goodly rumble of the bridge planks, and back. Once in third gear for opulence, once in fourth gear for humiliation. The event was, I thought, on par with the demonstration of Big Boy at Hiroshima. The declaration of technical superiority, that a propitious unconditional surrender will be accepted gracefully and with favorable terms. Uncle Jim saw it otherwise.

My father's selection of tractors solidified all doubts Uncle Jim had regarding them and all similar machineries. He could see the ink on Raymond's face already. That paralysis of character caused by tractors. Horses never set pride like that posture Raymond had motoring his WC Allis Chalmers. Besides, what if the tractor stopped running, what then?

A horse is a solid reality. You don't have to know how a horse works any more than you have to know biology to be part of it. Horses didn't involve the whole goddamn world. Horses came from mares and mares went with stallions and that is all it is necessary to know. Didn't have to know anything about spark gaps, bearing tolerances, shims, foot-pounds, gear-oil, spring tension or cold weather starting to understand horses. If a farmer understood hay and oats and not to water hot horses then he understood horses. Where did tractors come from? Nobody really knows, do they? How do tractors work? Nobody knows that either. Uncle Jim was sure they didn't, how could they? Uncle Jim understood horses; where they came from and exactly how. Had the when of the how marked on the calendar. What pasture to set the "how" loose in as the neighbor came over with the "when". Why, anyone can learn horses, but engines? No sir, America is built on horses and oughta stay horses. Why, there is no danger of explosive fuels or engines flying apart to shuck a man's bean in a moment of mechanical wrath. Horse don't fly apart. Might stun you at new shoes, but that's the whole heck of it. No sir, if there's god somewhere, whether in clouds or in the muck of the Boney Vieux, then he's a horse god. You wait and see, this tractoring will ruin everything awful. Why, even in awful bad years you can tend horses; where you at with tractors then? Buckled to Pennsylvania tars? I tell you, Pennsylvania is halfway to England already, in a hundirt years could be all the way there. That's what's wrong. Besides, what comes of a man breathing tractor gasses all day? When horse has the winds it's still breathable, don't warrant you try that with a tractor.

Uncle Jim was not fooled by progress. To his version only one sort of progress existed in the world and that's for a man and a woman with vows between them to advance. Everything else might be or might not be progress. Real progress was set up by getting chores done early, then supper, then blowing out the lights with the gloaming still on. Which was as close as Uncle Jim came to public smuttiness, and we kids took honor in being allowed to hear Uncle Jim at close range.

Even Pa admitted the WC Allis Chalmers was pretty experimental. Didn't have any machinery to match with it. A long tongue added to the horse-mower fit it for the tractor, same with the wagons. Pretty soon the binder got modified and hay rake. By then Pa was in a fix, whether to turn hard into tractors or continue to straddle the middle country between the two domains. He bought an Allis Chalmers combine. Did it, he said, 'cause he didn't like beer drinkers at his threshing. With his own combine he didn't have to worry whether the whole fool crew got drunk and his white oats at risk. The combine set Pa's destiny, after that he bought a used wire-tie baler, Harry Precourt rode it and twisted the wire ends when he was supposed to, putting the clipped wire ends in a tin can out of fear for what hardware did or might do to the insides of a cow.

The farm hung right there for awhile till Pa could get a cant hook into the shape of his own history. My sister was 14, my older brother 6, I was 2 and Gary, the youngest, just hatched. With three sons as a sign Pa was now able to make a wager on the future, three sons give a farmer decent odds. In 1951 Pa bought another Allis Chalmers, a new model WD, also a silo blower, an Allis Chalmers corn silage chopper and round hay-baler. We all had our picture taken with the last horse and it was summarily sold.

When Pa bought the second tractor something in Uncle Jim broke. His hope was tractors were a passing fad. By 1951 the evidence suggested tractors were not a drifting miasma in the farm sector. Minneapolis Moline, International Harvestor, Ford, Ferguson, John Deere, J.I. Case, Oliver, Farmall all had their wares and promises out at every fair and cross-road feedmill. The ages of the horse were done, from Genghis Khan to Sitting

Bull the horse people were done for. Uncle Jim knew it, saw it and with the refined vengeance of the vanquished, turned his back on the whole of it.

Meeting Uncle Jim on the town-road was a form of ritualized tragic opera. As a tractor approached, Uncle Jim pulled the team to the side of the road and stopped. Getting down from his rubber-tired freight wagon he walked around to the front of his team and stood with them waiting for the monstrosity to pass. His back turned on that evil. Uncle Jim was sure the tractor was evil. Steel axles, rubber tires, inner tube, timkin bearings, those were fair and worthy advances. But let civil-man be done with internal combustion. The petrol-engine had ruined the railroads, wiped the ocean of China-clippers and red-prowed Indiamen. All the cause of that fool engine.

Meet Uncle Jim on foot while hiking cows and he'd wave, pull his team over and talk the hour away, as likely two. In sure course he'd show off his new cabbage and a new marsh strain of dahlia. But be engine-propelled and Uncle Jim ignored your presence, your existence, your being, not once waving or calling out, instead his patent hunched-back pose never to honor the engine's passage. If three tractors had the town road aimed for the hay fields, Uncle Jim waited them all out. Sometimes he spent most of a forenoon traversing the 80 rods between barn door and pasture gate. Tractors had ruined his world. Tractors spoiled neighborhoods, polluted the weather and all the prime affairs of menfolk. Might take centuries, thousands, even millions of years, he could afford to wait. Within himself he knew he could wait out internal combustion, he and horse in a distant time will be avenged. Horses would be back. Folks would learn sooner or later that tractors were not a good idea. Nature never intended them. Engines weren't honest. Yup, horses would be back. Maybe horses are slow, and some given to wind, aye, but a horse never had need for a lamp under it for a winter morning start. Maybe they do hold back some if it's dark outside, but could a tractor offer any opinion of hay weather? Good haying horse can smell rain clouds far off as Kansas. In June all a farmer needs is a horse with a weather-nose and never again worry of moldy hay.

Good team of horses brings a man to twice as smart. Meet a stranger on the road and a horse can tell if a man were tramp, bum or hung out to dry. A horse could find its way home when the driver couldn't, yes sir. All the way from the Keene Postal Station and Tavern, try that, mister, with your tractor. Look what tractors done to the world. Never would have been world war if the earth were left to horses. Engines ruined the world. Was war that spilled the automobile. Uncle Jim was sure Wilson's war done it, done it to America, done it to him, done it to his horses. Democrats always start 'em. Don't mean to, but they do just the same. War gives a boy taste for liquor, fancy girls and hair oil; soldier couldn't see himself as debonair sitting out back of horses.

When the world was horse a man could hear himself think. Tractors are all noise and sparks, and pretty soon folks thinking they ain't smart if there isn't noise upholstery on everything. Uncle Jim knew where it would end; right back at horses.

He died that September at ninety years and four. Died in the upstairs room of the farmhouse he built in 1907. Slept in the same room, same iron bed, same east windows for fifty years. Never once a night away from his home and iron bedstead. Died in his sleep. So stiff by morning they said it was hard to get him down owing as the staircase is narrow and his body set-up. Had to stand Uncle Jim on end to make the turn. Said it was like he made the stairs on purpose so as maybe they'd leave him in the east room, with those morning windows and those fifty years near dawn.

In October they sold his team and captured and sold, too, the red stallion from the woodlot. Man had to shoot it to claim it. Nobody said so, but Uncle Jim's absence from the township was awful sudden. Dogs didn't have horseshit to roll in. We couldn't wait haying anymore for when Uncle Jim went out and the township knew haying was right 'cause Jim said it was right.

"I have followed horses all my living days and it has not broke bone or give complaint in ninety years."

THREE DOLLARS OVER

THE THING WAS RAIN. AND RAIN WAS A COMMON PAS-
sion uniting the townsmen. From Edmund to Lord Harold, Long Willie
to Uncle Jim, Grandfather Eugene and all his brothers, my father, my
brothers and myself. The village knew of the practice, as did every viable
and conscious merchant of the rivertown. Implement dealers prayed for
it, chore boys worshiped it and the entire township blasphemed should
it fail, from Bessie to the itinerant preach at his parsonage behind the
Liberty Corners Buena Vista Methodist Church.

From May to October only rain broke the drear bonds of husbandry.
Only rain canceled chore, boredom, delirium and the other unbending
habits of this rural planet. Granted, most observed Sunday as the Sabbath,
a day of Sunday school, churching, and in the laze of Sunday afternoon,
rest. Insanity might well have ended the human experiment long before
had it not been for the dictatorial god and the imposition of Sabbath.
For that reason, for the one Christian sanity, Sunday was obviously godly.

On their own, farmers would not have thought of Sunday, instead working straight through to their extinction. So it was their faith, and continued existence was secured by a god smart enough to demand Sabbath, this extended to children and farmboys who knew it was Sunday alone that separated them from pure abuse and early death. The damnation wasn't devils and sin but continuous chores. Let the preacher rage of future hell, every farmchild knew he had not taken chores into account. Don't tell a farm kid of black slaves or the smearing of Indian nations. We knew enough of foul intent. The city kid may well pursue innocence. Leisure was his. We knew there was god, if not maybe an upper case, capital letter god, but still a good and benevolent god, who salvaged our lives with the wisest, most generous thing the planet ever saw. No need to talk on nail holes, or rousing dead folks from the tomb. Sunday was holy. It found worship in every one of them, Lord Harold to Edmund, Uncle George and Grandfather Eugene.

Beyond the plain and obvious god of Sunday, one other existed, and it was rain. This was the capitalized, big G God. A drizzle wouldn't do, had to be rain. Thunder wasn't necessary, but wet had to be sufficient and hopefully excessive. A quarter-inch is of no help. Had to have more set to the teeth than that. Half-inch only approximated glory, an inch nearer lovely but one point five was both beauty and swoonful.

There were, of course, some dependent cases. Rain on top of spring melt wasn't worshipful. Even if it did take the frost out of the ground. Such a rain in the proximity of spring ruined dirt roads. Roads already had enough bother without rain on top of the melt. Anyways, spring didn't need rain to be marvelous.

Rain, to be honestly worshiped, had to enter at the portals of summer. The first chapter of rain worship is desire. I thought then and yet think this is a rule of worship. If you don't want it, you can't possibly worship the specimen. After the oats were in, the early potatoes, the maple leafed out, the oaks coming and the soil two weeks without, then we're talking possible worship.

The most worthy of rain happened in July when rain was more than miracle, it was loving. July rain had a wider congregation than all the brands of Jesus Book put together. July rain is welcomed and hosannahed by Papist, Methodee, water-dunker and Jerusalem artichoke. Summer rain brings out all the humor resident in the township's agrarians. A rain spending the night, still sprinkling at breakfast, invigorated with new thunder and redarkened sky after barn-cleaning did it. The day is baptized and devout. Our liberty was assured, whether towning or an afternoon spent wantonly in herbal confines of the haymow.

The surest sign of this emancipation is Pa dressed in new overalls with the list he had been advancing a couple months in his seedcorn notebook. Sickle blades, rivets, a new surcingle, strainer pads, grease in twenty-pound pails, window points, barn paint, a ten inch crescent, #50 roller chain, a ribbed front tire for the Allis. Beside each item, a notation of the expected cost. At the bottom the list was totalled. When Dad went to town he went by way of exact money. Every farmer knew the rule of exact money. Where the beatitude is preached to make it such a common lesson is difficult to say, but they all knew a wise man did not take an indeterminant fold of cash money to town. Not if he had dreams of empire and buying Widow Holiday's fallow forty or a new tractor. The fiscal potential of the farm empire they tended in their heads had only one ruin and that a rainy day libation. Which was why the notebook. A dollar more, maybe three. More than three and the man was a spendthrift.

Each farmer had his own favorite destination. Some went to Amherst Junction Milling, Bartig and Alm dealers for John Deere at Nelsonville, Laszewski Brothers Allis Chalmers in Plover Village, but most adored was the Fleet Farm store in Marshfield. Twenty miles west from the rivertown.

Fleet Farm was designed for the rainy day farmer. Ordinarily the store employed two clerks beside the owner, a plump, balding man. On rainy days four extra persons were employed along with the owner's wife. His genius was in understanding farmers and their needs. He had sickle knives to fit anything from a ground driven MacCormick Deering to an Oliver with hydraulic lift. Horse reins, bib overalls, soft rivets, stove bolts, carriage bolts, flat nails, cut nails, 16 penny, fence-wire, castrating knives, anti-suck calf masks, pump leathers in 2 inch, 3 inch and 3 and a half. Fleet Farm was a mercantile mountain. The building didn't have windows, the floor was gray cement with angle iron display racks from floor to ceiling. The shelves loaded with wares; piled in sizes, colors; caulks, paints, varnishes, brushes, pig bristle and nylon, light bulbs, posthole diggers, vee-belts, pulleys, cast and steel, set screws, thermos bottles, straw hat, winter flappers, chopper mitts. A farmer had to circulate the whole place a couple times to witness it.

The genius of Fleet Farm being the one aisle off toward the back of the building. The three dollar aisle. Toy tractors, wrist watches, flower pots, ladies nylons and garter belts. The ladies things in discreet little packages with half tone pictures of how they'd look when installed. Right behind the pen and pencil sets.

The wrist watches moved at Christmas time, pocket watches pretty steady year-round, garden seeds had their season, and flower pots. One other item had a constant pull, those nylons. Nice package with what's-her-name on the back. That farmgirl with the nice farm sounding name, Hayworth. A photograph of Miss Hayworth adjusting the item on her own limb was on the back side. The plump bald man thought it odd, how nylons sold on rainy days, at seventy-five cents each. Candy bars, licorice cigars, pipe 'baccy he could understand, but why nylons?

By noon the rain was letting up and the pickup trucks headed home and you know it's going to be a long noon-hour. Pa left the nylons on her chair next to the sewing machine so after he had gone out in the afternoon she'd find them. And when he came to the house from milking she smiled at him and shook her skirt showing Sunday shoes and twelve inches of investment credit.

Rain was worshipful in the township. I don't think the village ever really understood. They saw the pickups headed for town, the congestion at the feedmill, but didn't and couldn't know the dreams of rainy-day farmers.

On a rainy night with the clouds leaned into the horizon, I can feel the fields. Right there in the middle of the night, the world turns up at the edges. The more thunder the happier the curve. Tomorrow is a free one. A day in the haymow or to whittle in the woodshed. The girls spent the day with kittens in the window corner or among old clothes in the attic. Pa headed for town and Ma humming at the morning dishes, dreaming of the three dollar aisle at the Fleet Farm store.

OLD MAN WIGGY AND THE WOLF

HIS NAME WAS WIGGY, HE LIVED ON THE EAST AND west road long before it acquired a name in the platbook. Remembered for the black bib overalls he wore, his hair going decidedly gray, which came to his shoulders. His face was like the Moses on the Sistine ceiling; stony, yet inordinately gentle. It was generally accepted in the township Teddy Wiggy was crazy. Not a chair-breaking but a long hair crazy, a walking alone at night crazy.

Theodore and Joe Wiggy lived in the southeast corner of Section 2, Township 22 North, Range 8 East. The farm was a square parcel of a hundred and sixty acres; a small tidy house, out shed, barn, milk-house and a combination granary and tool-close. The front door of the house faced the town road and, as is customary in the township, was rarely used. Directly across the road from the farmhouse clawed the bruised profile of a crabapple tree. So situated, our intent on stealing apples had first to confront conscience before we could entertain sour apple bellyache. West from the porch spilled a benevolent society of lilacs, which when combined with a May breeze submerged the whole eastern half of the township in violet.

Joe Wiggy was a farmer and mechanic. For awhile he kept cows but in later years sold the herd and worked at odd jobs of mechanical repair. The Wiggys had come to the township mysteriously. Apparently they had no relatives in the area, which for the township is mystery enough. In 1936 they purchased the house on Section 2. Rumor had it they came from New York; actually they were from Chicago. The township's examination of strangers, while lacking in precision, made up for any lack of details with the rapid dissemination of what facts or estimations of fact were available.

"He was married."

"Who was?"

"The one named Theodore. Married to a socialite. You know the kind; willowy, bobbed hair, slinky dresses. Her family had money, I mean lots of money. She is supposed to have been beautiful. Her family made her leave him."

"Is that why he went nuts?"

"Yah, I think so; they say she was beautiful."

The fact was right as far as it went; she did leave him, the reason was not her family but a motorcar accident. The steering wheel crushed his chest and she was thrown out and killed. At first the deputies couldn't believe she was dead, she was that smooth and that beautiful. The car was a Model J Duesenberg four-passenger phaeton.

The Wiggys originally hailed from Philadelphia and a family thought well-to-do. As a young man Theodore was an accomplished scholar and in 1920 found himself in France studying literature and music of the Romantic Period. He fell in love with automobiles due to the embrace of a Type 35 Bugatti. While his family was under the impression he spent his time studying historical scores and chorals, he was in fact elbow deep in the nickel-plated complexity of a straight-eight, 2 liter, double overhead cams on needle bearings. Teddy had no difficulty obtaining a job at the Bugatti factory, in no small way due to his musical ear trained to cue the subtle difference of a connecting rod over-torqued and the engine slightly off key. When he returned to the States, Teddy searched out Fred Duesenberg and handed him a note signed by Ettore Bugatti. He was hired on the spot. Hired to deliver new cars to customers and as part of the price, teach them intricacies of a Duesenberg; the maintenance, lubrication and certain skills of high speed driving.

Teddy was impressive. Perhaps because he swore in French, perhaps his distinctive way of acknowledging the world, his slight turn and bow when a lady entered the room. He could recite a toast to Robert Bruce in Gaelic, or the balcony scene from Romeo and Juliet in liquid King James English.

She was a customer's daughter and they had been married three years when a vegetable truck sideswiped them. Teddy was not altogether blameless. The car had been traveling one hundred and six miles an hour and it was 2:30 a.m. But he had driven faster. Besides delivering new cars, Teddy ran-in new Duesenberg engines for 500 miles on the Indianapolis, Indiana racetrack before a coach body was fitted. The open frame J-Type Duesenberg on eight cylinders, 265 horsepower on 19 inch tires throttled up to a hundred and forty miles an hour. The SJ Model managed one hundred and seventy-five miles an hour with 320 horsepower from the aid of a centrifugal supercharger.

Teddy suffered a broken skull, fractured ribs, blurred vision and slurred speech. In time his vision returned, his speech never quite the controlled mechanism it was before. When he spoke French it hardly seemed to matter, that being the forgiving nature of the language. The willow-woman was buried in the family plot before he regained consciousness.

Shortly after, Joe bought the farm. The land was two dollars and seventy cents an acre, the improvements another 1100 dollars. Joe always liked the countryside, land was real to him and it promised a privacy a man could use in 1936, especially a man with a brother who woke in the night singing French songs.

Was Joe's hope Teddy would improve his mental health away from the city. The township offered the chance to put away long automobiles and anything as might remind Teddy of the willow-woman. At times Teddy was lucid. He'd glance over some broken bit of machinery and garble a few words about shaft wobble. Joe knew some day he'd be all right. Still his memory of things was out of round, he recalled her and the French language in the same momnent.

...conne on voit sur la branche au mois de mai la rose

en sa belle jennese, en sa premier fleur

rendre le ciel jaloix de sa vive couleur

quand l'aube de ses pleurs au point du jour l'arrose.

In another he'd recall how Bugattis looked like frogs from the way their suspension canted. How they smelled of castor oil. If the wind favored him Teddy could tell a Bugatti from any other car on the road, he smelled them coming and from the engine note, what gear it was in. Teddy didn't talk about Duesenbergs. He kept out of sight mostly, reading, sometimes working in the machine-shed at the little bench Joe set up. If Ted was unkempt, Joe thought he earned it. Too, maybe it helped to keep inquisitive neighbors away.

Wolves were thought to be extinct from central Wisconsin by the turn of the twentieth century. The last one had its photograph taken and printed in the Stevens Point Daily Journal in 1902. The caption read "Last of the Vermin." Few believed the rumor then of a wolf roaming the Buena Vista Marsh in the modern year of 1937. Some said they had seen tracks, others heard a howl. A howl even those uneducated in the way of wolves knew in their bones was a wolf. The marsh had coyotes, most folks heard one time or other the coyote bark and yawning sound.

The wolf was different. It was a separate vibration, an ecstasy between air and earth. In the dark the sound raised the hair on the back of the neck, hair most had forgotten had any erectile muscle attached to it. A few farmers were worried about the cattle and wanted to blow a hole in whatever it was as could give vent to a noise like that. It was, they thought, an indecent sound for a civilized country. Some took to carrying rifles in their rigs. There were arguments over who had actually seen it and who shot at what, and certain families no longer sat in a pew on the same side of the church with another family because the farm dog had turned up missing and a familiar-looking hide was stitched to the neighbor's barn door.

A wolf track is the size of a large man's fist. Kids lit on the idea of getting plaster-of-paris casts of wolf tracks. They pestered mothers to let them sleep outdoors so maybe they could hear the wolf and if they did, came running breathlessly to the house, unable to talk, unable to stop shaking. There were mothers whose mistake was thinking the effect was fear.

At the feedmill they talked of a collection to hire up a government hunter. The wolf, they thought, would attack cattle soon, and surely it was ruin of the deer herd, and hadn't they read of wolves killing grown horses and eviscerating children sent berry-picking. With winter coming (and winter makes everything meaner, they certainly knew that), it might be wise to settle the countryside down and get that wolf.

Was about this juncture someone took a shot at Teddy. A thirty-thirty lever-action fired at an unusual and hairy shape loping across the night field. "Well, he looked kinda wolfish. I mean, what's a man doing out there at that time of night?" The bullet passed cleanly through Teddy's calf muscle. Treated with rubbing alcohol and linen rags, the wound healed, leaving only the limp of scarred ligaments on cold days.

The bullet provoked something in Teddy. He felt the more related to what creature was out there, the incident had superimposed Ted and the wolf and their mutual fates. Joe told him, "Next time they won't miss, they'll shoot you dead." The advice fell without effect, and Joe knew it was useless to try.

At the Community Club the menfolk grumbled about potatoes at fifteen cents a hundred with the bag itself worth two. And whether they would ever make enough to buy a tractor, or whether tractors were altogether too complicated and too expensive to run. And they talked wolf. One said he had a cow go down and dragged it to the woods and poisoned it with three pounds of strychnine. He was sure he'd get the thing.

"I slit the belly open and hung the guts from a tree so the wind can catch the scent better."

"You gosh damn fool, you'll kill every farm dog, cat and runaway pig for twenty miles around with that fool stunt. Besides, a wolf won't eat carrion unless there is nothing else. My dad once told me wolves have a death talk with their prey before they kill it. He used to say the wolf and man are related. Once he had seen a wolf, and when it looked at him was with human eyes."

"I tell you an animal is an animal and a man is a man. I ain't related to any mangy wolf. You may know a bitch but I don't."

The women gathered at the coffee pot knew when the discussion around the stove had gotten overly tangled. Knew the signs of strain. Such as when no one was keeping a lookout due to the particular blue hue of the stories. Instead the menfolk were staring and sullen at the pit of silence between them. One of the women grabbed the cookie plate and coffee pot to loosen things up before a fist fight broke out which would over memorialize the Community Club Christmas party.

While the dairymen, potato farmers and milk haulers were reluctantly singing Christmas carols at the community hall, Teddy sat cross-legged in the SE corner of the NW corner of Section 13, cross-legged and wrapped in a frayed Navajo weave blanket. The sandy dune only a little above the muck moors of Buena Vista Marsh. The dune had been left by the melt waters of the last glaciation. A west wind drove his scent into the dense tangle of hemlock and balsam behind him, before him lay the marsh. He waited in the darkness for his eyes to adjust. It was about eleven o'clock when he began to howl.

A sound so like one he heard before. The howl of a supercharged Bugatti at 5 pounds of boost. You knew having heard it it was something powerful. The way the sound was warped and rippled by the landscape or the throttle.

At the community hall men were sitting on chairs and upended stovewood, smoking pipes, passing a small hip flask and still talking wolf.

"I figure to get the thing before Christmas."

"Like hell you do."

"I just bought a new rifle. Mean looking military surplus called a Springfield, thirty-aught-six caliber. Smaller bullet than the thirty-thirty but with a shell case long as my finger. I'll get the wolf I tell you. At a mile I can blow the top off a milk can."

"Pshaw. At a mile?"

"At a mile. If you can see it, the thirty-aught-six can reach out and smack it. Like I was telling, it's ex-military. The guy I bought it from said there're thousands stored away somewhere in warehouses and some day the thirty-aught-six be in the hand of every deer hunter."

It was a mile away when Teddy first saw the wolf. Against the snow the creature appeared no more than a vain whim of the winter landscape. Only the moon gave the wolf away, a depth of shadow to know it or something was there. Following the deer run as Teddy thought, the animal was smaller than he expected. Could easily be confused for a large dog, still it did not move like a dog. About it was a smoothness, a motion which gave the creature its name, lupus, canis lupus linneaus, concurrently the notion the creature could stalk and run forever. Against the darkness and the marsh the wolf seemed, well, civilized. Quite unexpected the thought touched him. Could a beast be civilized? Hadn't he spent years and other men their fortunes to achieve that same fluidity? That elegance of movement produced only by intelligence and civilization? Duesenbergs used copper-lined hypods filled with mercury to soothe the jerks of the 150 pound crankshaft. The wolf was like the Duesenberg, that same awareness, the refined acuity that can only be the product of mastered skills. In the automobile it was gauges; ammeter, oil pressure, fuel, water, temperature, revolution counter, chronograph, 150mph speedometer, altimeter, barometer, brake pressure and a signal box to indicate when it was time to change the oil, check the battery and that the self-lubrication reservoir was empty. The wolf had its like and perfect sensibilities. The wolf was an engineered design, of smell, eyesight, long shoulder muscle, tensile claw and silken hide. Teddy had read somewhere that 60 million years before, men and wolves belonged to the same family, both cursorial and carnivorous. Together in some ancestry both men and wolves learned the table-manners of canine tooth and power of clan and pack. He read that wolves live and hunt together, that the pups must be taught to hunt and to share. How sometimes wolves leave territory to let the game build up again like farmers fallowing land. How they scent-mark their territories to warn away strangers, as men might use tartan and flag. How wolves map their domains with scented roads so no wolf is ever lost. How bachelor wolves share in the child rearing. The pups play catch with a bone and are scolded for disobedience. How the pack maintains a population consistent with the food supply. And how they sometimes kill to excess and sometimes kill each other and sometimes commit suicide and sometimes climb trees and sometimes howl just to hear themselves howl and howl because they are in love or hungry or lonely. The Indian, he read somewhere, believes the wolf is holy because it is man's brother.

"Next time I'll kill them both. I swear, I will kill them both. I had that damn wolf in my sights when old man Wiggy lets out this howl that turned the wolf and sent it running like fire through a straw barn. I could have fired off a couple shots but not at 25 cents apiece, and I only have a dollar's worth. All because of that crazy Wiggy. I should've shot him and strung his hide from the barn. Somebody ought to put him away; he's crazy, ain't he? Besides, he looks like Karl Marx."

Within the week everyone knew Teddy was a Marxist or a Moslem or a cousin to Mozart or something awful. Not that it affected how they treated Teddy. In the township it was all right to have feelings but not at all correct to wear them on your sleeve. Why? Well just 'cause. Anyway, a machine might up and bust and they have to haul it over to Wiggy's for Joe to fix, and hadn't they seen Teddy pointing out something to Joe as if he was telling him how to weld it so they wouldn't have to buy a new one which cost twenty bucks and it was 1937 and a whole milk check would go to pay for it and week to get here besides? Hadn't they seen that, hadn't they?

Maybe Teddy was kinda funny and kinda crazy, still he was useful, and weren't they civilized? And if a man can't run off wild once in a while they all'd be shipped to the funny-farm. If Teddy wanted to invest his dark howling at a wolf it was his own personal business.

Teddy had a nose, perhaps because of all those years in France. He could smell the difference between any two kinds of beer, smoking tobacco or wine. They'd seen him sniff at a crankcase and say it was time to change oil. Teddy knew from the living room when Joe was putting too much black pepper on the fried potatoes. Smell is a language all by itself, he'd tell Joe. People smell different one from the other. A man spending the day in the woods gathering oak firewood smells separate from a man cutting pine logs for lumber. Without asking, he knew whether a woman had spent the day boiling chickens or weeding the garden. If he worked at it, he could tell if she was in love. In France, he told Joe, you read with your nose, you listen with your nose, and best of all you eat with your nose.

Didn't surprise Joe when Teddy disappeared for extended whiles. What bothered him was the prodigious amounts of water, tea and wine Teddy was consuming. Every time he turned around, Teddy seemed to be drinking some fluid. When questioned Teddy simply said he had been walking a great deal and must be sweating more.

"Where do you go anyway? You're up at the small hours, I hear the door close. You aren't back till mid-afternoon. Last week you were out the whole day. No, it don't bother me. But Christ, Teddy, there's people out there with guns and a few of them bear you personal grievance. In the dark they could shoot you instead of the wolf."

"That would serve."

"What?"

"Nothing." Joe and Ted were brothers and knew when not to pursue a subject.

"You mean to tell me you spent seventy-five dollars on that?"

"No, it only cost $32 but freight from Manitoba was 43 dollars and fifty cents."

"Why the hell d'yah spend 75 bucks on a dog?"

"It's not a dog, its a husky."

"Je's, looks big enough to pull a plow."

"Joe, don't tell anyone."

"What?"

"Don't tell anyone about the dog."

"Why not?"

"Just don't." Teddy used a tone of voice peculiar to the species when they come up against one of their foundation stones.

One car or rig parked on the town road is bound to attract the notice of a second and the second a third. The occurence was the township's definition of orbit. The first car stopped to borrow a logging chain and bring the kids a box of Christmas fudge. The second car stopped 'cause it was almost Christmas, and the man felt like talking. The third stopped 'cause he was afraid he'd slide into the ditch trying to get around the first two. Before the hour was out, three-quarters of the motorcars and half the horse rigs remaining in the township were lined up and down the road. They stopped because they thought it was a fire or a sawmill accident or something memorable.

The crowd was gathered at the windless side of Elias Mansavage's barn and looking at the hide nailed to the big sliding door. Elias stood in the center of the crowd holding aloft his rifle and demonstrated for the twentieth time how he lined up the shot and killed the thing.

"Easiest shot I ever made. Was gettin' stovewood from the woodlot pasture when I saw it coming. Was real careful to move deliberate so's not to spook it while I went for the rifle. Was loaded just in case, been loaded and waiting for all of three weeks. Thing never knew what hit him. Why, when the bullet plugged him, he folded up easy as a wet bransack. I bet that's the last wolf we'll see in these good parts. Which is a good thing. We can't have them sort of beasts in our woods. Look the size of it. Think your piglets be safe with those teeth running wild? Didn't I promise at the Community Club to make a rug out of it by Christmas? Didn't I? Though for awhile I wondered. Old man Wiggy was sneaking around so much; I think he thought to scare it off. Teddy's OK, I ain't meaning nothing at him, but a sane man doesn't howl, does he? And besides, I think the man has got a serious bladder problem."

The hide hung on that barn for almost three years, nailed in the historic fashion of victims. After awhile people didn't stop any more and the farmer pretty much forgot about it and never did make it into a rug. Finally one June morning he pulled the hide from the door with a pitch fork and tossed it into a manure spreader. The nails stayed behind and the hide left an irregular outline on the door till the barn burned in 1967. Old Elias did look at the spot from time to time and pleased himself remembering 1937 and the time he had the town road stopped up with cars and how he told them about the wolf and how he killed the beast with the first thirty-aught-six around. The distance with retelling went from fifty yards, to half a mile, to darn close to a mile, the wind blowing and the wolf running.

Well, almost a wolf.

After a while folks forgot how Theodore Wiggy had been heard howling and was once rumored to have had bladder trouble. Some of them swear on Christmas Eve they still hear a wolf, or maybe it is old Wiggy himself howling. How on a winter night the wind will work itself into a howl at the windows and howl too across the chimneytop. And there are those in the township who have come to think there is something quite lovely in a howl.

OLD SLAB

HAROLD EDWARDS HAD IN HIS LIFETIME AN AMALGAM
of dogs peculiar to farmers. The situation brought about by the typical
and sundry circumstance of dogs being shorter of life than their two-
legged alliance. That one out of five dogs wouldn't trade their lot for the
advertised elevation of homo-sapiens belies a prejudice. The statistics
taken, the average farmer during his installment works his way through
5.6 dogs. The nice thing about dogs, farm dogs in fact, is their whole
obedience to fractional mathematics.

Farm dogs are precise to statistics. Six-tenths of a dog can carry on
in natural comfort despite the adjournment of four-tenths of his corporal
being. The farmship is, generally speaking, rough on dogs. Mowing machines whittle legs, cows lend deciduous aspect to their teeth, tails get
wound in v-belts, pulleys, logging chains, their eyes are abbreviated by
sticks, stones, horse hoof, some lost to cat claw. Just why it is dogs are

inclined to nip the heels of a creation a hundred times their mass is lost to the mull of eons.

Harold Edwards had a dog, and its name was Slab. Slab because it looked exactly like its mother which was the previous edition and bore no semblance at all to the wild escort, of which there were several choices. Establishing the identity of Slab's breed would not have been possible with the most diligent research using laboratory techniques. Indeed disassembly of the animal would not have aided the quest. Slab was something of every dog, a jederman dog. At his face he was short-haired, his head and ears coiffured as an English barrister and his shoulders bore a ruff to glory the Tzar of White Russia. The precise hue of Slab was hard to determine being such a mix and stir the colors didn't settle. Slab's nose was short for a dog, and owing to the possession of two unmistakably blue eyes, Old Slab had about him the look of a pretty average citizen of that townshipif a bit warmly dressed for July, but still passable at the winter caucus, that is before the stove got warm enough for folks to squirm out from their coats. Seems the chimney of the institution had a stubborn draw which allowed anything dressed in a coat a chance to exercise citizenship. The reason the town hall and the electors of the town is mentioned is because it was at the winter caucus where one year Slab cast the deciding vote. Maybe it wasn't the deciding vote, but he voted, which is pretty good for a dog. For those with doubt, check the elector registry of 1953, Town of Plover; in it is named a citizen Slab Edwards residing on the Maine School Road south off the state highway.

The issue of the town meeting was whether dogs should be taxed and licensed at one dollar per annum. The habit had been the rage of the village and a nifty source of almost 500 dollars and all paid in cash. 500 dollars was deemed sufficient to pay the town crew except for any that were bound to work off their taxes. As a consequence a dog-tax was proposed and seized upon by the political constabulary. Here was one more excise they could gain as if ordained by heaven itself, or if that consensus was wanting then some passage out of Mister Darwin's sacrament.

The supervisors had anticipated consternation but not the temper the legislation precipitated in the township. Hadn't the village folks swallowed the dog tax easy enough, but things like hard roads and fire protection cause village folk to become a separate genre from their rural relation. After all, what's a dog's purpose in the village? Nothing but laps and parlor rugs. A farm dog tain't nothing like the sorry station of a village dog. His citizenry has account, that he can't hold property or run for office is an oversight in the law. Hence the special town-meeting was called to resolve the issue.

Now most folks more stable than milkweed fluff knew Harold Edwards of the Maine School Road south off the state highway. His place was the last of the highland, before the territory took a sudden disinclination toward farmers and farming in general and became the Buena Vista Marsh. A handsome place Harold's was, nice forty-cow barn, gambrel roof with a stone foundation. Nifty thing that stone foundation, being this was sand country and stones had to be hauled all the way from the moraine four miles east. A man has got to love solid a lot to build of stone in sand country. Which was pretty much the thing about Harold Edwards. Not that he was a perfectionist, rather when he set to something permanent he believed permanent meant just that. Boards were good for a hundred years, maybe even a couple hundred if of the best white pine heartwood. Paint he didn't have much faith in. Paint was for pictures and assessors, not for barns and granaries and chicken coops.

Atop his barn Harold established the largest mow ventilator ever constructed. About the size of a one-holer it was the major attraction of the township. People came for miles to see Harold Edwards' ventilator. Done in the most modern shape the object looked a great deal like something out of Mister H. G. Wells' literature, which might be supposed was the architect's intent. The four sides were galvanized steel joined together at the exhaust ring, above which projected a long conical declaration at whose point was a solid copper needle nearly three feet long. On this was balanced a wind-arrow of genuine brass on whose shaft stood, if delicately, a fabricated copper cow, all four feet agrip of the arrow. Whether the wind vane worked was never ascertained. It did point west, as good a guess as any for the locality.

The house sat east of the barn in its wind shadow and was more conversant with paint than was the barn. A tidy house, two-story with a south facing porch and bay windows on the living room. Another porch was situated east but of little utility other than a wintering room for squash. The upstairs room was never finished though it did have a handsome dormer with leaded-glass windows.

South below the house the land sloped toward the granary and machine-shed. Beside the granary, on the end with the feed grinder, was the family garden. Cultivated in the tradition of honorable English gardens everywhere the perimeter was handsomely fenced in with upright boards prescribing a secret acreage. It could be proposed the garden was sequestered out of reverence to the biblical precedence, which may have been the intent of the English, but surely was not the case for Harold Edwards. Harold was not into biblical symbols nor anything remotely connected to papists and their point of view on life or gardens. Of damnation Harold Edwards was inclined to be more the believer and had on hand a ready list of those he thought deserving. To his mind nothing was eternal, not man nor beast nor heaven or high water on the Buena Vista Marsh. By his judgment arthritis came as close to eternal as a thing could, and good heartwood boards and stone foundations, but all else was transient and had no right to be any the more.

Harold married late in life a red-haired lass of the Upper Peninsula, that pendant of sand and jack pine spewed out into Lake Superior which has caused enmity between the state of Wisconsin and Michigan for 150 years because Michigan kept the Upper Peninsula despite its solid attachments to the granite frame of Wisconsin.

Myrtle bore Harold five children in 21 years. All of them girls except at the last, separated by twelve years, a boy-child. Old Slab occupied this 12-year span when Harold figured his line was doomed if not genetically, then by sire-name. His misery was compounded by the Catholic hosts who circled around him, most of whom were of Polish extraction and were laying kids out at such a rate a common Englishman could not compete, even with a fenced-in garden.

During the lull of his progeny Harold continued to mind his farm and the one communal habit he allowed himself. There probably were several but for the sake of this tell we'll credit only one, that of taking cows. For those of a village reference, taking cows is the daily task of moving cows from barn to pasture and back from that position at the end of the day. Harld's pasture lay in line with the town road and as consequence he used the town road to attend the bovines to their forage.

Harold Edwards had one tractor, a Case Model DC. Common to the age, the Model DC had four cylinders driving two cast iron wheels through four headlong gears and one for retreat. A spring-loaded navigation seat was situated directly behind the steering wheel. Engaging a lever on the starboard side obtained forward motion. The tractor was fitted for all circumstance of farmers, those with short arms and even shorter legs could use the vehicle without undue hazard to themselves or the community. Those more long of frame used the implement by adjusting their stance, the result looked mightily like Juan Fangio straight-arming a Grand Prix Mercedes in the hot fatal dust of the Mille Miglia. Harold Edwards was the one exception to the Case Model DC. He could not fit the entirety of himself between the wheel and the seat with enough residue left over to establish his relish. So he stood behind the seat, one foot on the draw-bar, one foot on the deck, one hand on the steering knob, the other tending his pipe. With practice he found he could rest the front of his torso on the seat and gain considerable comfort. That no one else could or dare drive a tractor in the fashion of Harold Edwards enhanced the pose.

The importance of Harold's tractoring technique to the plot is the subsequently vacant seat. A prominence quickly analysed and seized on by Old Slab as the proper altar for his person. Old Slab looked a great deal like a person, if overly dressed for summer, but then odd things are wont to happen in the townships and particularly to those at the seam of the great marsh where freezing temperatures are in vogue any month of the year, so a man wearing a fur coat was not considered all that surprising.

Cows do not ordinarily move from barn to pasture or vice versa with any habitual velocity. Only exceptions being the first spring let-out and any atmospheric mix of cows in heat and those other fragrances of certain available licentiousness, a situation pretty much obliterated in the modern age of artificial insemination. In all but the first spring let-out, the cows took their time, and the Case Model DC never vented itself beyond first gear at 50% throttle, a decorum unchanged from pasture-gate to barn-yard.

Harold naturally reasoned Old Slab might as well do most of the driving, the road being straight and the steering linkage of the Model DC going through such a momentum of gears, followers, cast-iron shifters and narrow front-end as to prevent steering drift. All Slab had to do was put his paws on the wheel, that, combined with the native groove in the road, was steering enough. So Old Slab drove while Harold smoked his pipe, opened the gate and turned the tractor around at the end of the circuit. This policy continued rather matter-of-factly until village folk discovered to their delight this dog who could drive a tractor. Unfortunately the rumor spread, and Old Slab was pretty much a famous dog, which was all right, except folks wanted to see the real thing and parked their cars along the road just to catch a glimpse of Slab at the wheel.

It wasn't that Slab minded but the cows took affront and stopped dead in the road at the assembly of four cars and a clean pickup truck. Someone, to foster the action, tooted their horn which spooked the poor beasts and they split with the certain violence attending the species and

Old Slab

one, confronted with a handsome curved-window Studebaker, attempted to leap the impediment. Didn't make it, rather was short by half a car length and the roof of the new Studebaker was instantly conformed more to an impoundment of a stock-tank than a roof. The driver of the vehicle accosted Harold saying the incident was his fault and he'd have to pay damages. Now the only damages Harold Edwards ever considered he or any man liable to were those taking place outside the matrimonial stead. So he refused to pay. Even after three letters and a visit from the man's attorney, the case not advanced by the counselor's being of Polish extraction.

A trial date was set and in course Harold called to witness. The case seemed to be going the wrong way from the Studebaker when the man lit out it wasn't the cow's fault but that short fella who was driving the tractor. Seems the complainant had forgotten the initial reason for visiting the town road at milking time was to see a dog drive a Case Model DC. Instead his memory recalled only a short little man with a fur coat and a curious nose. This being in the age before artist renditions, the court was saved some deliberation. When asked of the identity of the mysterious folk in the fur coat Harold said he had to profess ignorance, knowing no little man in a fur coat. The client did not help the matter by jumping up and down, repeatedly shouting there was a funny little man in a fur coat and maybe even smoking a pipe and Mister Edwards knew darn well there was and had better gum up and tell the court who the furry little man was.

The sheriff's report was checked and rechecked but no mention could be found of an extra man with or without a fur coat. At which the claimant stood up on the courtroom table and yelled, "There is a little man in a fur coat somewhere," after which he stomped his feet and repeated the remark. It was the man's first almost-new Studebaker, and the big chrome bullet in the middle of the radiator looked awfully impressive when he first opened the garage door in the morning. And it was a pretty big pond smack dab in the middle of the roof and it did cost 33

97

dollars and 26 cents to repair, and doesn't it do something to a car to have a cow come down on it? It's never the same again.

After the man's lawyer helped him down from the table, the judge, fearing the hearing was not proceeding with the uniformity he anticipated, asked the lawyers to attend him at chambers. The aftermath was the dismissal of the case.

'Course everyone in the neighborhood knew who the little man in the fur coat was. None other than Old Slab. That no one came forward with the evidence suggested a contemporary opinion that a man bringing home his cows has a natural right-of-way. If village folk want to come and watch for their purposes it's OK, but cows are a little left-brained and cannot be counted on to hold their opinion when roused. Still, the neighbors thought it curious why any would want to watch cows come home even if driven by a dog on a Case Model DC.

The chairman asked whether a vote should be taken straight-off or if they wanted to discuss the issue. An hour later it was decided to vote straight-away. Those favoring the dog-tax made a show of 6 hands. Those contrary offered 84 hands and one paw. The vote was recorded as 85 to 6, opposed.

Another decade was to pass before a dog-tax came to the township, by then Old Slab was buried in the fencerow. Harold Edwards to his last days was proud of that dog. A dog who was a voting citizen of the township and the mystery villain in a crime perpetrated on a '49 Studebaker.

THE CRUISER

U NCLE NATE SAT ON THE EDGE OF SUMMER, THREW
back his head and remembered. A curious man, Uncle Nate. Not a genuine uncle, owing his weave to the family was by my sister-ogre marrying one G. D. Menzel of Stevens Point. G. D. being six foot six inches and Pattie a lousy five foot two, we didn't think they'd ever have kids on account of the obvious lack of fit.

Uncle Nate visited his sister in the river-city every couple weeks and in course of that visit drove out to the farm. That he chose to tour our hearts at one of the more dismal of violations of the farmkid endeared him to us. Without fail he drove into the farmyard at the exact incidence of evening chores. He lugged silage, he dumped milk buckets. He followed us into the haymow and took his turn with a bale from the top of the mow and tried to hit the chute in the one impressive "bombs-away" arc of mastery.

After supper the family retired to the front porch, sundown and Uncle Nate. He lay back his white head in an attitude that is the first supplication of memory, and smoked a continuous rhythm of unfiltered Pall Malls. After finishing each smoke he deliberately twisted the butts in the gravel, ruining any chance of that butt serving further purpose. Ma never said anything against Nate's cigarettes despite an obvious hacking cough that choked him up from time to time. When he spoke, his voice had the power of mid-channel river current, it pulled who ever was close right in. As he settled farther and farther within his own interior, he drew us with him as he mined the streak of memory deep inside. His voice became disconnected, as if piped to the surface. The words themselves seemed musty from storage, stinging with a newness of expression. Gone was Nate's flat urban voice and in its place the tongue of his grandfather, of Ojib and another way with words.

Nate spoke: "He could speak Ojibwa. Say, Good night and go to sleep and kiss me and what's for supper. Ojib is a musical language, like water over rocks, it bubbles, a rounded off language as if it is impolite for consonants to break the surface with their angular sounds.

My Grandfather Bruce was a timber cruiser, you could tell he was by the vain way he walked. Came of years walking the woods, sighting up trees and gaining new headlands. To be a cruiser was to be a prince then, those were piney days and Wisconsin about as far away from anything as you could get and still be on earth.

At 10 years he went to the woods as a cook's helper. His pa, my great grandad, hired him off for the grand wage of a dollar a week and the promise to give the boy a book-learning. By the time he was 12 he had read that new novel "Moby Dick" and recent writings of the eastern sage, Ralph Waldo Emerson. By 14 Bruce was a woods-buster and had his ripe height of five and nine. Caulked boots worn over two pairs of socks give him another two inches and he seemed suddenly a man. It was the hue of the woods on him that surprised his ma. The smell of pine pitch and smoky bunkhouse talk dismayed her. She complained he looked like a heathen, he was too tall, too limber and so sure of himself, more a deer than a Christian being.

Not all the jacks wore two pairs of socks, socks were then 50 cents a pair for the length coming to the top of the boot. Mullein leaves took the place of one pair. Mullein stays green all the winter, and its fuzzy leaves possess the approximate shape of a man's foot. They serve as insole, absorb sweat and grow in abundance on the cut-overs. Finding a patch of mullein, a jack picked a washtub full and hiked it back to the bunkhouse.

Lumbermen never knew of mullein leaves, they rarely came to the woods. Around Christmas sometimes, with their spoiled wives, bringing ham and whisky to the camp. They sent word they were coming and to lye-wash the bunkhouse so the wives didn't faint from the vapors. The lumbermen knew nothing of winter in the woods. What it does to a man's feet, how sweat collects in the boot and freezes if a man sits too long. .

Didn't do to steal another man's mullein supply or at least get caught stealing. The woods had its own justice. The first time they'd box the offender's ear. The guilty party made to toe one spot while someone took a free round-house swing at the man's ear. It was deemed permissable to wear a stocking cap, second time, no cap. Could break a man's eardrum and leave him dizzy for a week. Third time they'd hold his hand to a stump and crimp a wrought-iron nail around it so that man or boy stayed right there till he got cruel enough on himself to pull his finger through the nail. The square-cut edges of the nail skinned the finger slick. Sometimes the skin grew back, sometimes only a meaty scar leaving the finger stiff and useless on his hand the rest of his natural days.

If theft was substantial, the offender's thumb got chopped. Took of the hand he didn't work with. They weren't trying to be mean, just instructive. They knew stealing. Sometimes a man had to steal. The woods leaves a man forgetful what with his woman back home tending the farm and the kids sick and winter hard and the woodpile green.

Most jacks came to hate the woods. Hate winter. Those particular years when the winter and the woods were remorseless as a sawtooth. The sodden bunkhouse never aired out and near tubercular with shotgun bunks and vinegar acid socks hung over the rafters and the phlegm buckets filling over night from jacks with the cough.

They weren't lumberjacks because they loved the woods, instead they needed the money, they jacked to gain a stake. Four years in the wood paid off the farm with maybe enough left-over to build a barn and add a kitchen-lean to the house. Wasn't that the wages were good as much as cut-over land and barns were cheap. A dollar a day was good money. A keg of nails cost one dollar, a pair of mule leather boots were two and twenty, a buffalo robe at two dollars, a four-pane window 35 cents, boards enough for a barn cost 35 dollars, 16 dollars worth of shingles did the whole roof, bib overalls 65 cents. Loggers went to the woods to be farmers, not woodsmen.

Bruce fell otherwise, he fell head-long and heart for the woods. The woods got him, crawled in his mind and twisted up in his blood. The trees became his kinsmen. He could understand the woods. What others hated, he loved. When they grew bitter at long winter, the brutality and pain, he found pleasure. Winter in the woods was his life, his elixir, his meat and his bone. Alone in the pines, he heard his own blood pump.

Winter swallowed a man. If he needed to die, winter took him in an hour. Like times when a wound went green when a saw slipped and cut open to the bone and the bleeding stopped too soon, or a greasy needle stitched up the gash. Didn't dare cut an arm off, a man needed the chance, he was worse than dead without all his pins, and when the smell crept in, he knew his pyre was set. One cold clear afternoon he hobbled into the woods, sat on a stump and froze to death. He wore his best clothes so all there was to do was cork him up, penny his eyes and send him home in a new sawn box.

The winter woods didn't let the holler out. Instead passed it around, teasing an innocent jack with what he heard, or thought he heard in the woods. Toying at him. The woods had the stink of the undiscovered, those old trees might harbor things as didn't occur to science. He'd seen faces sometimes in the dark alleys, leering woodgrained faces of frozen loggers and Indians. Sometimes it was a woods full of thighs, soft brown thighs and privates, and he had to shake himself and bite off a new plug of tobacco to get clear.

A jack had to dress for winter, cotton long-johns under wool pants and a wool shirt. On a 10 degree day, a working jack rolled up his sleeves and worked bare-knuckled. The worst winters of all were warm ones, the sickness got passed around. Jacks said regular cold killed disease and fevers better than the apothecary.

At 16 Bruce swung an axe as well as any man in camp. His muscles smooth, he swung with the ease of a migrating bird, that same ceaseless patience was native to him. Bruce knew how to dress for the woods, how to bundle in a mackinaw after a hard chop and cool off slow instead of letting the sweat freeze. And never drink cold water in winter, instead tea; water rusts your bones. Tea of camomile and wild mint and Formosa black and wintergreen. Tea kept a man going, stood him when he'd rather sag in a heap somewhere in the middle of a logger's afternoon.

Bruce oiled his boots with pork fat, the boots a size larger and worn with a pair of light moccasins instead of socks. Moccasins didn't cost. Indians will swap half a dozen pair for a leather belt with a brass buckle. And as long as he was negotiating, he'd convince them of blueberries and maple sugar for the cook shanty in trade for bread and salt. Blueberry pancakes spilt humor among the loggers in the harsh muck before dawn. Blueberries and maple syrup soothe the rough circumference of the woods-jacks, and plug 'baccy kept the Indians happy.

Was a time he was lost; the night the camp-ox broke out, uncommon for ox, they lit diagonal to the country in the manner of wild cattle. The night was moon-crazed, and tree branches clucked like old women at their mends, the spilling shadows spooked the dull beast. Bruce set out while the tracks were easy to follow. Wait till morning, they told him.

But morning there be logs to nudge, bobs to shag and a river to gauge. He'd have that ox barned by breakfast. During the night the wind canted nor'west and it commenced to snow. In the woods a man keens his direction from the wind, figures wind to be a constant thing, dontcha know. By daylight Bruce was hauling through twelve inches of new snow and 22 miles, and it was late afternoon before he finally skidded that cow into camp. The crew hadn't worked whit, and when he came in belly dragging they laughed and snickered and wondered aloud if he'd been gone visiting the Milwaukee girls. Aye, they knew, every least one of them knew theyda died that night in the fen or had a woods dying fear overtake them or killed the ox and slung out its guts and clumb into the hole to avoid dying, the frozen dead dying of lost in the woods.

Bruce was a specimen. Not particular big, more middling size. He'd arm wrestle any who dare and as sure lose though he'd get groan of them 'fore they'd pine his hand.

At spring breakup, they'd hold a compeet. A race, from the bunk-biggie to creek, to snatch watercree and tear boot-tops and galooses back to the bunkhouse. Bruce, he'd out-snort 'em all. W' his peep in his yam the whole time just to make 'em mad, mad leaves a man tight and slow.

Came to the chopping, he'd worry a white pine as if born to axe. Start with a big vee, twist the axe-handle just a freck before it smacks wood. Whee-pine is wickedly explosive in the brittle of winter, chunks big as a crow flee off and afore ye ken the tree is ripe to holler down.

When the cross-cut came to the woods, the owners wanted all the trees sawyered because it was less waste and fast. Bruce never took to sawyerin'. Did admit it was a nice sound and leaves big square logs but chopping bring a man alive with the whole length of tree trembling. Sawyers hardly touch the tree, more of assassins, so qui't and calm they are. A tree should be hacked at. Fought toe to toe; axes brewed shoulders and flattened bellies. It felt good to get on the end of the handle and feel the arm cords ripple and the bone-stammerin' collision of axe against tree. Good chopper carried a leather tongue to clamp his teeth to lest the tree shake 'em free of his head.

They said there were lumber 'nough in the Pinery to last the whole countrie a thousand, surely a hundred years. Thousand years! Mind you! From high places all ye could see were trees. Whee-pine and red, hems, balsam, spruce, tammies, trees far as eyes could grab. The sky itself infected by the green of trees. Trees held the round world down. The open meadow and burns appeared unhealthy, neked, even frightful.

Some came to hate trees, hate the wide ransom they had on man and land. Bruce never hated trees.

Early in the Pinery a man cutting his own logs and sloughing them to the river to slay into boards with a gate-saw could make $10,000 in Yankee coin every year. With a reciprocating whip-saw in a wooden frame and a ready crew, they'd slab a thousand board feet between daylight and dark. About here some wit invented the spine-saw which didn't need a frame, it'd gnaw through 10,000 board feet a day. Finally came the "whirrin' terror," the circular saw and a daily due of 50,000 board feet. Some mills had three saws going, six days a week, 12 and 14 hours a day. Every day they tore out ten acres of prime pine. By 1863, 400 mills were hugging the big river with their teeth searching out the jugular vein of the Piney Woods.

The lands of the Piney sold for a dollar and twenty-five cents. The price rarely varied, nor the buyers. The Public Land Office's auctions were the lumberman's turf. Any brazen smart enough to bid a dollar and thirty-five found hisself escorted to the rears of the crowd where the auctioneer couldn't hear his voice nor see his hand if the roughs weren't already standing on him. The gov'ment never knew what it was selling under the Public Land Act and had no idea of how much pine there was nor any concern that it might last a thousand years. The lumbermen ken, ken the sections, the board feet, how far from water and where was the high ground for the lumber road. They ken because of the cruiser.

Bruce been twenty years when hired as cruiser. He could run and swim and read and cipher and chop and end an argument in the bunk-house with a slap of a double-bit on a plank table. If a main went lazy-crazy, he'd chop his muzzle-loading bunk, toss the pieces in the stove and fly his clothes into the shanty-yard. Bruce could set a bone and brew a tea to cure the "peenonee" and when a woods-boy came from town with the itch, he'd make a salve of boot oil, boiled pine needles and moldy potatoes.

Bruce was too good to waste at the bunkhouse. He was the kind to slay fortunes for other men. His pay went to five dollars a day, his job to note the 'proximate board feet in each section. How far the stand was from the river. How much was pine, how much hard. With a compass and axe he'd walk the line, blazing every tree in his way with a slap of axe leaving a bright scar against the rude woods.

He'd watch the river in spring to ken the when of high water. How deep and where the currents, and what rocks to catch the jam. His pay went eight dollars a day with a charge account at the local hardware and dry. He marked high ground, ridge and esker, drawing a line for the logging-roads. He selected the camps, a place near water but not so as to be mean with moskeets, a meadow nearby for the horse and ox. A spot where the shanties are warmed by sun yet tucked from the winter wind. He at ten dollars a day.

Bruce worked alone and wore the fit of cruisers. Woolen pants with button pockets and calf-high boots waterproofed with bear fat or stove lard. Lacing the boots from the toe to top took half the hour but kept a man from breaking a leg when scrambling windfalls. The shirt was the red and black sett of a Rob Roy tartan and he wore suspenders. Galooses because a belt puddles sweat and when sweat cools, the kidneys chill and a man gets the "runs" from cold kidneys. A belt gives bellyache when pulled sufficient to hold the pants on a man lean in hips. A belt was for store clarks, jacks and teamsters who need to tie in their guts to steer wide of rupture.

The axe were his badge. A light-weight double-bit, the handle three-quarters the normal length. I remember the way he used it. With a snap and hook of the wrist, slapping the tree. With his axe he drew lines and marked corners, squared woods to something understood in ledger books. A cruised woods looked like a page in a ledger; neat and precise, the figures just waiting to be subtracted. Was the cruiser who spilled a thousand prayer-towns and a million and ten pine coffins out of the piney woods.

All of it was in the axe. He sent the bit to Cleveland to have nickel-plated. The handle were blue beech and rubbed with oil till the stalk shone of waxed marble. The axe was a druid being. Had more energy than comes cell and grain alone. That axe spoke, it howled, it terrified the woods. The handle was shaved to a thinness, sly as a snake, supplicant as a village maiden's perfume. Bruce said he could blaze the opposite side of a tree from where he was standing without even leaning.

I seen him lash out with that axe. Smacking a tree with such suddenness and fury it stabbed me with fear. Sunlight gleaned on the blade as it angled through the air, the blade so sharp it cut air with thin whistles. The swing was lost into the shadows, then reappearing, the blade flashing fire. The blaze sent tumbling, black bark, white grain, black bark and white again. Was near to lightning stroke, such was his will with an axe. I do not know if the storm gathered in him or in his axe.

He wore a broad hat, wool felt of a smoky color. The hat smelled of tea and salt pork, the brim starched stiff to rebuff the whip of branches. Bruce put down his head and hatted his way through the middens of blackberry like a Roman army advancing on the protection of their shields. The hat was his roof. In the rain he'd back up against a tree, light his peep and watch the weather. At nooning he'd nap with his hat over his eyes. Asked him how he took sleep so quick. Because of the vapors, he said, vapors put you to sleep whether you want or not. Said he looked at the world through the vent holes. Lined up a morsel of sky and tree, a bird nest or of leaf and studied it as a painting. You can understand things better if you see them separate and off on their own instead of always submerged into what they belong.

Wore a bandanna 'round his neck. Tied so the fold covered the neck. The throat ought run warmer than the rest of the body otherwise it had a tendency to get sore, near choking a man with muscles in his neck. At midges, moskeets and no-see-ums, he'd dip it in water and tie it around his nose and mouth.

I went with him in the early summer before the flies got bad. He didn't walk the woods, he floated. I climbed and scrambled and ran and tripped; he hovered. When I was 'bout burned and thought to die, he'd decide to need me as a corner mark. Essential I stay in one place and not move, else he couldn't tell if the line ran straight. He'd find me asleep.

Afternoons we'd take tea. A small fire among stones, a green stick derrick to hold a tin can on a wire handle, filled with fresh seep, a pinch of leaves tossed before the water rolled. He be Scots and tea-time were the better fix than a meal. Tea, he said, is a working man's resurrection. Strong dose of black tea and scones about the time the legs went rubbery. We'd smear them with wild honey while he drank his tea from a china cup, the cup wrapped in a couple socks and stuffed in the tin can we used as a pot.

Camp was often no more than a canvas hung among trees. He slept in a wool blanket, carried a Bible and a small-print version of Shakespeare's plays. Could recite the funeral speech of Brutus and the part where Hamlet is talking on himself. As he cruised he repeated the parts he knew, and in that there was a strangeness in him.

He could talk Indian. Hunker around a tea fire and talk of the river and deep places. Indian hunkering weren't the cross-legged seen in picture books, more like squatting, the rear end never touching the ground. They'd rock back and forth to ease the muscles. Hunker and drink tea and talk the slow Indian way. A question not answered right off instead waiting so the response seemed considered.

He'd trade bags of salt for fresh meat. In the spring he'd swap for Indian sugar in bark cones, the Ojibwa word being makata. Thought Ma'd appreciate Indian sugar but she found squirrel bones in it and that spoiled Indian sugar for her. We borrowed the cones from the cupboard and traded them for marbles. Other kids thought genuine Indian sugar nice too.

He smoked a pipe, the stem stuck of his shirt pocket. Smoked once at tea and once after supper. Said, was bad form to smoke in woods. I think the smell of smoke in woods bothered him.

1871 was a dry summer and had been dry the winter before. Springs and creeks dried up, swamps caked over. Nobody was too sure how it started. A railroad crew had been north of the town and was standard practice to let the slash burn. And farmers were always burning stumps, a regular habit of farmers. The stumps sparked and smudged all summer, flashing with fire at every fresh wind.

Came night at 2 o'clock in the afternoon of October eight, 1871. Clouds hid the sun to a dusky light and ash sifted from the sky. People at first thought it snow from the slow lazy flight, then knew it was ashes, some still sparking. They started to wet down the shingle roofs, needn't have bothered.

Some knew right off it weren't no ordinary woods-fire. They got out of town right off and headed to Green Bay. Hesitation killed those who thought twice. A house at the edge of town caught. Some went to save it but by the time they got there another house was fired. Embers the size of stovewood fell out of the sky. A cry went up to run for the river. Some went god-crazy, praying and weeping and beseeching and holding their babies up to the hot wind.

In a matter of seconds the peaceful town of boardwalk, general-store, sawmill, shoe-repair, Episcopal Church, smithy, and hotel was veiled in a curtain of hell. People running, people hollering, people meowing and crying. People in flames, falling on the boardwalk, splattering like meat in a frying pan. Burning with a sooty flame, a ring of fire growling around them. The prettiest girl in town died in a flash of petticoat and yellow hair.

He had to dunk my older sister in the river every minute and pinch her nose and mouth and hold her wild eyes under water. They spent the night in the river as the town dissolved. Those too weary to hold themselves fell asleep and were drowned. One man, when he realized his whole family had been converted to ash and gas, ran headlong from the river into the inferno. As he ran his clothes, soaking but a moment before, steamed, then coughed into flame. They did not see him fall and doubted any whole part of him touched the ground.

By evening of the next day the sand cooled enough for them to venture out of the river. The sawmill was melted. All that remained of the buildings were heat-cracked foundation stones and tidy rows of iron nails which had been walls the day before. The fire was so intense the buildings were consumed where they stood, not falling apart and scattering the nails. They found heaps of white powder, then realized they were the pure calcium of bone, tooth and skull. Piled rocks around the remains thinking it might be a wife or brother or child. When help came with water and food they saved the tin cans to collect handfuls for proper burying. The wind scattered the rest. On his watch chain was the fire-sodden locket of his yellow-haired niece and the night in Peshtigo.

The company gave him the watch when he retired, solid gold case, the fob looped around the doorknob of a two bedroom cottage in the village of Park Falls. The deed for the house was on the kitchen table, cheese in the ice-box and twelve cases of imported whisky in the cellar. A bay-window with a stained glass panel and 320 acres of cut-over ten miles out of town. The parcel had a small lake and a spit of land that stretched out into the lake. On the point were a half dozen veteran white pines.

In the last years he'd go to the old cuts and sit on the stumps, counting rings and separate the good years from the bad. Find the year he was born, the year his father left Scotland and the years of his grandfathers before. In time, I think, he learned to hate the axe.

He was a cruiser, a Bruce and a prince of the woods.

SPUTNIK

Octover 4, 1957, Sadie, the first cow to the right of the self-closing door leading to the milk-house, birthed a heifer calf named Sputnik. Twelve hours earlier a reaction vehicle from a launch pad in the central Urals placed in earth orbit a cylinder containing a four-pound lead-core battery and a vacuum-tube transmitter. The broadcast was unintelligible in every language on the planet yet completely and instantly understood.

Six years earlier Sadie had stepped out of a cattle van along with three other Holsteins; Lady, Topsie and Sunflower. They were the core of Pa's agricultural revolution, a venture his father thought "risky and no account". For more than fifty years the dairy herd had been a Guernsey monopoly, the brown and white bovines originating from the isle of the same name in the English Sea off the coast of France. As a milk breed they'd been dominant nearly 400 years in Europe and known for 150 in America.

The world, it seems, has a vanity for cows, meaning bovines. Bison, musk ox, moose, English long-horn, short-horn, highland long hairs and a couple dozen others from Africa, sub-continental India and east Asia. Man's prowess, the very highlight of human achievement, is conveniently served and implemented by the presence of cows. Which is a lot of responsibility for cows, having to uphold the fame of humanity without a vote. I wasn't against giving the vote to cows since a few brands were already deified. I figured the vote wouldn't hurt nothing. I have no objection to cows being deified or holding public office. The Hindus have an admirable habit in their respect for cows, it nicely balances our respect for the human braincase.

Holsteins originated on the coast of Freisland, a product of special adoption as noted by Reverend Darwin's son. Grandfather thought no animal on earth was more pleasing to the eye than a Guernsey. Mild in both nature and stature, a white animal over-lain with brown spots. Some are prone to argue a Guernsey is a brown cow over-took by white spots; they are wrong and haven't studied the situation sufficiently. A Guernsey's milk is high in soluble fats and of a color approximating yellow.

The Red Star Creamery just below the hill where County J turned into the Valley Over depended for half a century on the Guernsey cow. Red Star handled all the milk of Valley Over, Valley Down and Valley Up. Except for those on the north prairie of Valley Up, who sent their milk to the creamery at the corner of County J and County B. Those dairymen dwelling west of the moraine supplied the Plover creamery.

The cow kingdom of Wisconsin was pretty much the product and imagination of aforementioned William Dempster Hoard. His elevation in the township could easily have gained Professor Hoard the favorite-son candidacy or, if he was willing, canonization. Hoard master-minded the transformation of the Pinery. A country by greed, saw blade and fate displaced, and through these same human qualities, turned into a visually useless going on wicked country, to whose scars, fugitives and tortures were applied the poultice and ministrations of good St. Hoard. His ecology and economy was none other than the milk-cow and the ability of its product to be honestly manufactured, conveniently stored and by all society, great and small, utilized. If Chicago was the backbone of America's poets and radical socialists and hog-butchers, if Cleveland were iron-monger, if Duluth was the iron-shoveler, then someone had to feed all those butchers, stevedores and union stewards. Fuel the hungry poets and fellow workmen in the pre-electric age. A food of easy purity and refinement, with enough energy to civilize the continent. That's where Grandpa, Hoard and the milk cow came in. After a modest career logging, whose father before raised sheep and funeral horses, Grandpa came to cheese. Four slices of homemade bread with two wedges of a barrel cheese three-quarters of an inch thick, paved over with a quarter inch of yellow Guernsey butter. That fueled America; then the hog-butcher's son graduated from college and went to work at the newspaper. The iron-monger's daughter became a secretary, the coal-digger's boy was a truck driver, and the tight web of William Dempster Hoard's yellow-butter farm on the cut-over began to slip and fade.

This was when Pa imported four black and white semi-mastodons. A move inimical to dairy farm's grade change from B to A, along with hundred-weight price increase and a hundred percent gain in fluid production. All, a response to the industrial catharsis on the American landscape. The sons of steel-drivers had little want for the 3000 calorie dinner bucket. They didn't want milk crusted over with yellow alluvium, and the Guernseys slid a notch toward extinction, and Freisland Holsteins advanced into the breech.

Sadie was stanchioned first on the right from 1951 until 1962. A handsome brute, Sadie maintained the highest individual milk production of any mammal in range on the township. Forty pounds per milking was routine, forty-five, forty-eight, fifty-two in a shot gun can designed for fifty pounds even. A container standing thirty inches high with a tight cover that needed to be lifted 52 inches off the ground and poured deliberately into a strainer.

The strainer set atop a self-contained milk-cooler referred to in local lexicon as a bulk-tank. The previous summer the entire milk-house had been extended three feet, the concrete can tank sledge-hammered out of existence leaving no like receptical for our frogs or fingerling trout. A water line from the house served the milk-house as per strictures of Grade A production. The barn was white-washed, the result which the cows would not enter until at the lapse of an hour's cajoling and finally oak whips.

Sadie was bred to H-31 named Morning Pride by Neil O'Keefe, inseminating technician for Badger Breeders of Shawano. H-31, whose picture was in the geneological cabinet affixed to the barn's south wall, was born in 1946, had sired 1200 daughters thus far in his career and at 4 years 8 months weighed 2700 pounds.

All the years previous Pa had maintained a bull in the bar-cage at the west end of the barn. A cell ten feet square designed with a steel gate and sliding dead-bolt keeper. I and every farm child hated that brute and all pretentions like him. I hated Joe Stalin, Japanese Zeros, the haymow in the dark and that bull. His name was Black, I thought it the description of his heart. Every night it fell to us to feed him. Like the sovereign he was, his moods were lordly.

At times he took to honest civility as if he knew no other adventure. Took his silage with grace, two scoops of ground corn and bran meal and the finest west mow alfalfa the farm could offer. Other times, and for no cogent reason, he'd roll his head in a rhythmic taunt. His eyes following your movements, picking his angle and, when in range, charging the bars with all his weight, his head reaching out in a teutonic swipe. The fork glanced off his head sending it flying, a missile of his vengeance. Sometimes batting his snout against my leg, rising purple welts before suppertime and a two day hobble. His dash against the cage bars shook the entire west end of the barn. Then, when his treachery was finished, he'd roll his eyes back till only the whites showed staring out in venomous vagrancy.

My faith in steel was at the time not immaculate. Nights and dreams I imagined the bars failing and that gloss black creat thundering over me, I smashed in the instant to thin smells. Neither was I sure sexuality was the greatest idea. If sex did to me what it performed on him, I didn't want the election. Even allowing for size and lack of education, sexuality as expressed by Black was totally suspect.

Sex was his purpose. Any fool could see sex was why he lived and breathed. Sex hung out of him. Sex providing him with an extra leg were his testicle bucket any longer. I was marveled and tried to find comparison between his accessories and those of my own property. I couldn't see any. We weren't in the same marble game at all.

His thing was even worse. Comparison? There weren't any. Human beings, when it came to peckers, were like the outhouses behind cathedrals. The size of the handle alone was enough to wonder what nature had in mind.

When a cow came in season, Pa kept the victim in the barn while the rest were sent to pasture. Only then did the cage open. Black already knew what he was supposed to do. His head had bunted at the bars for hours. Pa was careful with the bull, checked wind direction and called who ever was upwind, asking if they had any in season. If they did, Black was gated in the barnyard to avoid his going cross-country.

Never once were we allowed to witness "it." Nevertheless we found methods and did. The event surprised me. I expected open violence, it wasn't. The cow just stood there while the Louisville slugger slowly slipped out of the bat-rack and mystically swung at a slow pitch. Like a ballet dancer he reared and with only middle suddenness rode the cow, sliding a significant measure of himself into her. She just stood there. Sometimes moved for balance and chewed her cud. Other than that, there wasn't much to see. She bellered, he quivered, then slid off.

In a way it was elegant. No wild movements to establish fit of a thing long as a shovel handle. I was thoroughly disappointed. I expected clouds and thunder and it didn't even sprinkle. I imagined murder and puncture and it was hardly a scratch.

When Black ascended the ramp of the meat-truck I was glad to see him go. If any deserved killing he did. He was, I thought, built exactly opposite from what he oughta have been. Instead of being mean and energetic at the highest promontory of his life, he was undramatic. When he should have been gentle and content, he was vengeful and dark-hearted. If it wouldn't have been for dogs I might have given up on any exaltation of sexual chemistry.

Artificial insemination was even worse. At least with the bull there was an exchange of perfumes. Any maiming as might've resulted was balanced with the display. Neil O'Keefe wasn't any demonstration of anything as rich as what he ought to be doing. The way he did it he might as well have been installing ear-tags. Maybe Black had a few problems. He wasn't the greatest beast in the world and maybe did deserve to die with an eight-pound sledge hammer right 'tween the eyes. Maybe, maybe not, but artificial insemination was neglectful of cows. I know cows didn't show much enthusiasm but that's 'cause it was so public. I won't either.

You would think a company like Badger Breeders would know more about cows than doing what they were doing. Couple sand bags over the hips be helpful. Let the cow know what was happening. Some folks take an awful lot for granted, thinking any method will do as long as the result is the same. They see a cow and a bull as two gears and all that is required is that they mesh, forgetting lubrication. Neil O'Keefe oughta wear some kind of perfume. I won't say it matters awful much because, no matter what, in the end the majority of a thing is getting there. Still I want to believe technique counts for points or where are any of us? Might as well be a frog.

Look at the dinosaurs. They went out because they didn't have any art to them. I'm sure of it. Stands to reason, don't it? We know they were egg sprinklers owing as they're relative to the frog and crocodile.

Sputnik

Get something the size of a barn with no where else to go but egg sprin-kling and it's gonna go extinct. First 'cause they ain't fixed to be delicate. They probably ruined more nests than they populated.

Dinosaur was a good place for the world to start even if it was a mistake. Makes you wonder, don't it? That maybe God ain't so all-fired smart. Preacher said it's because of free will. Maybe, but I think free-form be more like it. Like painting a picture in the road during the melt using only mud. Can picture anything you want, only is, you gotta use mud. Some won't think it's anything more than mud when you're fin-ished, even if you're Mister Rembrandt, but it is. It's people and horses and liquid oxygen rocket ships and the last supper and angel tracks. You know, Tommy Soik said angels have feet like birds. Not toes but talons. I hope that's true. Should be when you think about it. Toes wouldn't be any purchase if you have to roost; seeing as they had wings they gotta roost. Can you see that at the Christmas pageant? Archangel Michael with talons perched on a telephone wire telling Mary she is PG.

Why ain't dinosaurs in the Bible? If they been included I'm sure there'd be a couple billion more Christian believers right now. Person can ignore lot of stuff, not dinosaurs. The way I see it, they could leave off the New Testament entirely. Instead, invest in an old, old testament. Served belief a lot better than the jesus chapters.

I didn't mind Jesus. Sometimes I thought he sounded a touch pathetic, maybe too much like a movie, nothing real is like a movie. I suppose the Bible is important to read because doesn't everyone feel that way some-times? A jesus, I mean? Like you're special and born out of more than your own ma and pa and feel like talking to what you really think you belong to. Like a moon night in May. When nobody understands you, nobody, and you don't even think Tommy Soik will want to listen and all there are left to talk to are the plowed fields.

I know the difference between Jesus and me. If I were nailed to a barn-beam I wouldn't be in a forgiving mood. I mean, what kind of person says, "Oh, that's OK, you go ahead and do anything you want, you're forgiven." Tain't natural. 'Course if you know beforehand they can't kill you no matter what, then you can forgive anything. I'd like to know what Jesus would have said if they killed him good and forever dead.

The whole New Testament sets cross-grain if you ask me. Like the whole thing was figured out in the beginning and all you have to do is follow the road-map of preachers and Sunday morning and you're gonna be right. Ain't so, just ain't so, not here, not on the moon, not as far off in the dark as light can reach and still touch anything. According to Jesus all you have to do is connect up with the one set of answers and everything will be all right. Maybe it is if you can turn stones to popcorn but it isn't if you have to hoe corn all summer before you get to popcorn. I don't think anything is born ripe. Some things can't be figured out no matter how long you're willing to sit.

Like dinosaurs. Why did they have to die? Are people any better than pterodactyls and triceratops and tyrannosaurus? Why did we get a soul and they not?

When Sputnik was born to Sadie, the Milwaukee Braves were in the World Series. Lew Burdette was pitching swell and Warren Spahn had a sore elbow. Pa give her the name and I loved Pa more for that. Didn't think Pa cared about stuff like that but Pa knew straight off Sputnik was more important than even the World Series.

Sputnik was a distraught Holstein. Ordinarily the black patches on a cow are smooth, like ink spills. Sputnik's patches were all chewed up. She looked more like an aerial view of the Fuji Islands with the freckles of sea-level reefs all over. Her appearance looked unfinished, even haphazard like she should've baked a little longer. We loved her more 'cause she was a curiosity.

Wasn't only curiosity that made Sputnik prime, part owed to being freshened on October 4 and part 'cause she was from Sadie, herself a handsome woman. I don't know why cows did it, the bull being gone. Nevertheless, they ran a regular beauty parlor, licking at each other's faces till they had regular salon permanents, all curly and shiny. No different than Ma when she gets frilled up with a new hair fix and her face done. When Ma comes home such ways, Pa has a new intensity. Don't take no high-up philosophy to figure why neither, when you consider she looks like someone else. I know exactly how it is. I'd rather do Tommy Soik's chores than my own. And his sister is a lot prettier than mine and he says mine is prettier than his. And Arlyn Clark's BB gun is better than mine. This is I think one of the most important solutions in the world I've ever come to and I'm gonna try and remember it.

Like being in Harrison Newby's woods which is the forty behind the heifer pasture. Harrison has the whole thing posted to keep hunters off. He feels pretty thick about his forty because signs cost fifty cents each at the hardware. A sign saying it's a criminal offense with a thousand dollar fine should keep a person out. You know it isn't that way at all, instead it makes you wanta see it worse than ever. The sign saying "can't" chews on your brain and you know sometime you're gonna take that fence; under, over or through the barbs but you're gonna take it.

Went in Mister Newby's woods a couple times. Felt awful and felt good all at the same moment. Good because I was seeing it and it wouldn't torment me and I knew where the north stream went and its little grove of white birches by the spring. Weren't nothing more than ordinary woods. Maybe not even as good. I've thought medium thick on it and wondered if I would have trespassed if the sign hadn't said I couldn't. Soon as I crawled under the fence I knew Harrison's woods was like any other woods. Less even, you can't make any noise. I'm pretty sure this is what the Bible calls adultery. Real adultery is twenty-twos and thirty-aught-sixes in Harrison Newby's woods, not BB guns.

Sputnik would have been a good human being. If we were to measure out humanity according to an assessment of character, then Sputnik fit right in. Instead, most folks think humanity is what you come packaged in whether deserving or not. Pa never had much time for Catholics, same as Harold Edwards. Catholics have too many secrets to be trusted, except for Leo Soik, who Pa figured was a special case. Pa says he can spot a

Catholic 'cause their outsides resemble the think they have inside. What he means to say is Catholics are more pucked-up than other Christian brands.

I don't know. Take the Pope. He's a plain ordinary old fellow, maybe he is some Catholic but mostly he is just another old fella like Grandpa. Probably has phlegm coughs like Grandpa and had to lift congestion out with alfalfa tea and a spit-bucket. I asked Tommy Soik what an acolyte was, were four of them at Eddie Sasarski's funeral. I thought they might have been fixed off the like of bull calves 'cause they don't act normal. Tommy says they weren't. Acolytes are regular kids only scrubbed. They ain't snipped? I asked. Nope, he says, regular hang underneath like anyone else.

Said he oughta know 'cause he were one and said it worried him some when the priest came and said he was now special before God and to serve God he had to be more than any other boy. Said he wasn't sure what was gonna happen next and whether to run or not. Nope, he says, acolytes were common kids and purity is only there to look at 'cause he thought some real awful things when serving communion and nothing happened. Holy Ghost didn't slap his face, altar didn't erupt with yellow fire. Whole thing is ordinary. They say it's the hand of God but it ain't. The wine comes out of a Christian Brothers bottle and the bread isn't peeled off of the bones of dead folks neither or fall out of the sky or nothing super like that. It's just plain flat bread that tastes worse than paper. Is that disappointing? Kinda is. Like when I found Uncle Jerome weren't really inside the communion table at the Liberty Corners even though it had his name on it and said, "Do this in remembrance of Ma." Like when I found out there wasn't anything beyond the purple velvet curtain behind the altar. All along I thought a tunnel led from the curtain to somewhere important. Instead just the same old wall. I couldn't decide if it was disappointing or not.

Sputnik followed the established routine on her way to cow. Nine months credit in the barn; first as a sucker then drinker, finally switched to hay and water. At the end of the year graduted to the heifer herd.

If I was born-again as a four-footed animal, I'd consider strong coming down as a heifer. Next to the Lone Ranger a heifer lives about as good a life as is possible to live and still wind up mostly legal. If a free-citizen exists anywhere who is more resplendent in freedom than a heifer, I'd like to see the evidence. Pa, I suspect, made it that way. He knew at the end of the heifer age, they were going to spend their lives stanchioned in one same spot. Without chance to move their head more than a quarter inch either way. Quarter inch on a three-quarter ton person tain't much liberty. And eat that way and sleep that way, get milked, breeded and medicated that way. If you would ask me, it's pretty awful when you think about it. Which is why Pa fixed it so being a heifer was the opposite sort of event. No, he didn't tell me so. Didn't need to because it is the obvious thing to do.

Every farmer, if he's near real at all, doubts the morality of his occupation. Doubts to such degree and permanence as to establish a petition even before he's guilty. Common pasture isn't enough for heifers, not when eight or ten years of stanchion service follows with the meat market truck after that, if not something even worse like the rendering-plant truck. Common pasture won't do at all when you know that.

Every farmer I ever knew in the town had a back-forty, or an eighty, and turned the young stock at it. Like as not the back forties tend to coagulate in the same place, owing mostly to geography. Instead of a forty or eighty acre patch the heifers of half a dozen farms have a thousand acres of low ground, fallow woods, sand meadows, bog, big timber, berry brakes and hazelnut clearings to roam and cavort. Taken altogether, the heifer pasture was the handsomest setup of landscape possible. On earth or anywhere. Heifer pasture was purely heaven. That's what Pa and the neighbor farmers had in mind though not a one of them talked of it outright, they knew the meaning of subliminal. You know subliminal. That's any of the whorls of branches of a pine tree beneath those at the top. Subliminal being what is that you don't see straight-off. What ain't part of the social breezes. What snow tends to break off, don't matter, knots are still there. You ever hold a pine board up against the light and see what light does to a pine knot? Pretty as a flower. Honest. All rosen and soft; looks the same as X-rays, the growth rings suspended in the flow. Look close and you can see grains of sand and the past deeds of wind.

Back-forty weren't forty acres but hundreds of acres. Creeks, springs, seeps, sand dunes, I know a white pine tree there maybe almost 200 years old and a white oak almost more than two hundred. Hemlock bowers, balsam fir, white ash and watercress, brookies and browns under Eckels' bridge. If you take it altogether it's a heaven sort of place. I mean, it's even better than heaven. Had to be, 'cause for the rest of their lives cows were gonna know steel stanchions and not much else, that's a sort of hell and farmers know it.

A heifer and a cow are really two different animals. Vulnerability is written all over a cow. On its own a cow couldn't survive ten seconds in untamed circumstances. The heifer is another thing entirely. A heifer can fairly compete with Bengal tigers, wooly mammoths or saber-toothed coyotes. The Neanderthal folks never tasted prime rib of Holstein or Guernsey. They supped on mammoths and wild rhinoceros but not heifer Holstein. A heifer is the fair match of anything under the P-51 Mustang with fifty caliber machine-guns.

A heifer can take the average four-strand barb-wire set in new cedar at four pace centers without touching the wire, the post or even shaking the ground. Cow can't. True, most of them might clear. Unfortunately the business of farmers is conducted with the portion which don't clear. Milking a cow with a barb-scratch in her tit is exactly like milking a tyrannosaurus rex, if they milked. Chance of maiming is about equal.

Quick? Nothing's quicker than a heifer. Seen it myself; heifers dodging so hard their own shadow is lamed and limps along after the original owner. Nobody minded that Gilman's heifers were with Newby's or Bannack's were with Isherwood's. Sooner or later they'd sort colors out as best they could recall. The system also doubled as herd improvement.

They thinking theirs was the one with the black spot looking rather like Greenland, or the glove on the left flank and yours was the one with the full white face. Both knowing it was the other way around.

Few delights compared with bringing in the heifers from the back-forty. Pa set off a whole day to do it, mentioning it a couple days or week before-hand so we could start training. Run to the school house and back a couple times every night. Ma got new laces for the Keds. Pa let us wear Keds when bringing in the heifers. Ordinarily, he didn't favor Keds and made us wear four-eye work shoes of brown oxford leather. For heifers we deployed the Keds. Sneakers at chores were forbidden because of cow-kick. What we wore Sunday afternoon was our own business, otherwise it was four-eye and three-hook. 'Cept for heifers.

Pa were a lovable man, not that we'd be prone to admit the opinion outright nor was he expecting, but he did teach us how to limber after heifers. It was the finest, most wonderful treat in our lives. Limbering after heifers was better than three dollars cash at the Amherst County Fair with fifteen cent rides on the Thrill Rocket.

Bringing home the heifers required every trick, deception, foul deed and perverse parry. To herd a pack of heifers who, in one short summer had acquired the manners of radioactive nuclei, back into their original forty, the first problem was finding them. The effect of this is the manufacture from farm kids some remittance and facsimile of trackers. Heifers leave tracks. In fact, they leave more than tracks, all cows do. A lot can be determined from a cow-pie. That's the house word, when out of earshot of Ma it's cow shit. People are funny about shit. I don't understand. In public we talk of manure, excrement, fertilizer, cow-pies, doggie-do, calf scours, runs, diarrhea and other lamentations, but not shit. It's all the same stuff. Don't make sense at all. Grown-ups are funny that way. They don't call dead, dead. 'Stead passed-on, departed, deceased, late; all the while it's plain dead.

Fresh cow-pie has a sheen. If real fresh, steam is still rising. When tracking heifers sometimes you need to ascertain how fresh. Sometimes the tracks give a clue. If the dirt is dark in the well of the track, it's newer than a track where the well is light. If you can't tell, the thing to do is cross-examine the cow-pie. Insert your finger far down as it will reach. Cow shit is little different than a loaf of bread. If warm on the inside instead of the same temperature, they were closer than if it weren't.

Best tracker ever was Willie Tech. He'd find heifers in the swamp quicker than a dog in heat'd find friends. Lots of folks called Willie when they wanted their heifers back. If they had any savvy they be done before October when folk here take winter meat. An extra heifer at herd in October might as never see home again and weren't no way to save it when the only identity remaining is hamburger and rib roast. Nobody did it, 'cause folks kept right and got their heifers out of the woods before October. The worry was Roodie Babcock. Roodie lived down on the marsh with his missus and eleven kids. House no more than a chicken coop for all of them. Roodie was kinda funny. He'd take October meat if it came to his woods, and he didn't even have heifers. A short, wizened faded-paint sort of a man. Never wore any but red flannel shirt, winter and summer. His eyes mucused and blood-bleery and a three day growth of uneven whiskers. Roodie looked like a bad spread of fertilizer, he needed more than meat and we knew it. If a cow went down and choice was rendering plant or Roodie, they'd roll the truck by his lane off the marsh road and ask if he'd want a lame cow. Actually that's not how they asked, rather if he'd help with a lamer, that way he could feel he earned it.

Roodie had a thing about Allis Chalmers tractors. Didn't pay to leave an Allis on the marsh over-night or Roodie'd have the carburator and magneto off. A Ford or Massey was safe. Somethin' about Allis Chalmers triggered him. We all knew he had a corn-crib full of gas caps, spark plug wires, crank handles, carbs and sediment bulbs. Didn't even have a tractor. Figured he was storing up for one.

Heifers in the woods after October were too much the temptation for Roodie so folks had 'em out. Invite Willie and his wife to supper the night before and ask if he was up to a little "heiferin." Willie at sixty-three years was always up to "heiferin." He knew the back-forties of ten different farms better than all the collective farmers themselves. We figured parts of the marsh and swamp never been seen or stepped on by white man or red, except Willie.

Heifers stick together, find one you've found them all. The problem was shagging them home. A heifer chase is about the best whoop-up and rip outside of the 4th of July and a thousand firecrackers. Nothing airs out lungs better than the heifer chase. Once the chase takes hold it's like nothing else exists. Only you, the heifers and the woods.

At first it is mannerly; you keep your shoes dry, and take caution on clearing the fences. After the while, after missing the top strand and now half the pant leg is torn off. After miscalculating the creek and touched down half-way over. From then on it's fun. No briar patch, soft muck, hot shit, creek or cut-bank is too acute to warn me off. I feel like howling.

Heiferin' is as good for the body as for knowing the woods. It's the only time you feel your lungs as the half cubic yard of absorption inside you. The brain is swollen against the case; every muscle, every joint, every secretion and gland is alive. Nothing else is quite like the slap of your own meat. It tests the seams in a person and you get a fair idea whether you'll live fifty years or a hundred so not disappointed when it happens.

Most farmers, if honest, admit they're a little scared of the swamp. Don't trust themselves to it. The way it goes all-green; fern and sphagnum, creeper and wild yam and air still enough to be a tomb. Most won't go without Willie. Heard of fox-snakes and blow-snakes, one once stretched full across the road south. Was only a single track but the snake had extra on both sides. They said it looked like a green branch torn off an elm tree; then it moved. That snake ruined its fair share of sleep before the week was out.

Sooner or later, we delayed as close to chore-time as possible and the heifers got routed to the lane. They didn't give up so much as they called time. We knew we didn't win. The heifers won; they just wanted us to feel good about it, before someone went for a shotgun and rock salt. Always was one delinquent who wouldn't be cornered, was as wild-eyed at four in the afternoon as nine o'clock that morning. We had the fix for such a heifer, the clearing west of Herman's woods funneled down and ended at a fenced-in farm lane. Once we had them in the clearing we damn well had them. We and they knew it. One always took exception and tried to double back. The idea was to give resistance. 'Course you'd see it turn and make for the corner between the trees leading once again to the swamp. Taking angle you'd head it back, all the while knowing it'd break again. Which it does. Usually this hiefer is a three-year-old and pretty wise and probably knowing this is the end of heifer heaven. By the winter it'd be bred and the following summer a calf and the rest of its life spent in the steel of a stanchion. I can't blame them for turning back.

It tries to run a couple more times, each time brought back, finally we let it go, but tear after it like the escape really counted. The heifer all eye-balls and tongue out, bearing down on the notch between the trees leading to the swamp and freedom. We kept a white oak 2 by 6 behind the tree for just this occasion. Was part of taming. Even a smart heifer won't notice the trap if you put up a fight and come hollering and running after it. It bears down on that freedom hole with all the liberation four legs can run after. When the heifer gets real close, whoever was hid in the trees drops the white oak 2 by 6 in place and gets away from the collision. The oak is neatly held between four burr saplings. Eight feet away the heifer isn't thinking leap, has no choice but to hope the 2 by 6 is pine.

The collision distends every muscle and fiber in the creature. We don't even bother to try and chase home what is left. The 2 by 6 is slid out of the way and it can walk whichever way it wants. Either take the chances of winter in the swamp and Roodie Babcock or a career as a cow. During the night it walks up to the barn, by morning it's drinking at the stock tank and still a little wobbly. We're some bloodied ourselves.

Sputnik calved in '60. Most heifers accept motherhood with grace, a few resist seeing it for the plot it is. What they don't realize is their own anatomy has been conspiring against them for the last couple months. Now they have an attached hobble that sloshes back and forth throwing them out of kilter with each step they take. A well-hung milk cow can not run in a straight line any more than a Mexican jumping bean. Neither can they whip the back legs forward with the great gallop they once excelled at. Most of a bushel basket's now in the way. Sooner or later the fact of being a cow tames them of its own accord.

The problem is the calf. Let a calf dry off in the woods and it believes itself constitutionally guaranteed the woods ever after. It possesses the nimbleness to defend the statute. A calf born a sodden miserable mass unable to stand on its knobby knees, much less raise its ears. Within an hour the calf is studying balance and making fine adjustments to gravity with the four more-or-less parallel devices. At two hours it has found supper. In three hours this calf is the fastest set of knees in the township, captured only by gang-tackles or a pickup truck in second gear. Let a calf stay an hour too long in the woods and the farmer might as well try and capture a deer with a butterfly net.

Pa kept notes on the heifers, and before one came due it was separated out of the cow herd and kept in the barn till it freshened. The calf neatly tamed and civilization assured. Sputnik didn't see it that way. She freshened all right and looked calm enough and might have stayed were it not for the southeast breeze with the wood's smell on it. We didn't think it a problem, the barn door being closed. She bellered. They all bellered. Sputnik looked out the knot hole in the sliding door at the end of the barn. They all look out the knot hole. The door is solid pine. We knew there was a disagreement when she stepped back one pace and lunged for that hole. Couldna been more than three inches across. Cow won't fit through a knot hole. The measure is off. Sputnik got her eyeball by, then figured the rest of her oughta fit. She drove her entire punctuation through that door. Exactly one cow width of barn pine turned to kindling and slivers. At this point a farmer has to decide which he needs more, a milk cow or winter meat. Pa was sliding toward winter meat.

He cooled some, and we tried again. This time we got her penned in and nailed boards on till they went right to the ceiling. Smugness was settin' in when we saw her looking out the window. No reason to worry about that window. Was a full four feet off the floor and a common 28 inch by 36 inch 9 pane window. "Get a couple boards over the. . . . " Pa said. Too late. Sputnik took one modest leap and cleared the floor, cleared the window sill, cleared the white board trim and cleat and smashed through the center of the window, spewing glass, spacers and window putty. The most beautiful act of obliteration I ever saw in my life. Just beautiful. Better than beautiful. Pa was now real heavy toward winter meat.

Last we saw of her she had cleared the barnyard fence, taken the four-strand ten acres south and was pulling at 30 miles an hour toward the far woods. Her tail straight up in the air waving back and forth in a taunting display of the Luftwaffe. Odds were awful heavy on winter meat. At noon Pa said he was going to call Willie after supper to bring her down, dress her out and give him the front quarter for the job.

Halfway through chores Sputnik stuck her head in the former window and bellered. The calf had set up a powerful din of its own all afternoon. Of vibrations I think a calf beller can be heard farther than any other. Better than church bell, steam whistle or police siren. Sputnik didn't move off when we came to the window. We rubbed her forehead, grinning like fools at about the smartest person we ever was to know. She came into the calving stall like the habit was routine, then we set her bull calf on. When Pa came to the barn, he couldn't believe it. He'd heard the beller stop and wondered if we'd put the calf on another cow.

Sputnik

He wanted to know which one, seeing as there were a couple we'd do anything to avoid putting a milker to.

When Sputnik looked at us it was of recognition. She knew who we were and she knew we knew who she was. Had proved it twice. I think that was her point. She needed to point out something missing in Genesis. Maybe she was a barn cow now, but we knew bloody well she was once a heifer of the woods. We could yip up all we wanted about human beings and upright and brains; she just wanted to let us know humans weren't everything. No sir, maybe not even half of what there is. Her look across the pen took down right inside us, she didn't need English or Ojibwa, language is language. She wrote it out for us. I don't think any of us ever forgot.

A calf beller is a hard thing to say no to. I don't understand why in the Odyssey when Ulysses is trying to clear the isle of Circe, the sirens are women. What's his name, Homer, should've used Holstein bull calves if he wanted sound. If I wrote the Odyssey, bull calves been my choice. Nothing lonesomer and more plain painful than a bull calf beller. The sound goes out in a mass. If you know what to look for you can see it; looks like gasoline vapors on a warm day, all blurry and a crowd of vibration. Watch a bull calf beller go across the field, weave over the jackpine, catch at the pasture gates, the fence wire carding some of it. When it passes the hollow where we hunt arrowheads, the sound disappears from sight. At the grove, that being the last high ground before the swamp, it dawdles at the horse-rake and moldy remains of the freight wagon. Finally the beller drops into the woods where it splits up and forages.

I don't think Pa ever intended Willie, Pa's slow to murder. He tied the calf up along the flank of the barn so the sound caromed off using the advantage of the whole length. If Sputnik hadn't come back, I wonder if he might have let her stay wild. I'm pretty sure; still a farmer can't have a wild cow in the woods. Hard on your reputation. Uncle Jim had a wild horse; that is different. The thing is a leftover from the Crusades, honest. Red-haired monster standing easy six foot at the shoulder, feet big as snowshoes. Nothing like that is gonna kiss up to a plow. No reason why it should. Wouldn't be polite even to try and harness it. Besides, it gave us the chance of being trampled to death by a real Crusader's horse, same as carried Richard the Lion Hearted. A wild woods needs a wild horse, same as bear. Place is wider and wilder for it. Trout fishermen are more honest how they treat a fence, and the wild red horse gave us a chance at trout not only them Saturday morning fellas.

Sputnik was the best cow in the universe. Not everyone might have thought so. The modern dairy couldn't have tolerated her owing as somewhere early she missed a fence and went from a four banger to a three titter. One of those three being about half of what was originally situated. Milking machine lost suck on that tit and it had to be hand stripped, the result was Sputnik heard more philosophy and political reaction than most cows.

If milking really wanted a try at modernism, they could redesign the tits. Long ones get stepped on; short ones lose suck. What they need is a knob on the end exactly like something else. The milker'd work better and the tits be out of the way of barbwire. A milker is a mean thing to attach to a cow. Every farmboy who isn't a liar knows the milking machine is cruel. You know as well as I do how they know. All you have to do is put your thumb in it to know. Don't feel bad till the blood gets all bunched up at the pulsating end, then it feels pretty uncomfortable. There's another reason farmboys know. That reason is the knob on the end. Fifteen pounds of negative draw is pretty convincing. Problem is how to get the thing off. Don't want to be caught that way. Milking machine don't feel at all as sumptuous as they look.

Sputnik started out at the end of the stanchions same as the rest. The best milkers worked their way to the dozen stanchions near the alleyway. Here they were first in line for the silage cart, feed cart and right next to the hay-shoot. Didn't have to wait for the chores to get their share as it fell right in front of them. Within a year Sputnik worked her way from a far end stanchion to the number one stanchion on the left, directly across from her mother. She knew very well the quickest route was lactation. Forty-five pounds of milk attached to a ninety pound kid lugged the length of the barn is going to be promoted quicker than a twenty pound collection. Fourth Law of Farmer Dynamics. Don't carry anything any farther than you have to. For three years Sputnik averaged forty-five pounds per milking. Three years she figured was enough to establish the alliance and she backed off to twenty pounds per milking. Any other cow would have been demoted to the far end of the barn.

She was the only cow who could converse, a few others talked some. Sputnik went beyond society and rumor into hypothesis and theory. Granted, her dipthongs were off of what is customary but ask her if she wanted a scoop of ground feed and she tossed her snout with inflection. Stop at that point without the second customary scoop and she looked thee in the eye stout as Lady MacBeth plotting night murders. Walk by without saying hello, she'd nip your work gloves out of the back pocket and spit them on the floor. Given timothy instead of alfalfa, Sputnik neatly catch the section on her nose and toss the insult right back in your face. Glaring until the right mix was brought. When she lost the front tit her product dropped to fifteen pounds per milking. The one behind went the way of a barb and tended to drain itself and Sputnik was at ten pounds including cover and pain and hand against the spring. Sputnik kept her place. If you gargled at her, she gargled back. Sneeze and she sneezed back. Toss her a ball, Sputnik caught it in her mouth and blow it back. She broke my nose in a staring contest. Twice.

In '67 she went down with milk fever. We tried for a week to get her up. The disease is a bone calcium dysfunction and some cows come out of it. Some don't. Dr. Cragg the vet lent us a vice to fit over her hip bones, tightened with a set of screw handles. Lifted her four times a day on two gang-pulleys. Rubbed linament. Injected penicillin. Massaged with hot water, sponges, ice packs. Finally electric stimulation. Nothing worked. We all knew we weren't going to beat milk fever this time.

Pa had his cousin Harry call the mink farm. They came and got her on the next Saturday morning. Dragged her the length of the barn on a stainless steel cable; dragged her by the leg over the gutter, up the cleats of the loading rack and into the dark mow of the truck. She didn't make sound, just her eyes, round and brown and solemn, looking at me. Looking at me like I failed something where nobody, nothing is supposed to fail. I felt her look searing through me. Minkman said she had to be alive or they could't pay the dime a pound. I know I should have killed her myself. I could have, knew well I could have. Those eyes hurt me like I never been hurt before. I'll tell yah, I don't want heaven for me but I sure hope there's someplace special for cows. You'd know it, too, if you ever saw a soul hanging on the end of a steel cable.

And if there's hell, then I know I'm going and I know what I'm going for.

Sometimes the worst place in the world is the farmboy.

MYRTLE'S KITCHIE

"**D**OGS CAN SPOT A BAFFIN QUICKER THAN ANY OTHER creat, reason is their nose. Whether they's cluckny, coofish or coot, depend on a howl to aim out the whereases before a person can cipher shoe-shine. A man can't 'cause thy has no possess of a nose. Wigh, d'ye ever watch a dog prowl after a new fella? How's they start off-ways then leans in, shoe laces, cuffs, knees, assaying him, anywhere a person comes together they nose. Stranger be the only temperature to stand for it. Any other hold to their honor and smack the dog right without even thinking insult. A strange or traveling can't tech a dog. Owing as they migh'lose hand or worse, what's available of family fortune, neither's seemly."

Harold Edwards' place is sequestered on the end of the Maine School Road. A modest square of biggins. The great barn, granary, pullet keep and scratch yard. The road is named for the cemetery, in turn named for the battleship late of Santiago Harbor. At the head of the road, west side as you're going south, is the town's original stone fire-house. The field behind has since been set up as a trailer park, spoiling any field chance the place had. East from the road is George Ivy's bleach plant. He started out in his garage, now runs two semis all over the state with gallon jugs of bleach. Few years ago, about twenty, he moved his house to the other side of the pine woods. Nice woods. A man used to raise silver fox, had forty acres penned in with eight foot cyclone fence and barbwire keepers at the top just like you see in prison movies. Looked wicked, I suppose that was better than pens.

Harold married Myrtle in '38. She was an Upper gal, meaning the peninsula, and had been cousining in the low country. On the way home they swung back via East Chicago and Des Plaines rather than try for the ferry. She had cousins near Stevens Point. Which was how Myrtle's folks operated. Sailing from place to place, from first cousin to thrice removed. In due course all members of the circuit got their share of violation. Any necessary repairs could be carried on while in process, which was the thing with Myrtle's side, their particular form of auto-mobile maintenance. Never in that family's history had they purchased a new car, horse, fence pickets or washing machine. Was as if they bore grudge against new. They considered new as both extravagent and dim-witted. Besides, second-hand allowed them to conduct their lives and residences in a relaxed fashion. Continuous employ wasn't the main thesis of the family. Instead kinda paddle from island of employ to island of employ. Knowing second-hand gave them more sheets in the wind than brand-new. All second-hand required was a bit of repair, a dab of grease and the deft probings of a screw driver. About the family was the sense they could, if necessary, repair anything and wouldn't even try until it was necessary, therein being the impulse necessary to succeed. The moral of them was, don't fix anything till it breaks. Preventive maintenance was considered sissy.

Like checking the dip-stick. Myrtle's brother drove from Ishpeming to Ann Arbor without once checking the dip-stick and the connected reservoir in his '23 Chevrolet Touring. The over-sight evident by Ann Arbor. A smattering negro music borne forth from the bowels of the engineering. Cure being oil from the differential added to the engine while the differential got a mix of water and sawdust. Good pine sawdust.

The automotive advanced as far as Stevens Point on the far side of the lake before again needing adoration. Any knowledgeable observer can admit the profundity of this achievement. Owing as machinery is not ordinarily deemed to survive on a regime of tar oil and pine-water. Least not in the digestive tract of the beast.

Which is how Harold met Myrtle. At the side of the road, her brother in the process of installing a new set of low-end bearings and crank-case gasket.

Harold was 32, Myrtle 16, going on 17 with braided red hair and amply endowed with certain female characteristics. She lay under the car holding in the throw-cylinders while her brother slipped the crankshaft back into its notches having just pasted antimony gum in the shyness of the crank journals. Her legs protruded from beneath the '23 Touring and were observed by Harold innocently bound for Plover.

Says he honestly stopped to help. Had a spare crank and bearings for a '21 wired to the garage wall and oughta fit. Six months later Harold and Myrtle married, she also three months pregnant. The situation being Harold's sense of fix.

In '39 they set up housekeep at the farm on the marsh end of Maine School Road, his pa having farmed there fifty-two years and the father before another thirty. The house was elevated off the ground in the standard practice owing to the proximity of the Buena Vista Marsh and a predictable pattern of high water. Genuinely two story, the second floor never finished but served the storage of seed catalogues, old sewing patterns and four years of Life magazine beginning with the December issue of 1941.

The two rooms on the north of the ground floor served as the winter bulwark for the better keep of the south side. Same as Harold's barn stood its backside to the leg and flank of the woodlot, January morning milking being benefited. Behind the front porch was the parlor, purple rugged and never used except for the laying out of his grandfather. The central focus of Harold Edwards' house was the keep of Myrtle's kitchie. A room of large dimension common to country kitchies, serving all the farm functions from bath to chicken killing and canning season. All this taking place on the down-side of the Maine Road gone to marsh.

If a dominance existed in Myrtle Edwards' kitchie, it was the titanic, cast-iron kitchen stove. The stove was bakery, bun and calf and kitten warmer, chick hatcher, water heater, yeast starter and battery thawer. Situated exactly on the equatorial meridian of the kitchie proper. Behind the stove reared the boding presence of a thick brick lum, told on by the knowing bulge in the plaster wall. Reserve capacity for the house was served by a second lum and nickel-plated stove in the parlor. The latter applicant rarely used except on the formal occasions. Of which were only two known possibilities, either funeral or a winter night in excess of 30 below. Otherwise all cordiality belonged to the kitchen-beast, all pageantry, from sovereign supper to all necessary swaddling.

The kitch was rarely without fire. In spring, twigs sufficed and only enough oak as was needed for bread. For summer fuel, corn cobs. Only in the most hideous of Julys was Myrtle's monument unvented. Otherwise the stove moaned and whispered, hissed, chortled and ruminated in its supreme and royal court. Invariably a sheet of cookies sat on the warming shelf. Perhaps a half dozen bricks of new-born bread, or a scrimmage tackle pile, the like of old time football, of succulent doughnuts. The vapors and tangs of Myrtle's stove twined and knotted throughout the near reaches of the township. Weren't sirens that lured Ulysses, were the cookie sheet. No council of war, winter snow, town crew and snowfence, no talk of spring tax or regumming the lumber blade was purely done and completed unless conducted in the circumspect of Myrtle Edwards' kitchie and claw-footed stove.

Excuse? Who needed excuse? Town crew needed an excuse. It was, after all, four miles back to the garage for a half gallon of radiator fluid. Cap wasn't right; was a 2½ pound cap and spring when it shoulda been a 3½ pound. There being the sufficient excuse why the pump of the townplow, six diesel cylinders hogging at four-drive wheels beneath a load of cruel gravel and by itself the profoundest machine in the township was parked in Harold Edwards' front yard and keep. More times outa ten during the middle morning than mechanical statistics might suppose. It was because of Myrtle's kitchie. The town crew and its citizens didn't know where Ninerva was situated, or Mecca, they did know it weren't at the town garage, nor at Elsie May Pope's red brick house a mile north with running water and television. But Myrtle's kitchie was awful close to the precise location of eternal goodness.

During snowfence time, the crew ran out of wire just south by a quarter from Harold's. Quite by accident. "Any old wire w'do. Any scrap, barb or phone-line, even a length of motor winding." Somehow they always ended up in the kitchen with coffee and a fistful of doughnuts.

The stove given only the modest throttle of early winter had the crew within minutes of arrival, two-thirds of the climb out of their overalls. Any failure to observe a slow strip in Myrtle's kitch caused such a damp that once outdoors violators were seen to visibly slow and calcify from the instant freezing of sweat glands and pores. Semi-nudity at Myrtle's was commonplace. The kitchen on any cold day became a vision of the metamorphosis not ordinarily associated with human beings. It was nothing in the least unique to witness a half-dozen grown men taking coffee from assorted cups, eating thick slices of new bread drenched with comb honey and with their fore-clothes rolled to their hips. Exposed torsos down to the red, cream and sweat-rusted woolens and sometimes the pink, snake-belly white and hairy upper pinnacles of their own naked selves.

The kitchie had the smell of rustic philosophy, of new and old sweat, lubrication oils, subtle manures and unsubtle manures, boot polish, pipe tobaccy and sweet rum-flavored chew. They discussed milk prices, the same as applied to bull-calves, methods of repair to a water pump or plow frog or Joe Stalin. Also the best way to saw white oak, the only way to saw red oak and any subsequent and township meaning of original sin. Also what might be night-killing the chickens and the current revelations of Senator Joe McCarthy, as well as suggestions of who else he could mull over as suffering the communist influence. They couldn't understand communists because communists weren't godly. Communism was as if someone said the Internal Revenue Service were holy and ought to be worshipped. A man can't worship government by itself for chrissake. Governments are things and accidental things at that. You can't really pray at government, any fool knows that. Prayer to make it count has gotta be aimed at somethin' vast. The IRS is wide but it ain't vast. Vast is more like winter and oceans. The snow plow driver could image themselves praying at winter or oceans. Sky too, night sky in particular. Communism is what happens when villagers outnumber farmers.

While the learned assembly sat, leaned, smoked and chewed, Myrtle progressed unencumbered with her chores. Round, endowed, red-haired and fully fifteen years younger than Harold, Myrtle in that mix of smoke and semi-naked men was exotic. Same as the calendar hung on the shop wall of the Laszewski Brothers Allis Chalmers dealership. Something flippantly female. No matter the month, the model wore no else than the least condition of summer clothes while posturing so as to reveal the constitutional majority of her biological torso. Yet when the townmen dreamed, what they dreamed of was somethin' nearer to Myrtle. Freckles, red braids and luxuriantly round. A mother kind of round. A pillow kind, a celestial kind of round. The round of Myrtle at the stove, Myrtle at milk stool, Myrtle with child and Myrtle with a full sheet of hot sourdough raisin cookies. They wished to bury their faces in Myrtle's round. They knew calendar girls might be nice but wonderful was Myrtle. The clean cut of her kitchen perfumes tore jagged holes in the atmosphere of 90 weight axle-lube, cow manure and the thin smarting stratospheres of ozone from the arc welder. She glided among the drifts of scent. Rubbed past their assemblies. They stepped back to let her pass, squashed each other's toes, were startled by a yelp, darted forward and rebounded from her, her roundness of deep-fry doughnuts and her laughter.

Only one mortal man came unwanted to the keep and kitchie of Myrtle. Only one in the hundred square mile township was honestly and duly hated, William Randolph Rogers, town assessor. Was said William Rogers came from a long line of assessors. That his fathers before were assessors far back as the Sheriff of Nottingham. Rogers did seem by nature provisioned to be assessor but his dad weren't one. He weren't no more assessor than anyone else even if his genetics seemed inclined.

William Randolph Rogers was a short man, narrowly missing the five foot mark. At six foot he'd have been several times dead. Once by pitch fork, another incidence of rifle bullet. Because he weren't dead didn't mean nature intended short people to be assessors, even if it is true some would've connected the axe-handle right across his ear if he were of larger size. And it also true any of a dozen punches could have landed smack along his jaw if he were taller; which he wasn't. Nature don't fabricate assessors. Instead they are birthed out on arbitrary constant. It's just that some don't survive.

William Randolph Rogers was the only son and issue of Archibald Liverworth Thomason. Scratch the issue, William weren't Archibald's natural. Something clogged in Missus Thomason and they never had naturals. They found William in an ammunition box on their doorstep the spring of 1902. April abouts. First off folks thought it a cranberry baby. Sometimes was a regular rash of them. From village gals who had gone to pick cranberries at a nickel a box. Never having been much weight with home and as there was a dance every night, with liquor as often and they not adjusted to it. Someone eyed them up-sides and down-sides even if they were plain as a shingle.

The Thomasons were known by all to be childless so whosoever freshened picked right. Thomason operated Pince's General Item on the corner of the second crossroads below the Green Bay and Central tracks. The store, since loosely affiliated with the International Grocer's Association, had for three generations pilfered and looted the pocket of local patrons. For one hundred and ten years Pince's existed as the only general grocery and software between Wisconsin Rapids and the fork of the Big Plover. The original Pince, his son and then his son-in-law, had no conscience against markups.

Others tried. In 1912 Hadley Smith opened a general store alongside his established feedmill. Smith never intended a store. Once too often his wife complained. Why she always did it before supper he didn't know. He could live with complaints, but not before supper. Smith hated bad news before supper.

How Thomason had charged a dollar-six for fifty pounds of single-grind white flour. Any perceptive customer knows the going rate of fifty pound single-grind in the river city were but eighty-eight, maybe ninety cents.

Missus Mother Smith had a treble of voice unusual in the human reference. As a girl she whistled between her teeth without forming the aperture with her fingers. When the situation required, she could add frequencies to her words that literally hurt any listener within half a dozen feet. When Missus Smith wanted she could ruin Hadley's supper juices. He had only a few attachments, Hadley did. Early morning, fishing, horseshoes and sandlot baseball with his boys. The one remaining prize was his supper juices. Work only had merit in that it primed a man for supper. He enjoyed the hunger building in him. He'd lug feed sacks himself to enrage it. His whole comportment and frame leaned toward the steamed kitchen window of his empire-style house one block back in the village. Third most handsome house in the plat. Double front doors of teak with cut-glass windows. Two glazed bays and a steam generator for electric lights and the only house in the village set on a block by itself.

No meal had the distinction of supper. The superiority of Christianity is directly related to supper. Communion wasn't breakfast, wasn't dinner, wasn't Saturday lunch or picnic; was supper. Supper was that important. Glorified by standing rib roast, a meaty pork loin or chicken legs bobbing in gravy and dumplings. Supper was a sanctum, a heaven, if only Missus wouldn't ruin it with her spasms.

To curtail invasion on his relic, Hadley Smith opened a small grocery in the corner of the feedmill. He didn't care whether it made a profit or not, as long as Missus was supplied with single-grind at eighty-eight cents.

Business bounded and even Smith was amazed. The first week he'd sold out a month's supply of flour. He ordered double. In three weeks he ordered again and Mother hadn't ruined his supper juices once. A grocery had been a rather good idea. He gave thought to sugars, a shelf for teas and coffee. Maybe soaps. Then the spring freshlet of 1913 took out the old mill.

Hadley couldn't understand how it happened. For near fifty years Smith's mill had stood against spring. Every flood rage and surge, tree root and wild boom, the mill stood. He knew the sluice gate was closed, hadn't he driven the nail in the jar-beam himself? Good new twenty-penny nail it was. No mere surge and ice plug could rattle it loose.

Hadley loved that mill. Each year after ice he'd pull the nail and let the river in. He liked to grind there sometimes instead of the new mill. Sure the village mill was faster, without the awful dust of the granite pucks. Still the old mill had its merits, didn't need engine or motor, only the river, besides, the old mill had such rich sounds. The crisp plunge of water through the gates, the elegance of the mill taking up the torque in the water and turning. He felt the old mill's foundations murmur. The whole building warping under the river flow, the twist feeding its way into the machinery, and the entirety leaning on the river, raw squeaks of the wood gear and catch pin; sure it was old, others would have burned the thing and sold the scrap. He knew it wasn't cost-effective, hadn't been for twenty years. Not since steam, not since internal combustion and surely not with electricity coming.

No point in even thinking the $300 in scrap. The flood had smashed it and plopped what didn't float in the river bottom. For awhile Hadley thought salvage. Then he realized he didn't want the 3 cents a pound for cast-iron, he wanted it back, the whole mill. Nobody missed the old mill but him. Folks didn't want stone-ground any more when they could have hammer-ground flour. Funny, though, that 20 penny should've held. The jar-beam was pine so's not to spit nails out the way ash might've. And the nail was crimped with a backside of a stove axe.

A week after the flood he saw Archibald, walking home on the side track. Seven-fifteen on the second Archy closed the store and aimed for supper. Sometimes they walked the track together, Archibald and Mrs. Thomason lived in the back of the village hotel. Most knew they didn't sleep together anymore, or thought they knew. Was said her delicate constitution didn't allow it. Known for a fact Archibald took a room in the hotel for himself, while she spent night in the family rooms of the story below. Everybody knew and Archibald was not of a mind to correct them. Indeed he did keep the far room in the hotel for himself. Had the key in his pocket twenty years, ever since he bought the hotel for one thousand dollars even, the thousand from his father-in-law as a wedding present. Was a wager, if he doubled the money in a year, Pince planned to give him the store, knowing his retirement and old age then be safe enough. If Archy couldn't, he'd sell the grocery to whoever offered the first two thousand dollars for it and the customer list.

Archy hired Betsy Wheelwright, widow Wheelwright, the second morning. She was the best shanty cook in the Pinery and had been slopping plates since 12 years old. Within a month the hotel was filled every night from Monday to Friday. Salesmen, rail-crew, circus folk, "Clean beds, hot food," said the sign. Archy ran the hotel at list price. First year he cleared 2,200 dollars and at January 1st his father-in-law, that being Amory Pince, handed him the true and free deed of the General Item.

Hadley Smith and Archy often walked the tracks. Been boys together. Archy told Smith he was sorry about the mill. How it musta been float ice in the race, then a sudden going. Or maybe the nail come loose of the jar-beam. Strange how precarious they all were. How a fire or flood or whim of nature might wipe a man the long-ways of the grave or worse, ruin his purse.

Archy remembered how when they were kids they fished from that second story porch on the river mill. Did he remember? Hadley remembered. How from the height they'd watch walleyes and trout below in the water. The river like a glass ball and the trout suspended in it. How a hook and line punctured that second world. The pane broken by the line then healed again. How they watched the bait, bacon rind and dead kittens. Was like having grip on destiny. Like being a sort of god. A Caesar above the Coliseum, rolling fate off their thumb. Knowing it was fate before it was fate. Did he ever feel that way too?

The reason Hadley's pa built the porch in the first place was for fishing. So's he didn't have to go to the river bank, and from the mill porch he could hear the machinery. It took something out of fishing when you see them coming. Same thing when the fish had gone upstream and they weren't there and even if you felt like hanging line for the sake of hanging line and no other, you still felt stupid even though it felt good. The knowledge of the porch kinda spoiled fishing. Hadley admitted he hadn't actually fished from the porch in what must be twenty years.

"You know how it was when they was biting and you couldn't get yourself to stop. How greed reared out and before you know'd it there's 20 trout more than you can eat all week."

Smith knew. He didn't really want to sell single-grind flour.

"Was me who pulled that nail."

Smith knew. No one else but Archy had the knowledge or the reason.

"Thought it was you."

"Soon as I pulled it I wanted to pound it back but was already too late. Was lucky to get out of the mill with my life. God-damn me Hadley, it were the most greetching sound I've ever to hear. I swear on my soul I'm sorry."

"Mill didn't have long anyway you know. The village committee wanted it out. I couldn't afford to put money in it seeing as folks don't care a whittle for stone-ground any the more."

"Hadley, I owe yah. On my soul I owe yah. Name it and I'll pay, whether my wife, my store or my savings account. I owe ya and I wanta be clean of it."

"How about twice-ground at cost?"

"Huh? I'm serious, you name the damages and I'll pay."

"OK, flour at cost for the next twenty years for all your customers."

Archy's mouth went off as if to complain. In a year alone he knew it'd cost him 200 dollars.

"Done," offered his hand and felt cleansed.

Smith didn't want to sell flour. The mill was gone anyway and weren't they both businessmen, anyway his supper was safe for awhile. Archibald Thomason lost money on flour but made up for the flour at cost by the increased traffic volume in store. Eight years later a trade magazine wrote him up as the founder of the "item leader." The merchandising technique of increasing profits by losing money on specific items.

William Randolph Rogers was the adoptive son of Archibald and Mrs. Thomason. The story we heard was the Rogers family had relatives in the township whose frame house caught fire on a February night. The blaze killed the parents and the new-born while William was with neighbors during Mrs. Rogers delivery. They thought to change his name to Thomason but decided against it, the reasons never clear.

William served in the First World War. During the war Archibald died and the village discovered he'd been writing poetry every night for nearly forty years. Poems about the village men and women. Poems about the preachers and yellow-haired girls. Poems with pencil drawings of people like you might see from an upper window. Boys in rented liveries with their hands under the chemises of the queens. Of tipplers peeing in the horse trough. And Sylvester Sharpinski who drowned in a trough, funny how no one heard him, being as it were right below the hotel.

They say Mrs. Thomason got the stuff back from the lawyer and burnt all the poems and the pencil drawings. They say, some of them were of her. Naked. Sitting in a chair, lying on the bed, bending at the window and her in the mirror, her with only stockings, hundreds of them, all in the nude.

William Rogers said he was artillery. The papers at the courthouse mention he was with the Expeditionary Force in the transport section of the General Pershings Boys as corporal. By 1955 William Randolph Rogers had been advanced by lore to a captain. That he didn't altogether look like an officer seemed all the better reason to think he was one. The promotion helped him write the tightest assessment ledger in the northern half of the state. They imaged Rogers machine-gunning the Huns in long dead windrows. He never offered he was only a corporal and a mule skinner. When he died at '61, Pince's grocery died with him. For a generation the store hadn't changed. As supermarkets followed the fashion of wide floor plans with refrigerated meat sections, he still sold cuts right off the animal swung out on a trolley from the cooler to chopping block. The dry groceries continued to be stacked in double rows so a ladder or ware-pliers were necessary to stock the shelves as well as shop from them. William Rogers was a better assessor than grocer.

Most thought he died from shrapnel that had come dislocated and lodged in his heart. At the village Methodist church they left him set up two full days seeing as more folks wanted to see him dead than anyone else in the village. At the funeral service Elsie May Pope sang the Battle Hymn of the Republic, lost track of the verses and so stamped out the vintage twice. The flag was too big for the coffin. Train went by during the scripture lesson; Green Bay and Western tracks but ten feet beyond the north wall of the kirk. Windows rattled, false teeth rattled, coffin rattled. Heard something like a pocket watch chime from inside the coffin, someone must've wound his watch because it struck the hour all the way back to the second pew. Pretty good watch figuring it hit the hour through two layers of bronzed steel, a lace pillow, whatever they do to a corpse and one 48-star American flag.

Only William Randolph Rogers was sufficiently cold-hearted to be the assessor of three towns at once. None better than "barrel-eyes Rogers," so no one else thought it prudent to run for office. Ever since his discharge in 1921 he'd served as elected assessor. Took an uncommon man, folks thought. If not fitted by creation to do it, it'd damage a man to try. Test was to note it's effect on your supper. Nothing touched Rogers. He'd count cows, argue improvements, license dogs and asked if saw logs were present. Fifteen cents on cows, twenty-five cents for a dog license and saw logs over a twelve inch diameter and eight foot long assessed at five cents each. Cut lumber passed without assessment.

Generally the citizenry didn't mind assessment, were the count that tortured them. Everyone knew a two-tit cow wasn't comparable to one with all four hangs. T'weren't right at all. Two tits is only half a cow. Behooved every farmer to explain the situation to the local assessor yearly if opportunity availed. Offering him an understanding of a basic mathematical reality. Two tits weren't a whole cow. They demonstrated. They exampled. They performed. Set milk-can by milk-can showing that half was half. "You come by at milking and I'll show you." Was a fool of an assessor who did. Why, every cow in the barn have to go on trial then and at that rate he won't finish the assessment roll till October next. "Tits make it a cow. If it has tits the State of Wisconsin Department of Revenue counts it. The book says to count cows not tits."

The demonstration proceeded. "Looka that. You call them tits? They're more raisins than tits." He pulls the pendants to show the lack of connection between lactation and orifice.

"A cow is a cow whether tits or nubbins. If she's so short of proper cow why don't you send her out?"

The remark bordered on insult. Here was a nincompoop assessor telling the dairyman to sell off his Sadie or Colleen or faithful Daisy. A cow in whose flank he's warmed his face a thousand mornings and narry a kick. Sell her? Could no more sell her than sell off the house woman.

Assessors were knocked down, tripped, shot at, spit on and propelled bodily out the upper half of a dutch-door. Probed with a pitch fork, splattered by warm manure and had their cars towed off while they counted.

The assessor dwelt within a remarkable shelter of Wisconsin law. No other being had the brevity and legal freedoms of the assessor. He could peek in windows, officially use spyglass and trespass without warrant and on Sunday. Not judge, sheriff or posse had equal practice.

They argued kickers; "Yah can't count kickers, whys they's hardly civil yet."

"I don't count civil cows, I don't count tame cows; I don't care if she's two heads, eats crocodiles or belches fire."

"But I only get half the milk of her I should before she rolls her impatient eyes and whether I'm vacant or not, rubs out the location with a kick to maim an ordinary man. The rest I have to tend off with calves else she'd curdle on me. You can't seriously count kickers."

William Randolph Rogers counted kickers. Counted anything with a milk purse. If a farmer slid his affection over a bovine and maintained her beyond useful years, William Randolph Rogers stood by to count her.

If a cow caught hardware and the dairyman kept on with her to watch the drama, to see whether the inning belonged to baling wire or the gastro-intestinal enzymes of a common hay-stoked cow, Rogers counted. Took a year sometimes. A year to kill or a year to survive and the farmer each morning fingering through her pie for the wire. The contest ruined her for milk even if afterwards she was right again. In the morning they'd find them dead in the stanchion. Rendering plant paid a dollar.

William Randolph Rogers counted her. They knew it weren't fair. No ways fair. Some didn't say a word to the man. Not hello, not fine how are you. The whole assessment conducted in the stillness of mortuaries. The moment both visibly and emotionally hung there, if violated it might have produced murder. Smart assessor didn't accept coffee, teas or even the hospitable glass of water. Silius Hardrum in Juneau County took tea and it killed him. Not outright. But that's what it were, poison, poison pure and simple. Don't take cookies, Boston brown bread or hot scones. Beneath the vanilla and cinnamon they'll getcha with madwort. Or juice of alyssum and before you can get yourself home to recuperate you're throwing your clothes off 'cause you think it's mites and fleas and bedbugs. Been assessors committed after being poisoned and witched by farmers.

Best time to assess is during a blizzard or spring rain. Good assessor kept rubber boots and macintosh. Count cows when countryside is in mirk, blurred over blue by storm. Don't give a care to what people think. Only assessors and devils love storm. The meaning is you can hide in a storm, climb on a yard-fence and count in comfort when even dogs don't bother.

There were alternatives for farmers. Precisely two. Either send half the heifers to the marsh pasture till April 15 or try and lie about the count in a face-up and sinless manner. It is true farmers are admirably practiced in certain falsehoods. Like bushels per acre. Every farmer had any of a half-dozen computations at hand for yields of corn, rye, oats, cuttings of clover and alfalfa and how many bales they put in the mow last July 11th, you know that fearfully humid day, 121 degrees in the sun, 145 degrees in the mow. Some tellings weren't lies, they were legends. But telling direct arithmetic errors to an agent of government seemed too separate a demarcation. Plainly, to lie in a man's face when he could count himself, lie to another Christian soul, was well, wrong; at least less than human expectation. Best alternative being to offer a slur of pronounciation.

"Milk cows? Huh . . . twenty-fouix." If put down twenty-four the farmer went two up. If twenty-six he was even and next time the slur hung on the previous syllable some bit longer.

The one weak spot of William Randolph Rogers came by his tendency to count cows all at one quick. In three days solid numbering he'd try and ledger the whole township from the wild marsh to the moraine. Problem being farm dogs. Rogers had no fervor for farm dogs, or any dogs that matter, whether lap, hunter, sicker or river-mutt. He didn't like dogs and they didn't like him. Dogs, he thought, were the major blemish on creation. Devil made dogs. Even the mildest of them can go wild in a moment. Come crust snow and marsh moon, any that's loose go deering. Dog is good for 25 miles per hour on March-snow while deer flounder and plow. Rogers seen 'em in his headlights and running in the field on a moon-glaze, wild and wicked as a million years previous. Tearing long-tongued after lean deer. Even honest well-fed dogs go off at the chance of bloodlust. Dogs made his skin crawl. Dogs are impatient with death. They begin eating before the deer is fully dead. The vision often soared within him and his testicles coiled against his pivot. God damn beasts!

William Randolph Rogers had seen his share of bones in the moonlight. During the war when most thought he was artillery he was instead a mule skinner, a teamster hauling water and Enfields. He'd seen bones alright, wagon loads of bones. Hauled from the war plains to the burial pits. He lied about being artillery because cannoneering seemed the more pure. Death ain't half bad when conducted at a distance. Wholesome, long-range killing, not mangled wastes of men, parts of them, virtual blood-swamps of riddled flesh and meat. He lied to convince himself of another existence. To keep his own mind and body from being forever buried in those bone pits.

They shoveled the bodies in. Wheel-barrows and dump wagons. Went through their pockets, straightened their faces, tried to avoid stepping on loose eyes. Heard the dogs circling. Seen them lope off with a prize; leg femur or severed hand. Seen soldiers gutted out because of dogs. What if they were yet alive? William Randolph Rogers hated dogs.

Dogs knew it. They can smell hate and fear and loathing. It precedes a man like an invisible bubble of his person. Fear is the easiest to smell.

Fear from sweaty palms, the smell of tense oils, thin volatile flags proclaiming instinctive fear. The depth of the vapor relates to how thick the fear is. To the farm dogs Assessor Rogers smelled exactly like a March-moon deer.

In Myrtle's kitchie Rogers met the host of the farm community. Wiggy, Whittaker, Pope, Cook, Holiday, Isherwood. Pa come to borrow a double hook logging chain, Ted Jensen needed 10 bushel of seed oats, Josh Whittaker looking for a brass rivet to fit a surcingle strap, the hardware was out of the item. Joe Wiggy because on Wednesday morning Myrtle made fresh doughnuts. Town crew had been hammering in weight-limit signs seeing as the frost been going out a couple weeks, and signs for the marsh roads saying the road was out. Didn't need a sign. With the thaw the old creek-bed ran water three feet deep and ten feet wide. Same creek as crossed the Maine Road 20 rods north of Harold's, only a foot deep there. By the time it swung south it included another 160 acres of drainage and had the right of way. What road remained didn't matter, nobody went west on the marsh in spring.

When Myrtle's kitchie was loaded to capacity a person weren't fully responsible for his actions. As one man raised his arm to eat his doughnut the angular intent eddied to either side in the line of his companions. After awhile folks learned to eat in synchronization. If on the up-beat when a stronger man was on the down, the food never reached your mouth.

Was not the sort of place where an assessor might gain comfort. The unison movements provided a wary prospect. As one man scratched his ear the two others to each side did the same, the two beyond half way to scratch. If one loosen his privates, the practice vibrated, minus friction, around the room. A child the kitchen learned all the habits of adulation without being told. Any one action drizzled as far as five and six folks away before it ran out of grip.

Myrtle's Harold had a face of geological origin. If not geology then more a gothic cathedral with gables, gargoyles and demonic rain gutters.

As he was already a practicing heathen the simile is best laid with geology. His face had escarpments, kames and stratifications. Within it were caverns and pillars, cauldra and vents. His face was a mischievous coagulant, never intended to serve as a billboard of humanity. When he pursed his lips his ears wiggled and his nose turned.

"Heifers?" Harold said aloud, looking at the ceiling. You could see he was ciphering. He shifted the pipe stem to the opposite set of molars. Withdrew the refractory, pointing the stem at some imagined set of numbers in direction of the ceiling. Scratched his chin, rubbed his cheek, looked at his hand while unrolling fingers as he looked through the numerizations.

Said aloud, "Betsy, Lady, Dunce, Orangutan, Spitfire and Messerschmitt," his voice drifting off, came back at "Critical Mass and Target Bundle."

"Twelve." Less said than growled.

"What?" Rogers eyes did look like gun-barrels. The riflings twisted right back into his mean soul. Everyone knew he was the best and only man for the post of assessor in the hard town of Plover.

"I said twelve, god-damn-it."

"Fresh heifers?"

"You counting those with blood in their milk?"

"I'm counting all heifers come full-term and calved." We all knew he'd been captain in the artillery. In that moment we felt sorry for the Germans at the wrong end of the cross-hairs from William Randolph Rogers' eyes. They still looked to be judging loft and trajectory, and in a moment setting loose a rain of death and crippling.

"Three, I suppose, one's got milk fever and I don't expect 'er up."

"Will she be here as of April 15th?"

"Depends on the road."

"Shall I count it three?"

"Yes, damn your hide, number it three."

"Milking cows?"

The dog from its stove corner was roused by a new and wonderful scent. After a stretch and yawn it came 'round the corner to study the source of the vapors.

Everyone in the room saw William Randolph Rogers for the briefest of moments turn his eyes. They knew. Credit was due Rogers for not staring at the dog, instead he kept a heavy pull on Harold. But his skin color went from a mellow cream to a crimson sundown.

Harold rolled his pipe, tasting the numbers, waiting for reinforcements.

The dog reconnoitered. Three feet off the port bow of William Randolph Rogers it stopped and again sampled the target. The dog knew those taints.

Rogers hated dogs. They always ate the soft parts first; the sex organs, the lower tract, the liver, kidneys, stomach...

That's when he felt the dog nuzzle his crotch. An insistent shove for scent, then a second opinion.

"Fourteen...and..."

The ledger slapped closed and William Randolph Rogers was out the door.

Everyone in Myrtle's kitchie knew Harold had a full eighteen milkers even if four had three tits or less.

Funny why Rogers left so quick, no arguing two-titters, hardware or the one with a twisted tract. Usually he'd argue the count...curious.

ADVENT

THE LIBRARY WAS TWO SHELVES. "ZANE GREY," "LITTLE Women," "Tarzan of the Apes," "History's Famous Women," Lincoln's "Concise World Encyclopedia" and Baden-Powell's "Handbook for Boys." The books were on the low shelves of my grandmother's secretary, stained so dark as to hide all trace of the oak grain. It nearly reached the ceiling with gothics and swoons. Its upper reaches complete with a mirror and colonnaded shelves on which resided Grandma's souvenirs of the Portage Railway and her three pieces of rose-glass, including one lettered in gold as a souvenir of Plainfield. A carved panel folded out revealing a small writing table. Inside were pigeon holes; for envelopes, ink well, faded photographs; below, the two shelves of books. Most had already served one generation, some were into their third.

Between them my grandparents and folks subscribed to a dozen different magazines and papers, not including farm catalogs, circulars and auction bills. Any list of them is incomplete; Successful Farming, Farm

Journal, Life magazine, Look magazine, Saturday Evening Post, Reader's Digest, Prairie Farmer, Hoard's Dairyman, the Agriculturist, the Stevens Point Daily Journal, Wisconsin Farmer, Better Homes and Gardens, Ladies Home Journal, Boy's Life and a greedy little publication of the Methodist Church as only included Methodees.

Upstairs in my older brother's room was the Colliers twelve volume set of encyclopedias. Bobby's room had four windows and a walk-in closet. The windows looked out on the porch roof Bobby utilized as a patio. Kept a pack of Lucky Strikes in the roof cornice. My room was in the middle, Gary's on the east. Gary's room had a closet we had converted to a chemistry lab. Only caught fire twice. My room had casement windows facing the barn. A brass latch opened them, meaning I didn't have to walk all the way downstairs to piss. Just open the window. Did rust the screen pretty bad though I believe it benefited the bridal-wreath below. The encyclopedias weren't any good at all. Only had two little paragraphs under "sex," and one sentence at "female."

I had traded a sack of cats-eye marbles for the book "Son of the Stars." Bobby had a copy of "Amazon Headhunters" with a recipe for shrinking heads and a photo of a woman suckling a baby and a dog at the same time. We kept that book in my desk. Pa's grandfather had it made of pine and behind the shelves was a secret drawer which opened by sticking your finger in a hole and pushing against the drawer. Kept "Amazon Headhunters" in there.

The house had a half-dozen Bibles including the great leather hided beast on Grandma's dresser. Inside were our names, our grandfather's, greats and great greats, a letter from the Civil War, another from Waterloo. That book swallowed lives like they was no more than the porch-light moths.

Each of us had a "Boy Scout Handbook" and we procured "One Thousand Electrical Experiments" from the Liberty Corners School, meaning we stole it. Door was open and the window broke, book set there a year 'fore we took it. Wasn't stealing, was adoption. Only problem, the experiments were supposed to be powered with a lantern battery. At ninety-eight cents each lantern batteries were beyond our resources. We used a tractor battery. The electro-magnet had more pull than what the instructions called for and the buzzer didn't buzz, it whistled.

I figured my older brother was a genius 'cause he built a shortwave radio from parts ordered through Allied Radio. Bobby was reluctant to let me listen to it till I bought for a dollar and eighty cents Werner von Braun's "History of Rocketry." Had pictures of Robert Goddard's first liquid- propelled church steeple. He wanted to read it pretty bad and I kept him off till he let me listen to the short-wave and tune it myself. He got 15 minutes of von Braun, I got 15 minutes of static. I didn't want to trade anymore after that. He said I should have known there wasn't anything to listen to till after dark and the atmosphere had cooled down so that radio waves bounce back.

I acted like I knew it, which I didn't.

The best book in the house was Grandpa Isherwood's "Illustrated Synopsis of Chinese Culture." The red binding was so thick it was near bullet-proof. Ordinarily you won't think a book with a title like that might attract attention. First, we thought it Bible of the Chinese. We were wrong, it was an awful lot better than a Bible. When we opened it, probably three hundred years since anyone had, the binding creaked like an old door in a crooked, unpainted house. Turn of the century gases were caught in the pages, by the smell they hadn't kept well.

Inside the covers was a frontispiece with a 2 by 3 inch piece of "mandarin silk." Green with gold dragons stitched in. The silk didn't smell like you think it might for being closed off in a book half of forever. Felt like running water. Cold when you first touched it, then it warmed up right in your hand. Behind the silk page were six double pages of maps. One for the Ming Dynasty, one for Ching, one for the Crimean War, the age of Mandarins and Warlords and one each for geology and trade.

The book went through China age by age. I never honestly tried to read the whole thing. Didn't seem polite, one person reading over 5000 years of people, a million, heck, a hundred million dying every time he turns the page. Sometimes nothing else was worth looking at. After I got tired of the Reader's Digest and the Post and if it was still raining I'd go find the "Illustrated Synopsis of Chinese Culture." Even Life magazine wasn't as close to good as the pictures in that book. When they told you about folks getting their heads cut off in China, they not only talked about it but showed how it was done. Buried the folks in the ground to their necks and clipped them off like they were rows in a cornfield. If a man steals or a son disobeys his dad, he gets his head whacked off. Shiss, just like that. They could sell him for a slave instead but it were worse than dead 'cause they took your name away. I hoped Pa never read the "Illustrated." When I was done with it I put it back on the shelf backwards so the binding didn't show and maybe get him interested.

The third chapter, page 131, the "Illustrated Synopsis of Chinese Culture" gave the exact recipe for gunpowder. One third saltpeter, one third sulfur, one third charcoal. The next best thing to Christmas in July were the directions for gunpowder. A Redwing crock in the basement had four gallons of rock peter. A bag in the granary had sulfur for when the cows had the binds, and I could make charcoal.

Didn't say any more than one third saltpeter, one third sulfur, one third char. Didn't need to. I'd been hunting the secret of gunpowder since I could remember and here it was; one third, one third, one third. My first try was a little dismal because I didn't crush the charcoal. The gunpowder smelled good but didn't burn, it sparkled some but wasn't anywhere near dangerous enough. I told Bobby and he said right off it was because the charcoal needed grinding. Used a rock in the bottom of Gary's coaster wagon. Then sifted it to separate out the grits. This time it flared and snorted pretty and I knew I was in approximation of the genuine gunpowder.

Advent

The problem was how to get what von Braun called thrust; compression is close but bang is the word. I could see gasoline was almost the same as gunpowder. A little goes a long ways but it has to be squashed in a cylinder coming to top dead center before it's any use, dontcha know. Firecrackers are no more than gunpowder and newspaper. Dynamite is close by. Pa had a box of dynamite in the granary for stumps. We knew it was in the corner. Knew if we touched it, if even caught breathing within three feet of it, we'd be buried in the sand to our necks and he'd drive the haymower over us. Ma kept after him till he buried that whole grand box of propulsion behind the old machine shed.

The problem with gunpowder is how to light the stuff after it is all rolled up in newspaper. Gasoline-soaked baler-twine fuse quit every time it got to the hole in the bundle. Hole snuffed it out. Nothing we tried worked. Went back to the picture in the "Illustrated Synopsis of Chinese Culture." Showed a man in a pigtail and bathrobe lighting rockets. Gary thought maybe we ought try pigtails. Little brothers are pretty stupid sometimes; besides, it would take six years to grow hair enough for a pigtail. With Grandpa's magnifying glass we went over the picture, if the artist was honest the answer was in there and not blurred over. Not the way Bible treats Mary on the way to Bethlehem. Next we see her she has the kid. No groaning, no afterbirth, no slime; if Mary on the way to Bethlehem is good enough for art, how come being born isn't? Some things decide right from the beginning they ain't going to tell the whole truth.

The fuse looked like an ordinary rope. So we tried rope. Nope, it weren't rope. Went back to the "Illustrated." Looking close, under the man's feet were little speckles. Dirt? Gravel? Nope, gunpowder. The rope had gunpowder twisted in the turns of the braids. Gunpowder wouldn't stay in twine, but rope held it.

It worked, whill-whee did it work. Ten seconds after it went off Ma came running around the lumber pile. White as a pullet, her eyes big as a cow's with the dish towel still in one hand.

"Whatcha boys been up to?" Pa, who'd been welding a stanchion link, came puffing up. He didn't say nothing, just looked at us like he was trying to settle on who he'd sell us to. "Gosh damn your hides, now whatcha been up to?"

They didn't believe it was the dynamite somehow spontaneously igniting. Spontaneous was Bobby's word, told you he was almost a genius. They kinda hesitated at it and we had another ten seconds to think up a second thesis. Bobby said it were an ether can we lit off.

"So where's the can now?" Pa says. We all shrugged in the unison chorus necessary for truth. "Blew it clean up, Pa. We watched it through the slats in the lumber pile and when it blew, the whole thing disappeared."

We knew the pressure was off. Ma looked at Pa like it was all his fault. "Listen, Florence, I gotta keep ether or I'll spend ten minutes cranking come winter." He looked back at us. "If I ever catch you guys fooling with ether again I'll tan your hides and hang what's left of you to dry in the calf pens." Why'd he have to mention calf pens? "By the way, they could stand a cleaning!" We headed in the direction. Bobby started running. Gawd damn it, meaning he'd get to watch the spreader while Gary and I had to pry and fork. It was only a little better than being sold.

Anyway we had protected our supply. We knew now to conduct research somewhere else and that Pa won't hide the saltpeter on us or the "Illustrated Synopsis of Chinese Culture." We built half a dozen rockets that summer from toilet tubes taped together. The biggest problem was some form of directional nozzle. Von Braun had the same problem. As a result our missiles tended to skid, meaning some days they went up, some days sideways. Once, in July, we set fire to an acre of bromgrass and jackpine. Lucky we were back near the creek. Took off our pants, soaked them in the stream and beat the fire out. Ma couldn't imagine what happened to our denims and we didn't enlighten her.

The ice-cone holder from West's dairy store in the village looked exactly like a rocket nozzle. A cone shaped cup was set inside the holder and you ate it that way. Supposed to leave the holder there at West's dairy store. We borrowed one. Wasn't stealing. Honest, borrowing is temporary, stealing is permanent. We would have paid a deposit but how can you explain rocket-nozzles to anyone who don't even know who Werner von Braun is?

The nozzle was ten times the size of any rocket we'd ever built before. Toilet paper tubes are maybe, 1½ inches in diameter. This nozzle must have been 3 inches across. We knew pretty well it was gonna come to this sooner or later.

What the heck, this could be our breakthrough. There was a linoleum tube in the rafters over the car garage. Spent two weeks grinding gunpowder, almost four pounds total. Whittled the nose-cone from a cedar fence post and drilled out the center to get rid of as much excess weight as possible. What we couldn't figure was how to fix the nozzle onto the tube. Didn't think harness leather cement'd hold. Maybe Uncle Jim knew. Wonder if he ever thought rockets instead of horses, kinda skipping internal combustion. Stove bolts spoil the gas pattern, von Braun said so, or maybe that was Robert Goddard.

Decided to let it try with harness leather cement. If that glue can hold two Pencherons, stands to reason it oughta hold four pounds of gunpowder. The perfect solution being aluminum irrigation pipe and rivets but we had to settle for linoleum tube and harness leather cement. Don't seem fair when you think about the breakthrough we had advanced.

No one wanted to light it. Ordinarily six inches of fuse gives us time to run the four rods to our block-house, really just a big elm stump we rolled on its side with a ton of dirt in the claws. We bored peep holes between the roots to watch from.

Figured we needed ten rods for this one. Oh god, was it ever super marvelous. We painted the rocket red with barn paint, the nose-cone white and four pounds of sifted Chinese-formula gunpowder. Sure learned a lot, it was two fizzles ago we found if the gunpowder is ground too fine the "burn" went out too fast for all of it to fit through the hole in the proximity of once. She blew, whee-yow, did it. Hurt our ears, even behind a hundred years worth of elm stump.

The three foot fuse took two minutes to burn. Dog went after it when it was only half and we had to call her off quick then hold her down.

She lit, we could tell by the sizzle inside, a stray of sparks, then a stream, then it was gone. A hundred feet up she blew the nozzle out and the rocket went hard west at an awful rate of speed. Accelerating, it disappeared over the cornfield. Uncle Jim's place being only a quarter-mile past.

We figured ten years each in federal prison if we lived to go on trial. Then we heard her go. Big rush of sound that bounded twice between the woods and the cornfield. With a lot of little echoes scattered over the swamp.

We quit rockets for awhile. Later we tried iron pipe. Didn't work. Problem was cross-section. What we needed was narrow tube an inch in diameter, with a quarter-inch hole. Best rockets we ever made were the used tubes from Roman Candles. Once we taped three together and modified the grind for each section. First layer coarse, the second finer, the third really fine. The idea being the faster burn maintained acceleration. Same white pine nose-cone. Never did know where that one went. Fissitt and it were gone. Just gone. Tried to find it with binoculars. What we wanted was twenty-two feet of cardborad tube. Or if the whole thing could be made out of gunpowder, so as it climbed it got lighter and faster.

Nobody has ever launched a satellite using black powder. We might have if there'd been more rock peter in the basement.

Best thing was, Pa never found out about the "Illustrated Synopsis of Chinese Culture." Sometimes I think he knew because there is a preserved maple leaf marking the page 131. The paragraph about the advent of gunpowder has a lot of dark tracks like other fingers have traced and retraced the ratios. "One third saltpeter, one third sulfur, one third charcoal." Maybe it was only us. Maybe not. Kid don't know and you can't ask. I liked it when they used the word advent. Same as at the Liberty Corners Methodist, means coming to be Christmas. Glad somebody else thought as highly of gunpowder as me.

WORK-UP

"A FIELD GAME FOLLOWING THE STANDARD OF AMER-
ican baseball using any number of players fewer than that necessary to
play team baseball. Object is to remain at bat with two other batsmen
while the fielding team endeavors to put them out. Once out a batman
goes to the outfield, usually beginning at rightfield, and works his way,
through the field position by position till once again at bat." [1]

The idea is to aim at the outset for what everyone else wants second,
which is first base. John P. and Dennis L. always got to home plate first.
Meaning at bat. So did Richard S. who had the desk by the door and
bubbler. All of B-group reading was by the door. That meant Dennis L.,
John and Richard P., Sharen W., Arlyn C., Salty W., Rose B. If you were
A-group reading you had to sit by the window. Houlihan said B-group's
real problem was the window. Not supposed to read the window.

1. *History of English and American Field Games*, Heratomus, H.
C. Wightwood, Cambridge.

Richard S. couldn't hit a bumble bee with a door-mat. Didn't matter if he was at bat or not. John P. and Dennis L. could and that was the problem. Maybe they weren't A-group reading or arithmetic or science but they were A-group baseball and everybody in A-group reading knew it.

John P. was three years older than the rest of us at McDill Consolidated Grade School. Then it's Tony B. who lives out on the marsh and flunked seventh grade. Was the only kid I knew who flunked. Don't know why they did it. Didn't make any difference. He was going to farm anyway. John P. was three years off 'cause his folks hid him at home. Didn't start school till he was almost nine. His ma said the Virgin Mary appeared to her and told her to keep John out of school.

The school was in Whiting Village a mile up the state road from Plover Village. Got on the map 'cause the papermill on the Big Plover River. Behind the school is jack pine mostly. Sand dunes are worse here than anything in Plover, grown over with sweet fern and hazel. Used to be some farms but they quit trying a hundred years ago.

John P. had a way of extricating himself at recess, foregone conclusion he'd be at bat. Eighth graders weren't supposed to have recess but we did. Houlihan let us out every morning at 10 o'clock if our 'rithmetic was done. No matter what, that arithmetic got done.

John P. didn't stop at his locker to get his Milwaukee Braves blue and red baseball cap or his fielder's glove. He didn't have a Braves cap or field glove. Peter M., who was in A- group everything, had a Milwaukee Braves baseball cap. The rest of us had to stop and find our gloves.

With three guys at bat, there's always extra gloves around. Some days John asked if he could use your glove, some days he didn't. Was all right anyway. John was six foot two and one hundred and eighty-five pounds so it was kind of an honor to share with John P. He being most of 17 years old and knowing what 17 felt like. I mean the animal chemistry of 17 years. John had hair and shaved every couple days. Not that I didn't shave. I did. First day of every month regular. Used my dad's Remington and his after-shave. Used it even when I hadn't shaved which I think is all right.

We all knew John P. and Judy H. had something on with each other. Judy's dad owned the Chicken-House at the junction of the state road with the federal north-south. She wore jeans to school before anyone else ever. Was the second person in class to have tits, Kathy F. was first. She and John shared a bag of potato chips every day at dinner-time. Wore her jeans so tight that she had to get up side-ways.

Linda B. played work-up with the boys. She was too good for the girls and good as anybody ever in outfield. At bat she was mostly singles. Too bad Judy H. couldn't play with the boys 'cause the way you have to stand in the batter's box would have looked good on Judy H., seeing as she almost showed through. Could tell she wasn't boy right off. Was something, but not boy.

Everyone knew John P. and Judy H. almost probably had sex. She let him touch her breasts at noon once. She dared him and he did. Would have been better if it weren't winter and she didn't have a coat on.

We knew it couldn't last 'cause John P. is Catholic and Judy H. German-Lutheran. Catholic can't marry anything but Catholic. Sure, they might date and touch all the way through high school but Catholics don't marry Protestants and Protestants don't marry Catholics. Not unless they turned. That's what they call it, turning. In 1958 Catholics knew if they traded in their religion for something else they were going right to Hell. Even if they ate fish every Friday after that. Keep a fence that tight and folks are going to stay behind it. No last rites, no purgatory, straight to Hell on a wild spring heifer. I'm glad my folks aren't Catholic.

Nobody skipped church if they were Catholic. Pa was always skipping church and either sleeping or mending fence. Sometimes he said he was gonna fix fence but we found him sleeping with his arms over his face instead. Even if they had cows Catholics didn't fix fence on Sunday morning. Pa could start fixing fence on Tuesday and not be done fixing if he worked a year solid. Three hundred and eleven acres and every inch of it surrounded by four strands on cedar, corner-braced. Every strand stretched tight then stretched a little more so the metal in the wire itself is slurred. Not everybody hung wire that way. Some just put it. Catholics mostly 'cause they can't fix on Sunday morning. First time a cow leans on a put-wire fence the thing goes limp and the corn is in jeopardy all summer. Pa strung fence like it was a guitar wire and supposed to hum. Sending tin notes for a quarter-mile either way. Seen heifers at full throttle collide with a stretched fence and it bounced them off bleeding and distended from eyeball to tail. Smart heifer learns right there to mind fences. If the first thing they collide with is a put-fence, they'll spend the rest of their natural lives trying fences. Good fences civilize cows. My dad said that.

Catholics, even if they were farmers, were in church every Sunday morning besides sending the kids to Saturday catechism. Pa would no sooner send us to a Saturday catechism than to the moon. I wouldn't have minded the moon. Preachers had to kidnap us at gun-point and fire a few rounds besides. By Pa's god Saturday were chores.

John P. knew about chores even if he was Catholic. He milked cows every morning before school, so did Louie S. Pa never made us do that except when he was sick and he wasn't ever once sick. Honest, not once. John P. had to milk eight cows every morning using only one milker. Eight took as long as thirty with three milking machines. His pa raised 40 acres of potatoes which is another way of saying they was Polish Catholics. You had to be Polish Catholic to raise more than a garden patch of potatoes. Pa thought any fool could raise potatoes. What he meant was the Catholic way of potatoes. By the second generation of the 20th century the only people with six or more kids were Catholic. Without kids enough you can't raise potatoes.

Before the country schools consolidated, the rural school system granted potato vacation, the most glorious and educational of occasions. The second week of October every schoolhouse north of Milwaukee let out for one week exact. Without it there'd have been no potatoes. If a kid needed town money it was available. We didn't have potatoes but there was corn-picking and the chicken house to clean and lumber to saw and lime to spread.

The lime spreader was built by the Little Giant Company of Lone Rock. A simple deal, two cast iron wheels about two feet in diameter with cleats bolted every four inches. By itelf the thing wouldn't stand up, but bolted to a wagon it sort of hung on. Thing strutted. Like you image a baby dinosaur walked, deliberate and ponderous, maybe a little pathetic.

Rotation was transferred through a bevel-gear toward two whirring disks on which ground limestone is shoveled. Needs two people to keep the broadcast even, otherwise you'd get bursts. Two keep the rate steady. The problem is staying on your feet as the wagon is towed across new plowing that is semi-frozen.

Cousins from the city got seasick when they tried the lime-wagon. One had stomach cramps and stuttered for an hour afterward.

John P. is a long ball hitter. If he connected, was either a home run or triple. John P. didn't gauge pitches. Didn't have to. Odds were one out of three he'd swat close enough to lay it off. John P.'s pop-ups were glorious enough to make the outfielders dizzy waiting for the ball to come down. John P. either struck out or put it in the trees. A single was an embarrassment. Long before it was fashion in the big leagues, John P. warbled and menaced us with the bat while anticipating the pitch.

We knew it was the noon bell when the janitor slid his mop pail out of the way. Old Ray, the janitor, knew to keep track of the dinner clock if he was somewhere between the herd and the ball-diamond door. Once he hadn't and John P. lit out with Hubert K. right behind at full throttle. John P. cleared the mop pail only to catch the wringer. Dropped him flat. Hubert went over the spread of John P. but hit a slick. Everyone else couldn't help but fall. They made us walk after that 'cause Sharon W. got caught in the current and broke her nose.

Dennis L. was farm too, Catholic and potato. He was the first installment of the Elvis look. Carried a comb ever since fourth grade, every half hour giving his hair a curry. The rest of us were still grizzes and flat-tops while Dennis L. tended a duck-tail. Didn't wear a tee-shirt neither and the only kid in class except Peter M. to wear Sunday shoes, black with two-tone wings on the side. Louie S. wore leather, they didn't count as they were farm shoes. Remember how different he looked the day he came to school in his first pair of Keds.

Didn't call them tennis shoes then. Didn't know what tennis was, besides, it took concrete. Keds were the only recreational shoe Shippy Brother Shoe Company sold. One inch of gum rubber glued to black canvas, white laces and vulcanized white patch by the ankle bone saying "Keds." Patch never lasted. Couple slides for second and it was gone. A month after school opened you could find a Keds brand rubber disk every ten feet or so.

Peter M. almost always got to pitch first. Not 'cause he was fast but he found his own mitt before everyone else and had 50 yards on us. Peter M.'s glove was as near the real leagues as any of us had seen. Chromed leather, the only glove in Portage County with a double-stitched web and Eddie Matthew's signature on it. Besides, it had paddings. Could catch a cannonball from Shiloh with it. And you didn't have to wake it up to make it look like a baseball glove. Thing was embalmed. Ours died when we took 'em off. Not Peter M.'s. Ours had to be breathed on and warmed and disciplined and the only place to catch a ball was smack dab in the middle of the flat where the fingers joined. Where all the bones are. Where a ball transmitted pound for pound all the swat of the swing. If you caught it, your hand vibrated for half an hour. Felt more loose after a good line drive than it did before. Forget the medal of honor and catch the ball on the first bounce.

Peter M. pitched 'cause he was the smartest kid in class. A matter of policy to let him pitch. Never knew when you might have need of him. Like capital of Afghanistan? Pete's lips saying Kabul, Kabul. In history when we read how the colonists threw out King George the Third because they didn't believe in the divine right of kings, we weren't so sure divine right were as awful as they said it was. And Peter didn't waste time with sucker-pitches.

John P., Dennis L. and Richard S. at bat, Richard S. mostly struck out, so then I'd pitch with Peter M. at bat, John already home and Dennis on second. No stealing. Peter M. tended to pop-up short or knock dribblers. He and Arlyn C. weren't built for acceleration and half the time got put out on the throw to first. Sometimes the throw went wide for the sake of the geography quiz in the afternoon.

Then it was John P., Dennis L. and me. We went five days once and they couldn't get us out. Wanted to change the rules. Louie S. got mad 'cause he was trapped on the infield with the village boys. We thought it an honest vengeance of manure pitchers, potato pickers and silage slingers. Houlihan said he'd make us start the rotation different every day. We knew it wasn't fair but it was glorious. And rules weren't always such a good idea 'cause then you're no farther ahead when trying to remember the capital of Afghanistan. Still, we already had no stealing. No sliding home as there wasn't no catcher. If the ball got to the pitcher before you crossed home plate you were out. That way we had a shortstop if we included Linda B.

Those five days John P. and Dennis L. and me showed 'em what farm boys were. Nifty little doubles, a smack straight at the shortstop, who'd duck. We laughed and everybody else booed. They said anything like that oughta be a direct out 'cause it went so close to a person. John P., he'd just lift them out. Finally John P. struck out. Was the Friday only half way through noon hour. Linda caught Dennis L.'s pop-up and I hit it right to Salty W. They laughed, three up, three down.

Once Arlyn C. and Louie S. and Salty W. held us off for three days. Arlyn had played Little League all summer and learned to connect. Louie S. was farm so he just levered them. Salty W. could make a double out of a single. His folks ran the rendering plant. Louie S. once broke the window in the principal's office. Never should have rolled that far but it did and was half way 'cross the street when a car pinched it just so with the tire and it went through the window. That was LeRoy H., he came out and stopped the game till we told him who hit the ball. Nobody was going to, till Louie S. said it was him. LeRoy took Louie by the ear. When he came back he had a bill for three dollars twenty-seven cents. We divided it by twelve, actually Peter M. did and said it worked out to exactly twenty-nine and a half cents each and we had to have it by Friday morning. Houlihan, when Linda B. told him, put in the three dollars, needing only two cents each. Peter M. said it was exactly two and a quarter cents and we had it up by Thursday morning. Louie S. asked if we could pay it in all pennies. Then Houlihan gets the idea of paying it in phennig, that's German. About a four hundred to a dollar. We vote it should be phennig. He calls the bank and asks, they told him to try the travel agent. All he has is 25 phennig notes. So we paid in regular pennies. Three hundred and twenty-seven pennies. Louie S. wrote, "taxation without representation" on it. LeRoy told Louie S. the cost was three dollars and twenty-seven cents not three hundred and twenty-seven cents. So Louie S. brought the sack back. Houlihan went to the office all of a sudden about as red in the face as you can be and not float off. When he came back he said the bill has been taken care of and the class can decide how to spend the three dollars and twenty-seven cents before our Christmas party. He said making us pay for that window was like making Joe Adcock pay for the window he broke when the ball went clear over the roof of Yankee Stadium in the World Series.

Richard P. always struck out. Sometimes he didn't even play. Richard is John P.'s younger brother. Where John was a mellow polish color and six foot two, Richard were swarthy and five foot three. Richard shot John in the back with a thirty-two caliber revolver one morning before school when John was combing his hair. Bullet grazed the backbone, nicked a kidney but missed the intestine. Houlihan showed us by pulling up his shirt and pointing right where the bullet traveled. Girls didn't even laugh. Stopped before it came all the way out.

John P. came back to school in ten days. They kept Richard P. in jail for almost a week, then he came back to school, too. Afterward we made sure Richard got only the best pitches, no suckers at all. Once he went the whole noon hour without getting out. We knew who shot John P. in the back and it weren't Richard.

CHICKEN FOOTBALL

I N THE BEGINNING WE WERE INNOCENT. IN THE END, IN-
nocence seemed too cumbersome to carry any whole distance. We gave
up on innocence.

Every country has a formula both defining and celebrating the farm.
Essential ingredients include the cow herd, haymow, silo, milk-house,
woodshed, root cellar, barnyard, woodlot, summer pasture. All serving
their purposes and certain diversions of purposes. Beyond these one other
resource stood singular, that of the chicken coop.

Chickens and their keep were dominion of my mother. The chicken
served and inflated all farm functions not directly financed by the pro-
ceeds of the dairy herd. The chickens were a secondary winding into the
magnetics of the capitalistic system. Sociologists have used various phrases
to define the result; pin money, cookie-jar money or the apron account.
Using the chicken my mother and all farm mothers before acquired the
graces of distant urbana. Chicken money filled the Sunday morning en-

velope at the Liberty Corners kirk. Chicken money bought the blue dress with white polka dots. With chicken money Ma got the fancy black lace brassiere haunting her ever since she read "Peyton Place," which chicken money also bought and secreted in the right hand drawer of her bedroom dressing table. Chicken money was the charitable ghost of Christmas. It propelled the substrata of the township; dog license, annual school trip, window curtains. The cows took care of themselves, the new tractor, the Model 14T John Deere haybaler, the orange throat and howl of the silage blower from Allis and Chalmers in Milwaukee. Cows bought groceries, paid taxes, supplied the pulse for the 1955 Chevrolet V-8 robin's-egg blue four-door sedan. Everywhere else was chicken.

The flock numbered approximately two hundred. The number always approximate owing to the daily inroads of chicken crisis and plague. Approximate being implicit to the chicken and the fluid mortality of the creatures.

Chickens were part of the tasks of morning and evening. In the morning after Ma helped Pa get the milking started, she tended chickens. Filled the mash-feeders hanging by a cob-webby wire from the hemlock-beam roof. Ma tended the water siphons and the oyster-shell grit-feeder, and collected the eggs. A similar foray came in the afternoon.

Every Thursday, the egg man from the Amherst Junction Egg Company coursed through the township. A tall, elegant man in wire-rim glasses not much given to discussion beyond the current weather. He attended the same route for 27 years and was the only man in my experience to wear a moustache. Each case contained 48 dozen eggs, three dozen to a layer separated by cardboard templates. The man's elegance was most discernable when he opened each case to check the count and color of eggs. Bending low he inhaled the egg carton's atmosphere to assure himself and the Amherst Junction Egg Company of the freshness of the eggs. Satisfied, he wrote out a check for the eggs with the regal seal of the Amherst Junction Egg Company on it.

Chicken Football

Chickens lived and died. It seemed to me they died considerably easier than they lived. If it weren't for the constant momentum of egging, I was sure chickens would have gone completely out of existence as a species within any successive ten day period. Chickens didn't waver between living and dead. They were either one side or the other. Cows kinda hovered. Lingered at death, sometimes for months, like when they had hardware and the swallowed wire coursed slowly through them. We fed bar magnet to listless cows hoping to catch the wire before it hit the heart or pierced the liver. Cows had faith in drama, chickens didn't. Even calves and kittens had a knowledgeable precaution regarding death. But not chickens, chickens were indecipherable. One day healthy, clucking, egg-laying hens, the next dead as a wet mitten. No subtleties, no peeking around the corner as any intelligent creature should. Just bang dead.

To us the cosmological inferences seemed straight-forward and plain. When it came to orders of creation, chickens were down among the weeds. Not even as high up as quack-grass that couldn't be killed with a pick axe, drain oil or cow piss hot from the receptacle. On a wide scale, chickens were of little account. If God didn't care for them any more than bang dead, we weren't about to rearrange the morals.

Should ever a totem of the American farm be legislated, the chicken would end up at the bottom. Injuns were pretty smart with totems. A vertical arrangement of animals and instruments arranged in order from the most primordial to the most important. The canny thing about their method is the least important stuff gets put in the middle. Not at the bottom, not at the top. The bottom totems were usually the contemptable creats. Contemptable yet weight-bearing. Like turtles, snakes, wolverines and badgers maybe. On the farm totem, the chicken was the bottom beast. Contemptable yet weight-bearing.

When a farmer wanted to take out a woodlot, he'd start by cutting out stovewood. The process wasn't fast and didn't require haste. After ten years of stovewood he bought a couple hundred extra chickens and let them have the run of the woods for a summer. Chickens can scratch and claw at a woods so not even oak whips or blackberry thorn survive. Didn't matter if at the end of summer he couldn't catch any of the chickens, they've done their work. The fox and owls could have 'em. Probably too tough anyway.

Chickens are a paradox. They have feathers and wings yet can't fly any better than a haybale. Whose fault was that? Who was fooling who? To our way of thinking the chicken was a form of experimental damnation.

Which is not to say all ceremony was denied them. When they died we had a regular bier for them. You wouldn't think it, but it is an honest bier and an honest ceremony. Granted, it was more fun than your average funeral.

Being as the barn is cleaned every day, dead chickens and any likewise thing got put on the manure spreader. Dead chickens, dead cats, afterbirth, a place reserved for each passing on the very top of the load. The alternative is throwing the dead chicken in the spreader before the rest of the sodden mass. The image is bothersome. Doesn't make any difference whether the chicken is dead or not, the impoliteness is too overt. Besides, a chicken at the top of the load adds delight and sensation to the chore of spreading manure.

For those unfamiliar with the apparatus of the manure spreader, I offer a description. Elementally the honey-wagon is a two wheeled cart. For five thousand years it was just such, a single axle vehicle with hickory pitchfork served the obligatory duties of the morning barn. Five thousand years. You'd think somebody would've figured some other way besides a pitchfork. They probably thought the pitchfork was an advancement.

Was a Mechanicsburg, Pennsylvania monger who applied the first geared advantage to the process of the morning barn. The man's name is lost to history as are most of those whose inventions solve the profoundest needs. Which is probably better as otherwise the man could have been elected President or Pope or anything else of his choosing.

The invention, once you've seen it, is simple enough, that being the way of solutions. Once done and built, the previous problem and lack of remedy seems whimsical and hardly to have existed at all. Beyond is the sense you were pretty stupid not to figure it out in the first place.

On a manure spreader a large wheel gear is engaged via a lever and service rod with contact made with an advancing cog that is connected to another gear, attached to a chain, the chain being driven with the turn of the wheel. All striving to move the field elixir toward the opening at the opposite end. Due to mechanical frictions and committees, the movement of the material toward the exit is glacially slow. Considering the alternative, velocity is not thought a rampant need after all.

History records all manner of farm childs who explored devious methods to speed up a manure spreader. History also records all manner of farm childs who discovered, in consequence, the physics of mass versus mechanical advantage. Finding, at least where morning barn chores were concerned, tonnage is more imminent than gear and cog. Enlightenment is in the form of shoveling out the entirety of the spreader's wealth with a six-tine fork.

No person is more alone in the world than a specimen deployed to shovel out a recalcitrant manure spreader. He has neither father, brother, friend, saint or god. Rubber overshoes are of no solace, nor gloves, long-sleeved shirts, or macintosh. The one sure result from a morning spent shoveling is caution. Sweet, righteous caution. Never again to treat the spreader to the hurries. Instead gently, reverently, with utmost deference to its delicacy. Were such a child ever brought to serve the Queen of England as parlorman, footstool purveyor or pillow consort, his comportment would without training be on par with any 5th generation pallbearer.

I admit I'm not telling the whole truth about putting chickens in the manure spreader. The reason they serve the top of the load isn't anything as sticky as conscience as much as for their entertainment. I've already detailed why spreading manure is not a full-speed-ahead sort of chore so some comic relief is useful. Knowledgeable practitioners place the chicken toward the front of the load so the beastie can be watched as it advances toward the flingers. The purpose of flingers is to propel the brown mass in an arc landing some distance from the spreader. The aim of this arc has not been perfected. The way the engineers designed it, the stuff was supposed to be hurled rearward. Obviously they never invested in the debenture themselves.

True enough, the fling is energetic but has no regard for direction. Elements and particles are spewed to the four cardinals. All morning chore practitioners hold to a law both mutual and inviolate. Newton didn't mind it but it is a universal law nevertheless. Always go up-wind. Always.

There are occasions when the wind doesn't and all farm childs knew the cursed becalm of the Ancient Mariner. No wind for mains'l and flying jig. Naught for tack and ply. Brown meteors rise in trailing arcs and incriminate our posture. Oozing missiles. We duck. We dodge. We reel and slink. The sodden organics hit the ground with a groan of expiration, likened to the imagined final noise from a jump suicide. The splat of nutrient. Of earth to earth and dust to dust. Cow shit, calf shit, oat straw, afterbirth, dead cat, dead kitten, dead chicken. Precautions? Pa wore his winter mackinaw. Harold Edwards turned his pipe upside down. Cousin Harry lowered his ear-flappers. So much for armament and preparation.

·   A dead chicken advancing on the whirring dervishes at the far end of the manure spreader is an entertainment. The slow reel of the manure gives the bird the elegance of a state funeral, least how we imagined a state funeral.

Reaching the beaters the chicken has a chance of being accepted by the velocities and sped heavenward. Rejection meant a short toss to the front of the load, there to recycle toward the exit once again. Hindus would have drawn great satisfaction from it. Rejected, rejected, caught, here the effect varied. Perhaps a minor low tangent or, on chance, a stellar incident. The glorified beast propelled with all resolve of mechanics toward the outer orbits. Wildly flung the chicken achieves pinnacle and purpose the poor beast never held in life. When the beaters have the precise grab the chicken swoons in a theatrical leap. A comfort to the eye. Never in life did it know such altitude. Then, in the moment, the feathers lose their purchase, the apogee wilts and the white apostle tumbles out of the sky. The impact ejecting one last cluck from the pilgrim.

As with chicken aeronautics, chicken football was discovered by chance. As documented earlier, Sunday afternoon was the only secure liberty in our lives. Only two known violations possible. One being bovine transgressions of Uncle Jim's line fence, whose fence served a rigid decorum. If stretched, broken or sagged, it had to be repaired at the moment. All other fences could wait out the Sabbath. Not Uncle Jim's line. His nerve fibers were connected to those four strands. If accluded by dishonest bovine, he'd come by and after minimal pleasantries say, "Your line is out." Pa had us there in the instant; spare wire, new post, staple bucket. The fence was Uncle Jim's god. Had to be. Fences were his general church. He was always at them, his horse team, the long grey reins and his fence wagon. The man had no need of any testament or creed beyond fences. Fences told all there was to be known of him. He wouldn't have a violated fence waiting out Sunday. More church than church, fences were. According to Uncle Jim, fences were the purest function a farmer could hanker after; get the fence right and everything else falls into place.

The only other moment to ruin a Sunday afternoon is the preacher coming to dinner. Once a year, if you ask me, is once a year too much. Had to leave our Sunday clothes on. Sunday clothes, churching clothes, aren't meant for such long-term installation. Told Ma it shouldn't be. 'Cause, well 'cause they're too rigid. Haven't been trafficked enough to soothe 'em. Steep clothes in piety every Sunday for six months and they're gonna be rigid. Sunday clothes had joints in all the wrong places. Same as what cow piss did to my sister's head. She wanted to be blond. Ma won't let her. So for a week she soaked her hair in a bucket of cow. That and sunshine did lighten her up some but nowhere near the Jean Harlow she were after.

My brother kicked it first. Coulda been Tommy Soik. Odds are it was Gary. He had a thing against chickens. Thought them more at reptile than bird. Being a Sunday we were off on our traditional amble, having shed our Sunday duds and partaken of Ma's voluminous Sunday sit-down. Voluminous tain't the word. Ma tried to kill folks with her Sunday dinners. An attempt to turn the human organism into one stove-up digestive tract. Pa fell unconscious from it and spent the majority of the afternoon under a newspaper. I think maybe such was her intention, that Sunday dinner should bring its own peace.

Gary kicked it first. Were dead anyway so the kick didn't count for nothing. We were headed southeast, past the stead and the pullet yard to the near pasture, thence beyond to the woods. Had five cheroots in my back pocket. Yup, the chicken was already dead. Cheapest form of dying on the planet. The kick precipitated the whole thing. The first followed by another, then for distance. In a moment we'd forgotten it started out as a chicken. It was now a football.

Rural football is habitually deprived of its mathematical components. Teams cannot be comprised by any even division of three participants. Our practice of the contest allowed one person on the defensive team, the two remaining were offense. After four downs the quarterback for the preceeding offensive unit became the center, guard and end for the former defensive team, the cycle repeating itself endlessly. No side can win, neither could it lose. The benefit I have subsequently thought ought be deployed on professional football. The object of the event is not the score. Presence matters more than arithmetic sometimes, I believe arithmetic as basically anti-human.

Chickens lend themselves readily to football. They look like footballs. Pointed on both ends. Same as fish. Besides, chickens have a kicking-tee built right in. Set on the pope's nose a chicken is poised for kick-off, inclined at an official ten degree lean toward the kicker. When it comes to the forward pass nothing is lovelier than a chicken. Slow motion replay is made for chicken football. Our conclusion was chicken football was meant to be so by the chief spook. Things like that don't just happen. Some folks call it fate. Tain't fate. Fate don't exist nowhere except maybe for Catholics. Thinking a person lived and strived all to die at one preset spot is dumb. Worse than dumb. It's swearing at the far end of everything from stars to rocks to the wild woods and the creek. According to fate, it tain't worth nothing. It's all show, a puppet factory. God wouldn't do that, whether there's only one of them or a committee or a bunch of committees. How come? 'Cause of prayer. If there's prayer there ain't fate and it's that simple. If it's all written down beforehand, nuttin' gonna touch it. The whole game is rigged. From the field creation don't look that way; the township is too elastic for fate.

Rigor mortis is vital to chicken football. Fresh dead weren't worth trying. The way to test it was to kick it; a fresh chicken flies obliquely, in an ungainly hinge of feathers and tangents. A ripe chicken inflated modestly by the ethereal gases is kicked forward at both rate and stature.

To begin the game we flip a coin, just like in regulation football, the local mint being a cow-pie. If landing face up they kicked off; warm side up we kicked off. Nice thing about cow-pies is you knew three feet before it touches the ground what way the toss will land and you could start walking. They ought use cow-pies for regular football, then everyone in the stands could see for themselves. If you ask me, some folks have an awful low gauge stick for upset. Not very democratic of them.

Tommy Soik was our kick-off specialist. His ma every summer bought him a new pair of high top leather shoes. The boot itself musta weighed four pounds without the foot in it. Add the foot and a certain Sunday afternoon vengeance and Tommy can kick a chicken thirty-five yards in the air. Not counting roll. Chickens don't. When they land, they stay put. Didn't pay to catch a chicken kick-off outright. Knock you off your feet. Just grab a leg or neck sticking up and rip downfield.

Same thing with the forward pass. Remember how the folks hold a regulation football, sort of in the middle. You have to be a well-tallied gargantua to do that. A chicken turns every kid into Y.A. Tittle. With a chicken, football is less forward pass than a hammer throw. Spectacular. No other contest had that opulence of the pullet streaming downfield. It was all we ever asked of ceremony. If the beast died ungrieved and unnoticed, it didn't stay dead unnoticed. Chicken football set a lot of things right.

The game continued. There were tackles, interceptions, fumbles and pile-ups. Fumbles admittedly are a problem. Both sides can gain possession of the ball but then the game is pretty automatically over. Doesn't pay neither for everybody to pile on the beast, inflated like it is. Once is lesson sufficient. A dull explosion and semi-consciousness for the players. Chicken football kept a civil contest that way. Unruly behavior takes care of itself. Break the rules and you break more than the rules.

Chicken football didn't need referees, because its rules were self-enforcing. Didn't need helmets, kicking tees, shoulder pads or silver dollars. And chicken football didn't need time clocks. When the game was over everybody knew it was over. And it didn't end till it was over. Since it didn't have a score, chicken football needed something. It didn't have shoulder pads to pump dull seismic thunder into the ground. Didn't have two minute warnings, though it did have quarters and halves but they all came at the end. If you ask me, and I know you're not gonna so I'm gonna tell you anyway, chicken football had conclusion. Conclusion, like opera had conclusion. The whole game was for the conclusion.

Throughout the contest the pullet slowly eroded. Near the end with the feathers gone, the chicken did look a good deal more like a football. A pimply white leather football whose pounds per square inch increased with each additional scrimmage. When it looked less chicken and more pterodactyl we knew the end was coming.

Sometimes it happened at the kick-off or at the wind-up for the pass or at the tackle. Best if it happened on the kick-off. If it happened on the tackle, we knew the chicken had won. Which is the difference between temporal victory and moral victory. Chicken football favored moral victories. It exploded. Kidneys, adenoids, pink lungs, sennica liver, purple gizzard, white intestines. If it was a tackle end, the gases brought near unconsciousness. One whiff of the ripe chicken and you'd spend the next half hour getting the smell out. Puking helped. After awhile we got used to it. Never quite. Which made it the game, don't you see. The chicken didn't lose. Not once. A dead chicken has only one place to go which is the manure spreader and ultimately the course of late-moon fox or wandering dog. To our perspective, this aftermath seemed neither cruel nor horrid. Because things just can't be awful.

Our lives were raised, decorated and nourished by the chicken. It was only fair it should also provide our sport. Maybe people didn't ship out on manure spreaders though many a farmer said it would be fair enough and he really ought to include the manure spreader in as part of the funeral cortege. None of them did. People often flunk from their own thoughts in order to fit them to what others think is pretty.

If you ask me, anybody who thinks they can find holy while sittin' in a white shirt on a Sunday morning, ain't gonna find it or even come close. There ain't no score in chicken football and there ain't no score in anything else. Tom's dad was dead, his sister, too, and we coulda been neighbors forever but knew it weren't gonna be 'cause his ma said they were moving to the village in September.

Of course the game was over and we went to the swamp to smoke.

SWAMP, POPPLE AND PERMANENCE

From the '49 Studebaker Pa went to a 1958 Chevrolet three-quarter ton, two eighty-three, three speed vee-eight with eight ply fifteens and two point eight final rear. The battleship gray pickup truck was by unanimous decision of his male offspring the wisest decision and purchase of the man's career. At the time the only better choice being Donald Campbell's land-speed record car with a sixteen cylinder Allison aircraft engine. Exact details of how we'd affix the 40 bushel oat bin to a 300 mph pickup truck was somewhat lacking.

In 1958 Bobby worked for Edmund Soik during the summer, picking potatoes and moving irrigation pipe. Right after the second hay crop, Pa let him go, Eddie paying 50 cents an hour with a dollar bonus for working Sundays. The relative availability of cash money on the potato farm versus its like presence on a dairy farm was to trouble my father's mind many nights between 1958 and 1960. The farm with a total of 60 head of Holstein dairy stock was grossing about twelve thousand dollars a year on three hundred and eleven acres; ninety marshland, forty swamp, fifty woods, the rest pasture and tillable.

Edmund Soik on a hundred and sixty acres planted to string beans and potatoes grossed twenty thousand in contract sales alone. After haying Bobby helped move irrigation pipe and crewed Edmund's new potato digger. In one summer Bobby earned one hundred and twenty dollars in wages, besides earning another 200 dollars peddling potatoes door-to-door that he had bought from Ed at a "special price." In the fall of 1960 I was a solid brown farmkid, fifteen years old. I asked Pa if after second crop I, too, could work for Edmund Soik.

Pa knew the implication of the threat; the 60 head dairy operation was hard-up against the new wage in the alluvial sands. The very next year we planted potatoes, twenty-two acres. John Maxwell of the village put in a high capacity pump, we bought a quarter-mile length of aluminum irrigation pipe at the horrendous cost of thirty cents a linear foot, along with a miscellany of elbows, main supply line and end plugs. From the Woodward Implement Company in Plainfield came a used wood-bin potato planter, a sprayer, wood slat bulk-box and a two section, two row potato digger with a ten horse Wisconsin engine and clutch. All these machines had seen better days and but for row crop primitives like us, would have rusted to their eternal reward behind Hank Woodward's shop. The machine shed was converted to a potato grading shed. Grandpa Isherwood had built the original three years after the barn. The dirt floor had no advantage so after laying a cement floor, thirty feet of two foot wide grading line was installed; uptake, sizer, washer, dryer, sorting table and end-bagger.

Pa figured he had gained at least a chance at the farm fathers's dream of margin of safety. From our angle, potatoes were the source of resource that did not first filter through Pa's account book. Early potatoes are the tenderest of vegetables. No other way exists to dig them other than using a single row digger and pick the tubers from the ground by hand into slat-boxes. Early potatoes bruise at anything over a whisper. Machinery is the ruin of profit as far as early potatoes are concerned. It was by this venue and vegetable combined with a 1958 Chevrolet pickup truck, a couple farm boys with will could make $40 a day, peddling potatoes in the metro-centers of Appleton, Oshkosh, Neenah-Menasha.

By late spring the potato cellars of Wisconsin, Maine and Minnesota were largely empty. The only available tubers being imported California long whites, so by early August a significant consumer fever developed for potatoes in the workman cities just two hours distant by Chevrolet truck.

Our choice had been to continue to buy early potatoes from Edmund Soik or attempt to grow and dig our own. With one further problem, a major shortage of slat-side potato boxes. True, the Antigo Potato Exchange had them at $1.50 each and those still needing some repair. Bill Feathers of Waupaca had quite a few but was not inclined to sell knowing new ones were up on two dollars. Pa's solution was to build them.

On the south of the swamp below the dune ridge lays a swale of muck woods grown to popple. One Saturday afternoon was spent cutting six solid twelve inch popple logs, a tree known to every forester as aspen and everybody else as popple. The very next Saturday the logs were hauled over to Harold Edward's mill. Wasn't till mid-afternoon the sawyering actually took place, the previous energies given to adjustments and two interludes in Myrtle's kitchie for fresh doughnuts and egg-shell coffee.

The popple was cut into two by six planks.

The next Saturday we converted the saw-rig on the WD to a motorized table-saw.

The two by six planks were first sawn into sections, exactly three-fifths of them twenty-four inches long, the remainder sixteen inches. In turn the sections were ripped into half-inch slats, neatly stacked and bundled together with baler twine. Corner brackets were cut two by two and one inch square. All the pieces carried to the back of the ice-house, buried in the snow and covered with a canvas tarp.

The next Saturday after cleaning the barn, Pa took one bundle of two footers, one of sixteen and asked us to bring along a bundle of corner frames. The two by twos he cut diagonally on the table-saw. During the week he had invented a jig to hold the corner braces. All we had to do was nail the slats on, leaving a grip space for the fingers between the top two slats. With the inch thick brace nailed on the bottom, the ends were ready to be nailed up with the sides and bottom. We had, in the gentle comfort of the furnace room, a potato box factory.

Every night for the next two months it fell our task to build two each. A dozen on Saturday afternoon. Under the tarpaulin the popple stayed soft and green so when nailed it didn't split and when it did finally dry, held the nails with a tenacity peculiar to swamp popple. Any leftover sections went back outdoors and the finished boxes were stacked in the north end of the machine shed.

After the barn chore and before supper we listened to the Lone Ranger and hammered potato boxes. We argued whether Hank Aaron was better than Babe Ruth, how far away Alpha Centauri was and at 100 miles an hour, how long it takes to get there. The challenge is to do it in your head and keep track of the zeros. Same as when mowing hay and mul-tiplying two by two, by two, by two and see how far you can get without losing track. We talked about what we wanted to be, how we'd know who to marry or whether it wasn't maybe more like pollinization, a wife sort of just happens to you. The last of the vacuum tube radios glowed dully, punctuating the Lone Ranger with the static we had a hard time telling from the gunfire. Around us the cleansing, vaguely antiseptic, smell of swamp popple.

By May we had two hundred potato boxes nailed up and stacked in nests of three in the machine shed. Pa knew we weren't going to ask to work for Edmund Soik or buy early potatoes from him because now we could pick our own. Pa said we could keep whatever we made peddling and he'd fill the gas tank besides.

That summer the farmer made half as much money on twenty-two acres of potatoes as on 60 head of milk cows and heifers. His sons thought more about girls. One smoked a pipe regular, in June he'd cut eighty acres of hay in one day from near dawn to half out of the gloaming and got to 67,108,864 in his head and dreamed about an MG.

Pa had taken up the gauntlet of agriculture. Whether of Edmund Soik or anything else out there. Least he'd have a chance now at what farmers hunger after more than a village man can ever know. Another generation with the sun coming to them over the same blue line of ice-hills. A good highland sand farm above the moors and swamps of the Boney Vieux. There, beyond the hemlock dunes, a swale of popple that don't split if nailed up green.

NANCY AT THE CREEK

SHE WAS ROB'S DAUGHTER, THE YOUNGEST OF FIVE. THEY worked the hill farm east of the swamp. The biggins set into the alteration of our geography known as hills. Called Berry ridge, unknown whether for Rob Berry or after that hill's habit for August blackberries. The ridge was the only real clue this territory had regarding the nature of its birth. Without the ridge not a farmer in a hundred would have believed in ice, almighty ice. With the hills laid out like a gryphon's fossil spine farmers believed in ice and grudge. Was ice that did it. Ice alone, from Berry ridge westward as far as Mehan station. Any farther and they weren't sure what to blame nor thought it any of their prime business. Yet they thought it curious. Wouldn't think this sort of vengeance existed in ice.

Nancy Berry was the best thing ever to happen to the Buena Vista Marsh and its perfect undrained soul. Nancy, for all being a girl, had the sublime implement of knowing what to do with the liberty of a Sunday afternoon. Nancy was good as a boy.

I won't admit it anywhere but here but sometimes Nancy was better than a boy. Particularly any village boys who didn't know nothing perfect as the swamp or nothing awful that wasn't plain mean. Village boys are excessive. Loose with a BB gun they want to kill any of everything that moves. If sparrows, they aren't content with one dying. Instead needed a gunnysack full to feel satiated. Neither are they satisfied to look at just one picture of an almost naked lady from the Monkey Wards catalogue. They got look at 'em all and all at once. Not saving a look for when they need pretty badly the look of another page in the catalog. The problem with village boys is chores. They didn't have none. Even less of any sort that count. Village boys are bothered by something and only village boys know what it is so I can't say any more on it.

Nothing bothered Nancy. After school she tended chickens, milked cows, lugged buckets. I told ya she was good as a boy. Better even. Better in her ability to dismiss those choices and proclivities she thought unsuitable. Nancy never cared for the swell which gets onto boys. If one of the tribe eats rhubarb, they all eat rhubarb. If one gets a hanker for lynching kittens, they're all of a mind. Armies are made of boys, hairy boys to be sure but still boys and to my thinking, armies and any of those things connected with armies, like neckties, polished shoes and white shirts. The collection is possible only because of what is in boys from the beginning. Whatever the source, I think village boys let it go beyond the bounds of honesty.

Every child knows a bicycle is the handsomest attainment of childhood powers. Myself I owned free and clear a Schwinn Model 24. Hoed pickles two years to get it. In the pickle patch that's about 258,000 days. Every one of them at 150 degrees Fahrenheit. Tommy Soik had a bike, my brothers, even Pa had one, which is hanging in the granary with cork handles, intermittant chain drive, wood rims and single ply tires. Everybody human has a bicycle. The motivation, meaning bicycles, is libeled by the dirt roads. Mr. Star, town chairman of Plover, had seen fit to service the town roads of consequence with asphalt. The problem being the rocks in the mix were too big. Mister Star, Mister Winslow Elias Star, thought a good proportion of big in the rock mix kept hard-road speeds in check. When Mister Star thought something it took place.

Nancy didn't see bikes as advancement. What did it prove pedaling home from the schoolhouse if you could walk home faster? Nancy's view was based on accepting the readiest solution, not the handsomest. The one which didn't attempt to kill yah for having apparently solved the problem.

Nancy was like her pa. Rob Berry was the last practicing farmer in the township to buy a barn-cleaner. Said he'd wait until they were refined and tamed. The pedigree of every farmer in that country depended on his scoffing at the ways of Rob Berry. If the world accepted Rob's principle, they thought, we'd still be in the caves using clubs. Everybody knew barn-cleaners had their distempers but when they worked they were handsome.

Winter, Rob Berry knew, had a thing against barn-cleaners. Sometimes you had to shovel the whole length and it won't have taken ten minutes forth and back if the cleats of the chain weren't in the way. Standing windward from the barn cleaner's fling arm with the wind favoring lift, there was no telling where she'd plop. Oh yes there were. With a hundred thousand cubic feet of available vacancy and only one cubic occupied by tender innocence, the odds favored the attending kid get splattered.

Manure in classic formulation is a semi-solid mass, brown to dark brown in color. Odor, if any, depends on its edition. By itself the material is listless, only given transport in combination with oat straw. The best manure is laid directly in the pasture. Sunshine scabs it over but for a couple days it vents downwind opinions into the atmosphere. Given proper seasoning, a pasture cow-pie is a pure artifact. Useful as the four bases in a game of baseball. Regulated baseball uses canvas containers filled with talc and sand to add excitement to the game. Regulation bases are held to the ground by a steel ring and iron stake driven a minimum of twelve inches into the ground. Otherwise the bases be skidding all over the field and the game wouldn't be the same.

Too bad they can't move the bases. Baseball could use improvement especially if you're three runs down. That's the problem with sports and church and grown-ups, too many rules. Rules burden the activity. Denies exploration. Rules are good so as folks get to the right pasture but sometimes rules ruin the possibilities of a thing. The Saturday Evening Post had a talk about Margaret Mead at Samoa. She went there and found the society loose. A society where boys explore . . . well . . . explore, she said, "their sexual nature." I know what sex is. Don't know why she had to go to Samoa to look for it. The Post said what she found only applies to primitive societies. I lost my faith in Saturday Evening Post at that. "Sexual exploration goes against the fabric of western culture," they said, "leading to disease and moral decay."

Seems to me it's the same as baseball. You can't learn anymore about baseball than what there is if you can't move the bases around. Saying what a thing is don't always grip hold of its sublimer possibilities. Calf scours for instance. Doesn't sound bad, does it? Calf scours happens when a calf is at suck too long. Pale, yellow and fluid. Attached is a sting of bio-chemistry as smarts the eyes, assails the nose, burns the throat and vulcanizes a boot. Ma don't mind the freckles and accidents of manure at the table but calf scours meant a clean pair of pants and a hose-down. Meaning you'd be lucky to get any fair share of supper. Calf scours have the habit of glue. Put on a tire, it will ride along despite the best of centrifugal force to throw off the substance. Of manures, calf scours are the worst.

Manure gives me bad dreams. Every farm kid had his own version of damnation. I weren't bothered by the hot versions. Magma, caulders and lavas aren't punishment. Neck deep in calf scours, that's how I imagine it. If I keep a tighter moral orbit than other folk it'll be for sake of my revision of the damnation sport. The preacher can linger at the heats and smelting if he wants. My vote is for insipient rubberous yellows, toxic, limpet petro-smells; glues, amalgams and cosmic rays. No fooling, them's calf scours by only half.

Rob Berry cleaned barn by hand. No fling-arms, no breakdowns or freeze-ups. Just ten minutes behind an eight-tine fork. Said it gave his sons shoulders and his daughters lift.

Nancy had lift. Two of 'em. I've never understood nature. Why would wisdom as old and practiced as nature and nature's god put them right out in the open like that? There's only one conclusion and I'm not gonna venture it in public.

I knew where Nancy Berry's lift came from, pitching manure for a half hour every day. Puts staves in your barrel, Rob said. Staves and a couple bongs besides. Other farmers might buy machines, motors, inclined planes, jack-shafts, conveyor belts to save ten minutes but not Rob Berry. His neighbors thought he was a fool for work.

My pa got a silo-unloader from the local equipment manufacture in the manner of experiment. Before the arrival of this "labor-saving" implement, it fell to me or one of my brothers to pitch silage. A pleasant task, being as it was a good distance from view. Pitching silage proceeded at a pace of personal choice. Even if it was work, it had a leisure. Pa said maybe we ought to put lights in the silo. We said acid would eat off the insulation and we would be electrocuted. Truth of it was we just didn't want Edison in there with us. A silo owns a darkness three times the proof of the surrounding night. A handsome darkness you got to stand in to believe, any thicker and it'd float you off, once you got over the hiatus of it being dark. Folks are funny about dark. Being so-wise myself I can understand. The problem is a failure of the learning system. They teach phonics, sums and algebra if you're lucky, and spelling words you never use and avoiding those as have possibilities but not once in discussion of world affairs do they mention saber-tooth tigers are extinct. I know they say saber-tooth tigers once were. But have you ever heard them say, they aren't any more? There is too a difference! How am I to know Edmund Soik's woodlot doesn't really have saber-tooth tigers in it? I mean, they coulda slipped up. Didn't they find a fish in the Pacific Ocean trench they thought extinct and it wasn't. Was there all the time. Reader's Digest said so. Had a picture of it. More teeth than your average fish. I think they ought to be careful in this extinction business. I mean, if something's extinct and you know it's extinct that's fine. But if they say it's extinct and you acting like it's extinct and it ain't, it's gonna be heck. Besides, there are places in the Buena Vista Marsh nobody's seen yet, not even Indians.

Rob Berry said the Boney Vieux has places not even God has seen twice. See it once and you'd know it was true, too. Mostly swamp and low woods, bogs and yellow sand, dunes and swales whose tight-buttoned corners ain't had the erosion of eyeballs on them yet.

Which doesn't mean you should be smack-feared about every counterweight the universe turns on. Darkness is one. Most folks can't abide dark. Problem is they haven't given themselves enough lubrication to shut-up their own hinge. Which is why I love pitching silage in the perfect of dark. A dark so pure you get lost in it.

In the silo you can't help but think what it's like being dead. A Christian dead, where you got a soul nothing can stamp out and that's all there is to you. I don't know. It might be nice and maybe I won't mind, but what if you get bored and it's only you forever? That's almost too awful to think about. The more I think about it only thing necessary is dark. Deep, wide dark. Pure as a star. If God is a thing I think he's darkness. Not light like the Book says. The Book ain't explored darkness honestly, least not from an open silo in the middle of a winter dark.

A silo is a telescope. A regular barrel pointed farther away than you can even think. I like what a silo can reach. Lean on the fork and wait for the eyes to sink in. Same as climbing a ladder, the longer you wait the farther off you get. First the fat stars, then more distant sparks till the whole business kneels. Bows and bends right over a Wisconsin winter silo, a hundred thousand stars from a million light years out. I know I ain't nothing, nor is the planet, solar system and even Washington, D.C.

ain't nothing either. It's the best and worst feeling all at once. In the silo you know you're no different for the bugs and trees and summer rain. Some folks don't want to admit that, and if I was to offer any salvage I say religion was what got us out of kilter in the first place. Religion's chief fascination is not the almighty prospect of God or the shelf of saints or mister jesus. The real idea behind religion is man, the glorification and polish of ordinary folks who don't want to admit the possibility they are nothing. 'Course it means they're scared of nothing, nothing at all. So they invent something to be scared of, when it's really nothing.

Night spoils a person's importance. You can't lie at the night. Against it you know how much you're worth and it isn't even bubble gum at Wentworth's store. The denomination don't get any smaller. I don't know, I think it feels good. I wonder if somebody up there is halfway through chores and is looking up at my spark.

Mrs. Gilman said it wasn't so. Said if I were a good boy and'd been listening instead of pulling hair I'd've heard. Couple times probably, what the Bible said on it. And since the Bible didn't say nothing about other folks around other stars it wasn't so. I can read it for myself, she said.

I suppose she's right. I mean if the book don't mention it then it probably ain't so. Still it didn't say nothing about dinosaurs and they were and it didn't say a word about saber-tooth tigers and they were, so maybe the Bible don't know everything. I wouldn't say that out loud, least not in the hear of Mrs. Gilman. She'd have me signed up for a one way tour of hell.

Which is the thing about silos, they are off by themselves. I can sing if I want and the sound goes straight up and nobody ever hears. Singing is easier if nobody has to listen when you've forgot half the words and need to make up a new batch.

If there is someone looking down I bet they're in the same fix I am. Knowing someone might be out there who is just like them, at least as much as what matters and neither of us able to talk about it.

199

Pa put in an automatic silo unloader. With three motors, two claw chains, one hundred and ten feet of electrical cord and a pitching rotor. It would be swell in the winter time, Pa said. It would've been if it worked. It was supposed to pick and fork and pitch. All it did was sound like a tomcat in the motor oil barrel. Couldn't hear yourself think much less dare a look at the stars. I didn't care for the machine. It had to be pushed and levered, all with them chains going around at nine million miles an hour and only the sparks it chewed off the wall to see by. Thought often what it'd be like to get chewed at by that chain. Had a pretty good rendition of it. Kept telling Pa that machine wasn't a good idea. How it spoiled the silo and the night.

I couldn't rightly tell Pa to have it out because it scared me, could I? How it ruined one of the finest jobs and places there was in the world, or how singing didn't matter any more because of that banshee scream. And seeing yourself going by in little bittee pieces the same direction as that nine million mile per hour chain.

I hope you won't tell anybody, but I killed that machine. Killed it dead and I ain't ever said it before. Took the iron post we pitch horseshoes at and stood it against the wall and let the machine swallow it. One gulp and she blew sparks, spun backwards and died. Was just like killing a dragon. I felt awful, and I felt good. Knew I was gonna get caught but I hated the thing too much to stop. When all the noise settled, I climbed back up in the silo. T'were a mess. Two of the motors smoking, the gear box bleedin' oil, the pitchin' rotor wound up with the claw chain and turned off at an angle. Was dead all right. I spent half an hour extracting the horseshoe post which was pretty well chewed off.

Buried it behind the ice house. Was next spring before Pa wondered where the other shoe-stake went. Had tooth marks on it and he woulda known so I let it stay buried.

Nancy Berry's pa wasn't even tempted by a silo unloader. Why should he, when he had three sons and two daughters who had a place at the supper table anyway? Besides, pitchin' silage gave boys shoulders and girls lift.

The Berry place was one of the original steads on the ice ridge. The federal route turned at an angle by their barn to catch a shallower rise of the moraine so the road passed within 50 yards of Rob Berry's buildings. The road might have ruined the place except for a solid line of broad-hipped oak trees sheltering the house and garden. From Berry's place it was a good view, the swamp to the west, north the sand outwash left by the ice. The house sat on higher ground while the barn stood half on and half off the hill. The north side of the hay floor was at ground level while the south side had the milkhouse and cow floor. The object of the architecture, the milking stall was protected from the north, open to the south and insulated from above. The strategy was of the sort you'd expect of the Stategic Air Command. The portion of the milk room in the hill was buried behind two feet of solid rock wall. For Rob Berry, expansion was never a temptation. In the sweep to the west between the house and barn stood the chicken-coop, a couple sheds and the slat walls of the corn-crib. North of the house in a spill of level ground was the family garden, fully two acres. Rhubarb, asparagus, strawberries, a tangle of raspberry cane to the back. The garden surrounded by those two lines of hairy-chested oak trees. One was festooned with a porch swing, one with a tree house, a third had a poster for the loser in the last congressional campaign. Rob had been persuaded with two dollars to hang the poster at the far end of his garden. He said it kept away flies. The campaign worker had not envisioned the payment but when confronted with the squat, terse manner of Mister Berry who felt the poster was not guaranteed by any district law and might besides offend the vegetable patch. When asked what he meant by that, Rob commented a good garden needed talking up to. As ground, it did not abide lectures, speeches, sermons or contracts, though to theorems it might listen. Political rhetoric had not been demonstrated to improve the crisp of cucumbers.

The campaign worker knew the north tree was in a deft position for south-bound traffic. And Rob Berry could hold a pose longer than most, his jaw provisioned with a plug of Red Man Chew the size of a wild butternut. He didn't once threaten the political pilgrim with physical violence though he did spit in some proximity to the man.

Rob had spit tobacco and various other juices for 50 years. Chaw, he claimed, cured the common cold. Didn't just improve the misery of it, rather eradicated the whole infraction. A man wasn't round in his orifices if he didn't take chaw. Chaw improved the digestive tract. Should the internal windings slow their transport, all a person had to do was swallow the oyster. No matter if it's man, woman or child, chaw improves the vigor of the breed. Chaw got a person going in the morning, unlike coffee, person didn't have to heat-up chaw. His came in a pouch and cost 14 cents each at Raymond Fletcher's grocery and merchandise. Rob hadn't bought a pouch of Red Man Chew for 10 years. Not since the man from R. J. Reynolds, direct from South Carolina, came by and wanted to paint a sign on the east wall of his barn. Ordinarily they satisfied themselves with the slogan, "Chew Red Man," done up in black letters on a white background. Rob Berry's barn at the rise of the hill had more potential than black on white. Those south-bound on the highway came on the barn with a startled suddenness. The road curve caught the unwary, who believed for a partial second they were going to motor straight through Rob Berry's mow-floor. Which was why the tobacco agent thought the barn might favorably serve his company. A sign for Red Man Chew right there on the barn's east flank, using the entire thirty-eight foot facade. Rob said he wouldn't want the stones of the milking wall covered with paint.

A crew from Milwaukee came special to paint it. A portrait of the original Red Man in full war bonnet, real right down to the ermine tails dangling from the eagle feathers. Thirty linear feet of solemn Indian right off the bow of the car.

Rob Berry thought kindly of the advertisement and when they came to discussing remuneration, the man had the wit to notice Mister Berry took leaf himself. Thereafter and twice yearly the R. J. Reynolds truck stopped at the Berry farm and delivered two cases of Red Man, the Christmas allotment included a Carolina smoked ham complete with a note of appreciation.

The deal lasted until 1962 when the Wisconsin Department of Transportation thought to improve the federal route, so moved it away from the hills to four lanes crossing the flats and moors of the Buena Vista Marsh.

Nancy had the same charity common to most farm bairns, the free use and liberty of Sunday afternoons. All the pains of servitude, all the chores, the dank bins and feedmill were forgiven if bestowed the equity of Sunday afternoon. From nooning till even-tide, youth might be fancied and spent.

The general rule among farm-kind is the worship of the bicycle. Nancy being of her pa had other estimations. Not to purple Schwinns but to a square-legged horse of indeterminant breed. Her horse was a wary vehicle of genetics, half Clydesdale, a half Morgan, a pitch we thought of donkey as well as the sincere parts of rodent, lizard and bat. The horse, as a result, was well fit to all purposes and circumstance. Nothing could be asked it would not do, with profusion if not precision. The horse leaped four-strand fences with the splendor of the finest steeplechase horse in the world. Should it catch the top strand, the wire snaped before the oaken legs of river Clyde's child. Scale a creek bank, leap a blow, run the length of the creek at 80% throttle and wind enough to plow home without diminution. That was Nancy's horse. We surely would have burned our bicycles before that horse if it might have gained us a copy. Unfortunately, our bikes didn't burn.

The creek bottoms of the Buena Vista were the finest expressions of childhood. Any of a dozen environs existed. On the sandy dunes were hemlock bowers directly connected to the retreats and hospitality of Robin Hood. Gothic spires of balsam-fir enchantments, maple groves, oak burns of white and burr oak at least half a million years old and the haughty white pine, the sovereign leige of Wisconsin. Pine whose muscle and fortitude are the house boards and barn timbers of every man, woman and bairn within the next thousand cubic miles. The moor had bogs, peat cracks and muckings; ponds, puddles, streams, creeks, seeps and meanders. The Boney Vieux had more diversity of occupation than any ten other territories put together. Its streams were wildly removed from the impositions and services of the regular world so the tendency to run naked is involuntary.

The whole membership of the Rattlesnake Patrol did it. We piled our clothes in the cut-bank where the heifers came to water. Being an opening where the sun had ample opportunity to warm our clothes before our return. Warm clothes were more necessary than frivolous after an hour's dalliance in cold swamp water, the creek having just escaped the ice hills. The ice of its origin was obvious. No need to read geology to know ice once had them hills; had them yet by our measure.

The frigid water invigorated our delight and we set off in our game. A blend of steeplechase, mud wrestling, pole vault, marathon and war. The only rule was, no clothes. No shirts, no socks, no sneakers or cottons; no protection whatever. The leader was simply the first in the water. The task of those who followed was to overtake by tripping, sheer velocity or choice navigation. The boundaries of the contest included the streambed and as much woodlot beyond as our pale insteps could tolerate. The effect of spring water on our anatomies was subtle and had we not been born boys and become used to it the shrink caused by cold water might have redefined our sex.

Never occurred to us we might be observed. The purpose of watching a six-pack of boys in various stages of adolescent hang and jangle fulfilled no purpose in our estimate of what was worth looking at; and we felt secure. Besides, Sunday afternoon every adult within our diameter was asleep or visiting relatives. Never once did it enter our minds a girl might quest the same revelation as did we, if offered the chance. We were fairly certain girls were not physically equipped for cold water. What their precise designs were we neither discussed nor imagined. That girls were different was a thesis. It withstood all the criteria we could bring to bare. Of course we knew about tits, or some subterranean cause for female lumpiness. If girls had the impulse and need for naked abandon on a Sunday afternoon they'd be here.

Girls, we believed, did not have any similar device to note motions of the earth nor the splash of 43 degree ice water. There was on girls, according to our communal construct, nothing to move. What exactly there was we weren't sure, as no clinical document existed.

Arlyn Clark said his older brother had a "Sun and Health" magazine detailing the female fashion. Jimmy Soik had a pen and ink illustration of the "female part" we had thoroughly examined by campfire light. We weren't sure what side of the diagram was supposed to be up or what friendly purpose it served. I said it looked like a balloon seller at the county fair. Didn't look at all the like of something attached directly to a person, least not without laming them. Being mostly venturi tubes, and carburators had venturi tubes. Mechanics Illustrated said air sucked in the venturi tube was accelerated to the speed of sound. The shock wave atomized the fuel droplets. What something on that principle was doing in a woman I didn't know nor did I want to find out in person.

Had my suspicions. Dogs got stuck together. Better even than glue considering glue don't work on dog fur. Was the time our best-ever farm dog got tied up with a shaggy itinerant and the two of 'em spent the morning in the front yard. When Ma saw them she spent so much energy in denial and vilification we were pretty sure this was the drama involved. Never seen her so worked up over another batch of puppies, most of whom would not witness daylight in any of its broad implications. Just a few hours of respiration until Pa steeled himself to the drowning pail. It's logical all right. If it not for drowning pails the planet be carpeted in dogs and cats. Anyone could see that sure enough. Because it's logical, don't make it easy to put innocence under water. Gotta do it before they learn to swim. Dogs are quick to swim. We knew to leave Pa alone after a drowning morning, even if he asked some fool thing like a mile of fence mending or two weeks worth of ground feed. Only natural he'd want to bruise the world after drowning puppies.

Somewhere that venturi tube probably had its event on human folks. Looked dangerous. Worse than getting caught in a corn picker. I didn't think it looked safe, even if you were married.

Woulda been simpler just to pollinize. Use air-borne fertilants. But then marriage wouldn't have amounted to much. Pa says it was God himself who invented marriage. I don't know. Maybe he did have it in mind when he built woman, hydraulics and all. Still, I wonder if God might not've been more considerate if he just left off at the flower method. A great deal less mess. Every spring there'd be all sorts of pollen drift and if folks wanted children, they'd simply expose themselves.

Roger Precourt said if we did it like flowers folks wouldn't know what they were getting. Couldn't have that. Why, he said, everybody would be cousins and you'd be related to someone half a world off. I don't know, sounds pretty good to me. I didn't see the logic and said so.

What if it were black man's pollen and china man's pollen and jap pollen and commie pollen, he says.

I hadn't thought of that.

"You could have a family," Roger was getting warm to the task, "with four different colors, six blends of hair and eyes at three separate slants.

"Which is why there's venturi tubes. Otherwise folks'd be running indoors every time the wind changed."

Ma tried a water hose on the dogs. Like I said, it was better than glue. Why she bothered I've no knowing. Since the window is already broken, why burn the bat? Of course she did it for us. Hosing down the dogs being the moral thing to do. Too, she thought it would calm our ambitions. She need not have bothered. I weren't going to mess with anything with a grip like that. No sir.

Finally she took a rake handle to 'em and he broke off relations and took up the road. Didn't look like full-speed to me but about all the thrust he could manage at the moment. For awhile I was worried he might have broken off more than his lineage. Ma seemed satisfied. Too satisfied. She wasn't even that angry when the cows violated the tomato patch. Regular righteous, she was. Like the devil, Beelzebub and Mephistopheles were sent home without supper.

Whatever it was I didn't want anything to do with it. I'd live the life of a hermit somewhere in the Buena Vista Marsh before taking a risk like that. Which was before I saw Nancy. Nancy taking Sunday at the creek.

Must've been July. Was hot and twice as thick as hot. Had been hot all week. We haying the whole length. Highland alfalfa from Whittaker's forty and Puznach's. Eighty acres in with another hundred to go. Had to take turns in the haymow, being July, was like taking turns at dying.

Ma's cure for haymows was ice tea, brewed bitter and brown and perfectly balanced between refreshment and pain. So bitter it smarted your eyes. Did cure thirst for awhile. During July, drowning seemed a peaceful way to die. All bloated and cool. We'd hold our heads under the water in the stock tank till the inside edges of the brain started to turn black from lack of air. Was so hot Ma didn't make us go to church. Because it was haying with a hundred acres to go and church clothes were no release. Her and Pa went to the Grant picnic, Gary went too. I had four slices of bread and a jelly jar in my official Boy Scout backpack. Bobby and Jimmy Soik were off in another section, smoking cheroots, I figured. Wouldn't have minded a cheroot myself if it weren't so blamed hot.

Was laying on the north side of the creek bank 'neath the butternut. Weren't doing nothing but tending sky and herding clouds. The dog heard her first, Nancy and Fencebender. Was Nancy's holler all right.

Nancy had lungs and nothing else makes a splash like 1500 pounds of horse at forward throttle right down the middle of the creek. She'd done it before. We seen her often enough to know it was her. Thought to pelt her with a handful of pea-gravel and was about to wind up when I realized I wasn't costumed for battle much less discovery. So I just peered over the bank to watch her.

Straight off there was something different. Nancy reverberated, all the way across Finnessy's clearing most of a quarter-mile away. The horse submerged between splashes and above it I heard her yodeling, she was different. Was as if the horse carried a spark, a honey of light and condensation.

She got closer and I knew why. Nancy was all the way naked on her red hair horse. Riding bareback and I mean bareback, bare front and bare bottom with only a pasture bridle on Fencebender, naked as an angle worm.

Nancy weren't at all what I thought. I knew about them. You know, them! The two of 'em. Udders. OK, OK. Tits. I'd never seen 'em real. Just in the picture of what was in the Genesis chapter of the Precourt Bible at the kirk. Didn't look like the pictures. Don't suppose they can paint a picture that honest. Besides, they moved. Maybe the word is jiggle. It's more than jiggle, more solemn than jiggle. I don't know, I thought them holy from the first time I seed 'em. Right there I did. Yup, they was holy. Seen holy things before. As holy as anything in the Book. Holy as the big white pine in the west woods. Holy like the drowning pail and chicken axe. Holy like the haymow on a rainy night and thunder in the township. Holy like a BB gun and holy like being alone. I knew it and I felt it and wasn't going to tell anyone, but Nancy Berry's tits were holy. Coming down the creek on Fencebender, nothing could have been more alive and wonderful than Nancy. The splashes turned her to fire and stars. Nancy, better looking than the comet I'd seen over the handle of the Big Dipper two years ago.

FOUR STRANDS ON CEDAR

I F THE EARTH'S CIRCUMFERENCE IS SOMEWHERE OF 25,000 miles and I know it to be so, then the true and actual perimeter of the farm is half that. If all the laws of mathematics apply, with primes multiplied, factored and heifer fence added and squared, the yield is a genuine circumference of 12,000 miles. At least. Easy. No fooling.

This chore never ended. It ranged before our lives, before our leisures, like the specter of violence it was to boy energies and boy time. Grinding feed ended, even if it caked lungs and left a fortnight of itching. Calf pens, chicken coops, they too ceased.

Mending fence stood eternal.

The fence and its mend never ceased. Every field, wood edge, creek turn, far and middle distance, had one. Each in local disrepair and bereavement. A broken strand, a rotten post or rusted staple. Whenever my father wanted to be rid of us, the command was simple, "Fix fence." Its services were never complete, nor its winnings victorious. Should we miss a chore, leave a gate unsecured, tarry at a duty, get caught BB gunning chickens, we knew the words of banishment and censure, "Fix fence."

In the kingdom of agriculture before the four bottom plow, aluminum irrigation and the advent of tractors possessing more than 50 horsepower, dwelt a formula of farming mindful of barbwire. The average field was ten acres. Smaller fields still in the back corners, five acres against the woods, seven at the creek. Every field had its lane, a fence on both sides, four strand and double-barbed. The posts were cedar, white oak, tamarack and where white oak, cedar and tamarack were absent, steel posts of two patterns. Impediment is the word. Steel posts had to be driven in by sledge hammer from an unsteady wagon-rack into sod ground so crowded with alfalfa roots, glacial gravel and subterranean impediments as to weary any kid so sent, precluding the ability to hit the post smack in the face in the first place.

Jubilation was not our habit, when at any moment fencing could enter its viscous evil and what was an original injun whoopup day went the way of four strands on cedar.

Lest one suppose the escape must then be through cedar posting instead of knuckle mashing steel, let it be known all appointments with fencing were kept with a post-hole digger. Powered by the same .001 horsepower farmkid. As luck had it, a dull post-hole digger and a sudden layer of hard-pan. The blades curled up rheumatically so the hole itself was as quickly encouraged by digging with bare hands as with the tool.

Fixing fence was good for us because Pa said we weren't human beings yet. Nobody, he said, starts right off as a human being. We didn't know that. We thought a person came naveled as the human sort. Nope, he said, humanity is earned. Evolution ain't the full and only measure of it. You're the raw stuff all right. Pa knew cows who had come awfully close to being human and a couple horses that actually made the grade.

Now I don't know where Pa got his notion. It weren't biology, nor were it the Bible, but he held to it all the same. I think it were something to do with fencing. After a half million miles of fence a person is ready to become human. The way I see it, you start out being mammal, which is tea-warm blood and fur and tits. I knew right off I had a problem. On my own inspection I couldn't find evidence for two of the criteria. And if they did show up, I was going to have real troubles at the irrigation pit. Tits wouldn't be anything advantageous to have attached to you if you're a boy. On Nancy Berry they looked about as good as a pair of bumps can look and still be entirely mortal. I asked Ma once if angels had tits. She gave me the strongest look. She didn't say. The way I figure it, if angels have tits and wings, they are about as set up as a creature can get when it comes to heavenly. Tits are handsome but wings are more the handsome, they're beautiful. Myself, I wouldn't want tits but I wouldn't mind wings. And if it is the way Pa says it is then I have a chance. You start out as a baby, which is as useless a heap of mortality as a thing gets and not be a stone. If you ask me, stones are better than babies. After being a baby awhile you become a kid then a teenager than an adult then a human being. Pa says some folks never become human beings. Hitler weren't one. Joseph Stalin weren't either. Pa thought Joe McCarthy was, and a pretty good one. After becoming a human being, a person still has to work his way up to angel.

I like the idea, not so much for its purity as those wings. Wings are worth anything. I asked Pa once if hawks and bluejays are the angels of gophers and tadpoles. He looked at me like I just ate a turd. Seemed logical enough to me.

Heaven, I figure, don't have fences. The other place, I'm pretty sure does. At least 5 strand. But then maybe heaven does too have fences. If it had gates it probably oughta have fences or else why a gate? I thought about that a long time, I mean heaven and fences. Heaven wasn't a nonentity, whatever an entity was. The preacher used the word and I found it had a nice swoop to it. Which was one of the good things about Harold Edwards. He didn't have much else, but he had lots of words with pretty swoops. Cuss words and swear phrases without repeating themselves. Like comets, Harold could string out a lingering tail of words. Pa said Harold had more words than a priest caught in a paternity suit. I wasn't sure what it meant but was a handsome line. Instead of saying a person is sick, Harold said, "Looks like he just had a warm glass of cow kool-aid." I knew what he meant and its a lot better than plain saying a person were sick. Harold said heaven is the basic propellant for most of humanity even though most of 'em were headed in the wrong direction. Harold didn't think heaven existed.

It hurt when Harold said that. Because if Harold said it, the chances of it being true were considerably better than if anyone else said so, including Pa, the preacher or even Uncle Kingsley. Till then I figured I would get to see heaven. Any bird-brained son of a cow-kick could. Heaven hung right there in the sky. Until Uncle Harold, heaven had withstood logic. Sure, there were a few doors in the hypothecary. Like I seen airplanes from North Central Airlines pass right through clouds. Didn't spill out angels or prophets, least not as you could see. Sunset was another time I knew heaven to exist. When the sun grew crimson and swelled orange and red light over the whole township. I have wasted more time on evening horizon than any other thing excepting maybe night itself.

Life magazine came on Saturday. It was August, we were half way into haying and Life magazine had a cover photo of Marilyn Monroe behind a blue towel. I looked at the towel for the longest time. It was almost like a sunset and close to a heaven. Ma didn't see it that way. She hid that Life magazine, first under the davenport and finally hauled it to the stoveroom where it would have met a kindling fate if we hadn't rescued Marilyn. I traded the cover for the contents, exchanging the innards of Life for those of Saturday Evening Post. So when Ma burned Marilyn, she did it with satisfaction. I too burned with Marilyn and satisfaction.

I knew there were problems with clouds as heaven. You could see clouds turning and rolling on a summer day all the way from the ground.

Either angels hover a lot or have to run to keep pace. Stalwart prophets in bathrobes lost some luster when imagined at a-gallop on their terrain just to maintain their position because of what a hot July is capable of doing to clouds. Didn't fit the pose of saints. Still clouds had to be it. Wouldn't do to have heaven on Jupiter. Nobody would want it or plan to go. The real reason folks wanted heaven anyway was for the invasion of privacy. Imagine floating over any township of your choice, prevailing winds being the exception. Would be like taking a smoke in a church pew. The only reason besides wings that folks might want of heaven is to spy on their neighbors. Harold said heaven was the only place mankind can sin with impunity. I'm not sure what impunity means. Suspect it has something to do with not being shy of what you're looking at. And what an angel can do in public and a mortal can't, like the August issue of Life magazine with Marilyn Monroe on the cover. It's not that I want to look at that blue towel, I have to look at it. Like stealing cookies. I can steal cookies and not even be hungry, same goes with new bread. Marilyn Monroe is the same magnetism, like Uncle Jesse Grant's electric fence when he has the voltage turned up. You can't let go, you can think let go, you can try letting go, but you can't. If you can, you're rusted metal in the first place.

Did ya ever drink out of a mud puddle? Ever been that thirsty? Ever get your hands so cold as to put them in the back door of a milk cow? Marilyn Monroe and a blue towel are a lot like that. Everything has fences, even heaven. Some fence you in, some fence you out and sometimes you can't help being where you are.

Two kinds of fences. Those made by compass and those made by land. Pa went by compass, Grandpa Fletcher went by land. Neither could understand the other's allegiance. Were simple enough in fact. Pa was outwash, Grandpa were stone. I don't rightly know how Pa got the fence so straight anyway. First he'd sight them then walk his paces between the post holes, ten paces even. More deliberation was spent in the pacing and count than reconnoitering where he was, still he came out true. I

213

think the compass was in Pa. He woulda made a compass fence whether on stony land or sand. Was his nature. I've imagined Pa on Ulysses' boat sailing by the isle of Sirens. Pa have no need to lash himself to the mast. Pa would have wiggled his ears at the Sirens. Why do they call naked women Sirens? At that point they don't have to make any noise. Like mosquitoes, if they learned to touch down without their motors whining, their mortality rate decrease by half.

It's hard to know whether to love fences or not. If you want to be alone all you have to do is grab the staple bucket and walk the strands. A fence is a good place to think, which is why, I suspect, there are as many of them as there is. People don't really mean to fence, instead it's a sort of recreation. If it weren't for cows needing four barb strands to hold their attention, a fence wouldn't be a bad thing. The idea that everything behind the fence is yours had a good feeling. Even if Uncle Harold says it ain't 'cause the assessor really owns everything but our breath and has a lien on that. A fence is a good thing and every place has one. The cookie jar, even Marilyn in a blue towel. A fence measures off something even if you don't know at the time what it is. A fence is kinda alive because it always needs attention. What I would like is a trained badger who learned how to dig straight down. A little crooked be fine. Could plant a crop of rutabagas and collect white grubs for him if he'd agree to an hour a week.

I know there are machines to do it. What I want is a badger. Nice quiet running badger. 'Course if we could communicate with badger, we could communicate with the brown thrush at potato-bug time. When you think about it, man ain't so smart, instead of learning Russian and French we should be trying to learn marsh wren and ovenbird. Think of the crew you could get up. Crow be good too. Had a crow once.

ALL NOVELS ARE LIARS

I F NOBODY EVER WHISPERS, IT IS CURED RIGHT OFF. RUMOR is what gives a kid the idea. Hadn't been for the village boys, was too, I might never known. They said yup it did, yup it does, yup ain't nothing else like it.

At first I didn't give the village boys much intelligence on the matter. Why, what do village boys know anyhow? About anything? Chores? They said chores was what they did at home, five minutes with the garbage-can or walking the dog. Chores? And work? Their work is cleaning the car-garage on Saturday morning or carrying golf bags. That isn't work, that's walking. Work is walking and filling the bag at the same time. Edmund Soik pays 50 cents an hour for picking potatoes. A condition I thought pretty fair till I knew the village boys.

Hardest work ever is bloated cows. They bloat on account of spring pasture; once inflated all they want to do is lie down. They do and they're dead. Puuf dead.

What you have to do is walk 'em till the bloat wears off. Yell, holler and switch at them with oak whips. Everything you can think of is fair; BB guns, dogs, firecrackers. Otherwise they're dead if you don't.

Pa has a mixture, half kerosene, part sulfur, raw eggs. It is supposed to work. From the sound of the mix it ought. Problem is getting the slush down the throat of a bloated cow. Like I said, bloat as far as cows are concerned is puuf, dead. Try and pour a cure down the throat of the cow while keeping it moving at the same time. Gary sitting on Pa's shoulders tried, with Bobby holding the funnel fixed to length of a garden hose, this stoved down the cow's throat. Do this and keep up with the cow who has to be moving or it'll lie down and die.

If the cow does go down there is only the last cure to try. Stick a knife behind the fifth rib and with a sharp thrust, pierce the stomach. If it works you know. Whee, jesus horses does it work. Nothing like it. Soon as the knife hits the stomach, it flies off from the pressure. The cow looks exactly like a balloon let go. The bloat venting out the knife hole. Everything within twenty feet plastered with cow cud. All the while the cow is wiggling and shaking all over as if no more than a dish towel on the laundry line. Must be 150 pounds per square inch inside the cow; pressure is what kills it, lungs can't work nor the heart. Seen the knife go in, hit the rib, by the time it's pulled out and restuck the cow's dead. Sometimes the stomach wall boils out the hole with the pressure still hung up inside. If it's fixed, the cow can stand up in a couple minutes though acting dizzy for awhile.

Two summers ago, Gary, I and Tommy Soik were under the bridge listening to the rain, smoking tiparillos, and my stomach started to ache. The worst hurt I ever had. Worse than green apples and rhubarb, worse than when Sputnik broke my nose, worse than when the bee stung my eyelid. Lot worse; knew I was gonna die and from my view it couldn't come soon and quick enough. Never felt that way before, that much hurt. Always thought dying was the last thing a person might want. Heck, it isn't that way at all. Sometimes dying is nearer to Christmas than anything else a person could want. Needing it so much, wanting to go meet it somewhere so you don't have to wait any longer. Like holding your breath under water, not wanting to breathe water but wanting to breathe all the same, holding off till you don't care whether it's water or air as long as it's a lungful of something. Was only appendicitis and me wanting death like it was Christmas.

I did so have the idea before the village boys said it were so. My brother-in-law gave me "A Manual for Young Men." Dark blue covers and one hundred and fifty-six pages, all about sex. On page forty-six and fifty-two were two pen and ink drawings of the male and female sex. Took up the whole page. With numbers to indicate the separate parts. The opposite page had a key to the numbers. Weren't no enlightenment whatsoever. If they hadn't labeled one as the "male sex" I couldn't have told the difference, though I did think the side-view looked sort of familiar.

I had hoped there was more distinction between the sexes. What point is served by being a man if what separates you from being a woman is the road turning right instead of left? That is assuming you're holding the map right-side up to begin with. I can't see why creation went to all the expense of separating the races right down the middle of the male and female flavor if the difference didn't amount to more than that.

Straight off I figured "A Manual for Young Men" wasn't telling all there is to know. Or else they didn't know themselves. What they did say was there are tractors and engines in the world, what they looked like and where to find the spark plugs. They said nothing at all how to drive one. Or whether it had a tendency to quit in the rain, or how to stomp hard and pinch the brakes to bring the front end around for square corners at hay-time.

Sunday, the Reverend Ribbs talked about the Christians and the Romans. How the Romans fed the Christians to the lions because they were Christians. I've heard it before but I'm not sure any more. If I knew I was about to be fed to the lions for spectacle beause I was Christian, I'd give up the Christian habit. If what Rev. Ribbs said was the whole truth, the Christian brand ought to have died out a long time back. Leads you to think what really happened was some off of what Rev. Ribbs said.

Rome probably weren't no different from the Liberty Corners Method. Ain't a grown man over thirty with his eyes open at the end of the sermon. The womenfolks are looking at each other's dresses or counting the links in the chain of the ceiling lights. Announce any who show up the next Sunday will be fed to lions and folks find other places to go.

Only reason people like Sunday is because it is free. When God said, remember the Sabbath and keep it holy, work in the forenoon if you must but take a nap after dinner, visit the cousins and otherwise take it easy. When God did that he was one heck of a smart God.

I figure I could've been born any of half a dozen different sorts of Christian, Hindu or even Catholic and not known the difference. My choice would've been Sioux if you could choose. I think if I was born in any of the top ten animals of the world I'd be just as happy. A whale, bear, grizzly or polar, otter, three or four kinds of hawks, wolf for sure. If being Christian isn't any more difference than that, then it's either real good or real bad. Every person there is, thinks their religion is the onlyest and mightyest and finest specimen available. Problem is folks are comfortable where they are, and when you think on it that's the best religion can do. Accept bow-ties for Sunday as quick as shrunken heads; religion has to be a pretty fertile level piece of ground to begin with.

"A Manual for Young Men" gave me the idea. Weren't the village boys at all like I said it was. The book said it happens, almost everybody did it and if they didn't, it happened anyway. Can't get any better endorsement for a product than that.

Said it wasn't something to be trifled with. Take it seriously, don't abuse it and it will add vigor and health to the practitioner.

For birth control the "Manual" recommended condoms. Whatever condoms are. From what I can figure, some method of umbrella or tarpaulin. A precaution, it said, from pregnancy and disease.

218

I wish they said more about the disease business. Instead they left off at the most dangerous stretch of the river, supposing everybody knows how to swim. Disease of what? From what? Is it better or worse than leprosy? Said the signals are a rash. Jesus holy cow christ, rash. There's rash with oats, new alfalfa, sawmill dust. If they are going to tour the country, they ought mark the map better than that.

They never touched back at abuse neither. I don't mind limits, but tell exactly where the fence is. Between the burr oak and the telephone pole south of the road culvert. Like thou shalt not steal. I mean once a day, or only after four times? Tom Brownson has a quart jar full. Only took him three weeks. Said it smells some.

Was in the haymow. Nearly everything good that ever happened to me happened in the haymow. Read "Son of the Stars" in the haymow. "My Life Among the Indians," "The Red Car" and "Laughing Boy." Became blood-brothers with Arlyn Clark in the haymow. Shot Tommy Soik's arrow in half with my new birch arrows on Christmas afternoon two years ago. Gave him one and glued the broken arrow to a pine board to hang in my room. Rev. Ribbs' daughter showed me hers in the haymow. Good thing I saw it otherwise I still wouldn't know what side was up. She wanted me to touch it. Said I'd rather just look which was a lie.

At first I thought womenfolks were cheated from the ordinariness of it. Weren't. The more I looked at it the less I thought they had got cheated. She wanted to play doctor. I wanted to play archeologist.

Most people probably wonder what it feels like to be in the other sex of creation. I wondered if maybe men didn't get cheated. Men look the more rough-sawn than women. Creation should have sent the man sex under the finishing plane one more time.

What I don't understand is why women aren't better at baseball. By the looks they should beat boys on account of streamlining alone. Boys look like a gentler set of eggs than women.

Fell out of the haymow in 1955. Straw bale stuck in the alley-chute and I jumped on it to keep it going. Done it a thousand times before; no problem. This time Pa saw the bale from below and forked it loose in a manner of helping. Right when I had myself cocked, primed and launched, he pulled the bale out. I went through the chute like a greased snake in a deer-mouse nest. Tripped on the bale going about half speed and landed smack on my head. Broke. From here to there and once more cross-ways.

Dizzy isn't the word. Whole farm circulated around me at forty rpm. Started puking, blood, supper and more blood.

Ma put everything in quart jars so she could tell Doc Benn exactly what was happening. He told her to call in the morning. Went to the hospital the next day; the rpm had slowed half of what it was the evening before. Stayed three days. A hospital is the most awful excuse for healing; being a Catholic version I didn't think any remedy they knew could work on a Methodist boy.

Pa stood at the window crying, afraid I might die. I knew I wasn't gonna. Didn't feel like dying. Didn't feel nowhere even close to the breeze death has, or the smell of it coming long before the mail itself.

Ever watch a cat with a gopher as ain't dead? Off-hand a person think the gopher be trying and screwing away from the cat. It don't. Sorta lies there with the cat 90% around its life. Gopher has a distant look. Like it is watching itself. Studying the whole thing and pretty impressed with what it sees. Felt the same way after the skull fracture. Like I was at my own movie even if in the morning they were going to take me out and shoot me. Me anxious for the movie to end so I can go home. Same thing with the gopher. The same look. In a minute the cat is going to complete circuit and that gopher watching like it is his cousin Harry getting wiped out. An honest story needs to kill the hero off right in the beginning once in a while, or have the girl move to Michigan. Movies are liars. All novels are liars. Nobody is good all the time; not Jesus, not Moses, nor Werner von Braun. Tain't no helping it. Truth depends on where you're standing and what day of the week it is. Too much hovering and circling going on as to say the truth is right here, at this patch of vegetables, when it's closer to the woods.

Harold Edwards told me you better be able to tell the truth and lie with just as much ease. The lie, he said, is for yourself. He said it weren't his idea; the saints had used the principle a couple thousand years.

Pick your lie careful and tell the truth easy, he said. Like Tommy Soik when his pa and sister got killed coming back from groceries. Tommy said God wanted Leo worse than his ma wanted Leo. He knows it ain't so. But it let him stand by the grave hole when they buried Leo and his sister. And take Plover town dirt and throw it in the hole and hear the plop against the coffin lid. And watch the dirt slide off the polish and trickle into the dark ground underneath. I watched him take a second handful and drop it in. He was watching dirt. It weren't a funeral, weren't his pa; were only dirt, dirt too dry to stick to the coffin lid.

I was dizzy. Never would have believed this sort of vibration was in me. Most amazing thing I'd ever felt in my life. The stuff looked like oatmeal and to think the beginning of people is dripping off the rim of my hand, a thousand, a million different persons. Some slow in arithmetic, maybe even some who hated books, or wanted to kill everything like Warren Southern. Some like me, most of them more different from me than like me, and girls too.

I guess that is why "A Manual for Young Men" said to save it, 'cause you didn't know who you might be wasting.

It's a lie. You can't save it. Nobody, not Rev. Ribbs or Father Przybylsi at St. Bronislava in the village. A hundred million persons slid over the edge every day and there's no stopping it.

"A Manual for Young Men" says too much makes you forgetful. I think it's a lie. "Manual" said the Bible admonishes against it. If the Bible can't understand jackin' off any better than to admonish against it, then it don't want to tell the truth neither. Makes you wonder exactly how difficult this truth stuff is to get at in the first place.

COLOPHON

Designed by Moonlit Ink, Madison, Wisconsin

Illustrations by Jim McEvoy

Copy editing by Robert Frankenberg

Type set in Trump Medieval Book by Impressions, Inc., Madison, Wisconsin

Printed and bound on 50 lb. Warren Sebago, cream white by R.R. Donnelley & Sons, Crawfordsville, Indiana

Published by Heartland Press, an imprint of NorthWord Inc., Minocqua, Wisconsin

Also from NORTHWORD
PRESS, INC

ABOUT COWS
Sara Rath

About Cows is an affectionately humorous tribute to the domestic animal which produces 20% of the agricultural wealth of this country. Anyone with any connections with cows will love this illustrated collection of cow history, trivia and nostalgia. Sprinkled with anecdotes from farmers, cheesemakers, veterinarians and others who have crossed paths with cows.

About Cows features 32 color photographs of cows in their natural habitat and dozens of fascinating black-and-white illustrations.

$14.95 • 9¼ × 7⅞, 256 pages, paper • ISBN 0-942802-75-6

PRAIRIE VISIONS
Robert Gard

Author of thirty-eight books, Robert Gard is the premier storyteller of The Heartlands. *Prairie Visions* is his autobiographical journey into the heart of America. The book distills the stories and legends of mid-America and masterfully captures the mystique of the Heartland and its people.

Prairie Visions traces the steps of this award-winning author from his boyhood home in depression-racked Kansas to New York where he developed a regional theater program and to Wisconsin where his literary talents took firm root. Besides providing an intriguing record of the places he has been and the people he has met, *Prairie Visions* presents a spiritual profile of the Heartland itself.

$14.95 • 6½ × 9½, 320 pages, cloth • ISBN 0-942802-54-3

ALL-SEASON GUIDE TO WISCONSIN'S PARKS
Jim Umhoefer

"There are more than 70 state parks, forests, and trails in Wisconsin, and author Jim Umhoefer has visited them all. The guide is useful, informative, fun to read, and suited to all seasons, melding together commentary, maps, and photos. A browse through the book reveals the state's highest falls, best fishing holes—enjoyable regions to spend a few days. Bikers will find indispensable maps of the state's bike trails; hikers, campers, picnickers, vacationers, and anyone wanting to be outside will find this guide more than worth their money."—*Wisconsin Trails*

$9.95 • 8½ × 11, 80 pages, paper • ISBN 0-942802-00-4

CALKED BOOTS & CANT HOOKS
George Corrigan

Through Corrigan's eyes you can follow the evolution of the logging industry from horses to tractors and from cross-cuts to chain saws. Having worked dozens of woods' jobs, he describes the evolution with detail and accuracy as well as compassion. He loved the woods and the assortment of people who worked with him. With an ear for language, he has captured the character of the lumberjack.

$11.95 • 6 × 9, 288 pages, paper • ISBN 0-942802-14-4

FIRE & ICE
Don Davenport and Robert W. Wells

Combines two deadly disaster epics under one cover. "These are shocking tales of nature's fury: the 1958 killer storm that sent the big ore carrier *Carl D. Bradley* bubbling to the bottom of Lake Michigan, and the 1871 holocaust that charred bodies and blackened the landscape in Peshtigo, Wisconsin, the most disastrous fire in American history.

"*Shipwreck on Lake Michigan*, by Don Davenport, a Great Lakes scholar, is the kind of story a reader can't put down. Robert Wells tells the searing story of *Fire at Peshtigo* with the sure hand of a veteran newspaperman."—*The Milwaukee Journal*

$13.95 • 5½ × 8½, 450 pages, paper • ISBN 0-942802-04-7

LUMBERJACK LINGO
L.G. Sorden & Jacque Vallier

Over 4,000 terms and phrases fill this unusual dictionary. "*It's five a.m. and the gabriel blows. The bark eaters fall out of their muzzle loaders and head for the chuck house to bolt down a pile of stovelids with lots of blackstrap, some fried murphys or Johnny cake and maybe some logging berries.*" That's the colorful language of the lumberjack. Anyone with an interest in forestry or forest industries will enjoy reading this reference work, page by page.

$9.95 • 6 × 9, 288 pages, paper • ISBN 0-942802-12-8

To receive our free color catalog or order any of these books call toll free 1-800-336-5666. NorthWord Press Inc., Box 1360, Minocqua, WI 54548.